the dog walkers

MICHELLE DAVIS

To the amazing dogs I have been blessed to know …

Susie

Aspen

Jake

Samantha

Kelly

Burton

Mollie

Max

Abby

Mia

Mac

Callie

Bella

Coda

Obi

Chase

I am grateful for the joy each has brought to my life.

"Dogs have a way of finding the people who need them and filling an emptiness we didn't ever know we had."

– THOM JONES

"I think dogs are the most amazing creatures.
They give unconditional love.
For me they are the role model for being alive."

– GILDA RADNER

"Dogs are not our whole life, but they make our lives whole."

– ROGER CARAS

CHAPTER 1

Glancing in the rearview mirror, I see a woman whose green eyes sparkle with hope. She's happy, content, in control. Ali Doyle is more than ready for the next stage of her life.

Normally reserved, I can no longer suppress the joy for what my future holds. David and I leave for Costa Rica in twenty days. I've packed most of my clothing and booked our daily activities, excursions, and dinner reservations at the resort. Plus, I'm two weeks ahead at work. I've never been more prepared for anything in my life.

For months, David's promised we'd go away. Sure, we've traveled together, but only for long weekends in the tristate area. Between our demanding jobs and his having partial custody of Caroline, whom I have yet to meet, David always claimed life was too busy.

But last Christmas, he surprised me with a week's stay at a private villa at Nayara Gardens, an exclusive jungle resort in Costa Rica. We're going white water rafting, exploring the rain forest, and indulging in amazing spa treatments. And the restaurants at Nayara Gardens look incredible. But what I'm most looking forward to is seven days alone with David. He assured me this trip will be special. Yet I have a feeling it will be more than *just special*. I think David plans to propose.

Thoughts of engagement rings and sunny Costa Rica fade as I return to the present. Tonight, like most January evenings in

Pennsylvania, it's dark, cold, and damp. According to the Volvo's dashboard, the temperature hovers at thirty-three degrees.

Although yesterday's snowfall melted earlier today, black ice is bound to be lurking in previously shaded areas. Slowly, I pull into O'Malley's parking lot. It's packed for a Thursday night, and the only available space is in the rear, next to the dumpster. Scanning the backup camera for shiny spots on the asphalt, I carefully back my car into the open spot, conscious of the rusting maroon trash container situated too close to the fading white parking line.

We said we'd meet at 7:30, but it's 7:37. No doubt David will be there, waiting at our table, drinking a manhattan, and perhaps eyeing his watch.

Every Thursday, David and I meet for dinner at O'Malley's, a small pub in Haverford. Actually, it's where we had our first date, almost two years ago, shortly after I left my job at Teleco to begin working at Genesis, a small company specializing in telephone software. I was tired of commuting downtown, captive to the train schedule. But it was much more than that—large corporate politics frustrated me.

Initially attracted to this industry by the innovation it offered, I was naive and thought being smart and working hard was enough. But I didn't anticipate the hierarchy—one that I, as a female, didn't fit into.

Then I met Miles Becker at a software engineering conference in Washington, DC. This fifty-nine-year-old balding man introduced himself to me after the keynote presentation. Surprised to learn the company he founded was located in Bala Cynwyd, only a few miles from my apartment in Narberth, I began to ask a lot of questions about his firm. But it was his mission statement—*Teamwork, ingenuity, and creativity: how we develop superior software packages designed to meet your needs*—that piqued my interest.

One thing led to another and before I returned to Philadelphia, Miles offered me a package I could not refuse. I promptly resigned from Teleco and then immediately began my new position, reporting directly to Miles. This past November marked my two-year anniversary at Genesis.

My life could not have been better. At age thirty, I worked for an amazing boss at an incredible organization and earned an extremely competitive salary. I had it all.

At least that's what I thought—until David. I know, it's kind of cliché, but how we met was magical.

Twenty minutes late to work—I had slept through my alarm—I sprinted into Genesis's lobby to catch the elevator before the doors shut, asking the person inside to please hold the door. When the elevator reopened, there was only one occupant, a tall, thin man with short reddish-blond hair. Dressed in a pinstriped suit, he had a somewhat angular face that appeared perturbed with the momentary delay, but quickly his gaze turned warmer. I remember how it felt when I first set eyes on him. My face flushed, and tingles coursed through my body during the entire fifteen-second ride to the fourth floor. Even with heels, I was clearly much shorter than this stranger. As the doors opened, I nervously looked up at him and offered an awkward smile before exiting the elevator and dashing toward my office, as our team had a meeting scheduled in five minutes.

Once inside my office, I quickly glanced in the mirror that hangs on the back of the door. Realizing my long hair, slightly wet from my morning shower, looked disheveled and a bit unruly, I tucked brown strands behind my ears then used my hands to smooth my hair into place. Not having seen this man before, I assumed it was only a happenstance encounter, and it didn't matter what I'd looked like because I'd never see him again. But two minutes later, as I entered the conference room, there he was, sitting right next to Miles.

Miles began the morning's meeting by introducing us to David Hendrix, a newly hired lawyer at the law firm that represents Genesis. Miles continued to share that David graduated at the top of his class from Tufts University and that he would be providing legal assistance in the development of patents for our newest software, my team's responsibility.

After the meeting ended, David approached me in the hallway outside of the conference room. Small talk ensued, turning into flirtatious banter. Before I knew it, I gave him my phone number. And now, two years later, I'm headed into O'Malley's to have dinner with the man of my dreams.

***

"Tough day?" David rises to kiss me hello after he sets his glass on the cocktail napkin imprinted with a large "OM" in dark green, a hue matching the stripes on the restaurant's plaid wallpaper. While I'm a bit over five foot six, David's six-foot, two-inch stature requires me to stand on my tippy toes to meet his kiss.

"Yes," I say then sit down in the heavy wooden chair next to David. I drape my black woolen coat over an empty seat to my right before picking up the menu. Why I bother to look at it is a mystery because I always seem to order the same thing—a pub burger with sautéed asparagus and a house salad. I begin to play with several strands of my hair as I wait to see if David asks about my day.

But David doesn't probe, or perhaps he's not interested—sometimes I'm unsure. So without hesitation or invitation, I share the events of my chaotic day. I begin with a recap of our team's rush to meet today's deadline, then transition to how Carole, my administrative assistant, had to leave work to take care of her sick child. Finally, I tell David about the three-car accident that shut down Montgomery Avenue, requiring an unexpected detour, thus explaining why I am seven minutes late to dinner.

David doesn't say much. He seems preoccupied, not his normal self.

"How was your day?" I ask in an upbeat tone, wondering if he, too, had a hellish afternoon and that was why he seems a bit off.

"Work was fine." He takes a sip of his manhattan before continuing. "I received a text." David pauses. "From Julia." His eyes move closer as slight wrinkles form on his forehead. This makes him look older than thirty-nine.

Knowing a text from his ex-wife is anything but good news, I patiently wait, hoping he'll offer more.

After taking a long swig of his half-drunk manhattan, David finally speaks. "Apparently, she is headed to Los Angeles next month and needs me to take Caroline from the twelfth through the twentieth." He shares this in a clear and crisp manner, not showing any sign of regret nor anger. It's merely a matter-of-fact statement.

Immediately, there's a huge weight on my chest, as I realize that's the week we're supposed to be in Costa Rica, over Valentine's Day. *It's when he's going to propose.*

"What did you say?" My voice cracks and my eyes blink several times. It's practically impossible to contain myself, though I habitually do this whenever he discusses Julia or Caroline. But now beads of perspiration form on my forehead and my hands become clammy. I take the napkin from my lap and dab my face.

"What could I say? She's my daughter. I have to take her." David's voice is monotone, showing no disappointment, no remorse, nothing. David takes another sip of his drink, seeming to savor the liquid before swallowing.

My throat tightens, but I manage to ask, "What about Julia's parents? Can't Caroline stay with them?" Panic begins to rise, causing my heartbeat to quicken. I clear my throat as if I'm offering a natural solution to the dilemma.

"You know Caroline won't sleep anywhere but at Julia's or my place. It would be utterly traumatic for her." David's voice becomes stern and his nostrils flare. Is *he* chastising *me* for being selfish about cancelling the trip? Could he actually be suggesting that I'm putting my needs before his ex-wife's or his six-year-old daughter's, whom I have yet to meet?

"But this was my Christmas present," I say in a measured tone. I offer a small smile, hoping he'll change his mind. "I don't understand how Julia can drop this on you last minute. Why does she have to go to LA then? Can't she change *her* plans?" I fight the urge to raise my voice, restraining my Irish temper from showing. "I'm sure Caroline would prefer to be with you, but perhaps it's time for a babysitter?"

"Allison, you've always known Caroline comes first. As much as I want to be in Costa Rica with you, we'll have to go another time. You understand, don't you?" he says as he tilts his head and raises his slightly opaque eyebrows. He then gives me a controlled grin, as if that will smooth things over.

But it won't. I'm pissed. David is not the least bit upset about cancelling our week in Costa Rica. In fact, he seems absolutely fine with calling off *our* trip—the one where *he* is supposed to ask *me* to marry him. And while I've accepted David's protective nature regarding Caroline, I cannot comprehend why he will not introduce me to his daughter. It's not like we only started dating. It's been two years, and we practically live together, except for every other weekend and Tuesday evenings when he has Caroline. Oh, and of course, any time it's inconvenient for Julia to be a mom.

The server appears and asks if I'd like a drink. I order a glass of the house cabernet without looking in her direction. My attention focuses 100 percent on David right now.

"David, I've been looking forward to this trip. Isn't there some way we could go? What if Caroline came with us?" Yet what would a romantic getaway to Costa Rica be like with his six-year-old daughter who has no idea that Daddy has a girlfriend?

As if he read my thoughts, David says, "You know I prefer Caroline not know about us. I think it would confuse and upset her. I'll call the travel agent tomorrow and ask that she take care of the cancellation."

Frustration overrides my attempt to remain calm, and I finally say what I've been holding back for some time. "So when are you going to tell her about us, David? How old does she have to be? No doubt she's aware of the men Julia's been dating." The waitress reappears with my wine, and I down a good third of the glass right after she hands it to me.

"None of that is good for Caroline. She needs stability in her life, not a revolving door of her mother's boyfriends." His voice begins to fade as he finishes his sentence.

"But you and I are stable. This is not a one-night stand or random relationship." My mouth hangs open longer than it should. "I want to meet Caroline. I think it would be good for everyone." There, I've said it.

"Don't push me." David finishes his manhattan then signals to the waitress for another.

"I don't think I'm pushing you. I wouldn't suggest anything that would be hurtful to you or to Caroline. But if you and I are going to be a couple, well, it's important I get to know your daughter."

David takes a big breath before speaking. "Allison, I haven't introduced you to Caroline because the chances are that at some point, we won't be together. I thought you realized I have no intention of getting married again."

My heart plummets to the beer-stained hardwood floor. Did he really say he has no intention of marrying me? But what about Costa Rica? That's where he was supposed to propose. I try to speak, but it's as if my throat is constricted by a vise, not only suppressing my voice but also preventing my breath.

David notices my reaction. But instead of showing any sort of regret for the harshness of his words, he shakes his head and says, "Allison, what were you expecting, that I propose to you in Costa Rica?"

Damn him. Barely able to speak, I choke back tears as I nod my head.

After a loud sigh, David softly says, "I don't want to get married again, not to you or to anyone else." His eyes focus on his lap as he slowly shakes his head. "I don't do the marriage thing very well. And I certainly don't want to have any more children. That would destroy Caroline."

With that double statement, I gulp as tears spill down my cheeks. I grab the napkin from my lap and quickly blot my wet face. Being the youngest in a large Irish Catholic family, I've always wanted kids. But I thought I'd have them later in life, after I'd established my career. And despite what David claims, I don't remember him mentioning he didn't want to get married or have any more children. Had he said those things? If so, was I not listening? Or did I not want to hear?

His second manhattan arrives. David eats the cherry then lifts the glass to his lips. But before he takes a sip, he replaces it on the table and looks directly into my eyes. He reaches for my hand and says, "Allison, you and I have a good thing. It works." He gently squeezes my clammy fingers. "You have a demanding job, and so do

I. Marriage would only complicate things. And are you truly ready to be the stepmother to a six-year-old girl?" He attempts a chuckle, but I find none of this funny.

"David, maybe all along you've assumed I didn't want to get married, but you did not clearly share your feelings about this topic with me. What was I supposed to think?" I take a big sip of wine, perhaps for courage to say what must be said. "For the past two years, we've been together almost every night, except when you have Caroline. Why wouldn't I expect you'd propose?" My voice grows louder, and the couple next to us stops talking to face me before quickly turning their heads back toward one another.

David looks down at the white tablecloth, sits back into the chair, and says, "I'm sorry. That's all I can offer." Stillness fills the air as the distance between us expands though neither one of us has moved.

"You're sorry … that's all you can offer? That's the best line you can come up with?" My normally gentle tone has a nasty hiss to it.

"We should go." David once again signals to the waitress, but this time for the check.

After ten minutes of complete silence, the waitress returns with his credit card and slip. David signs the restaurant's copy of the receipt, and we promptly leave O'Malley's. He instinctively places his hand on my back as we walk into the parking lot, but I pull away. I'd rather fall on ice than have him touch me.

"Allison, you're tired. Why don't you go home and get some rest? We can talk about this tomorrow when you're more yourself." Plain. Factual. Heartless.

"When I am more myself?" I say as bile rises into my throat.

"Yes, when you've had some sleep and are calmer, more ratio-nal." His tone is degrading. Is this how he always speaks? Am I only now noticing it?

"I have never been more myself than I am right now. And I *am* perfectly calm. I'm telling you what I want, David." I stand tall and put both hands on my hips.

"What *you* want?" he asks as he tilts his head and stares at me. I definitely have his attention.

"Yes, what *I* want. This entire time I've gone along and allowed you to keep our relationship from your daughter, did my best to understand how you were trying to be a good father. But I don't think that's what it is. I think you are selfish. You want me at your beck and call, yet you do not want to invest in us. But I want more. This—what we have," I say as I wave my hand in the air, "well, it isn't enough." Something inside releases as I finally declare my truth.

David takes a step back as if he's been slapped. The lines in his face appear to sharpen. His lips create a straight horizontal line, no hint of sadness nor victory. He is emotionless.

"That's it?" I stammer. "You have no response?" Heat rises through my body, and the Irish temper I've worked so hard to suppress feels ready to blow. Inhaling deeply, I try to keep the lid on my emotions. Ali Doyle maintains control at all times, even in a dark parking lot when on the verge of ending a two-year relationship.

"Listen, I'm fine with how things have been between us. It's you who flipped out when I said we had to cancel the trip to Costa Rica. Then you admitted you assumed we were going to get married. Really, Allison? What gave you that idea?"

His words reverberate in my brain. *What gave you that idea?* Staring straight at him, I am speechless. I have no idea what gave me this idea—I just felt it, assumed that was how it was supposed to be. Why would I continue in a long-term relationship, at thirty-two, that was going nowhere?

But I cannot say this, for doing so would only make me look weak and vulnerable, and I am certainly not that. No, I'm dependable, solid, and decisive. I would *never* waste two years of my life with a man who has no intention of marrying me. Or would I? Have I? My breath releases and the power in my chest deflates.

Apparently, when it came to David, I'd broken every rule I'd established for myself. I let my guard down. I lost my discipline. I failed.

Knowing no words can rectify this situation, I turn sharply toward the Volvo as I fish for the keys inside of my purse. Clicking the unlock button, I pull open the door then jump inside, focusing solely on starting the car and getting the hell away from this place … and David … as fast as possible.

The Volvo starts instantly. Barely glancing sideways, I slam my foot on the accelerator, and I speed to the end of the parking lot. But before pulling out onto Montgomery Avenue, I pause for a moment to fasten my seatbelt. That look on his face, when I told him what we had wasn't enough, haunts my mind. He showed no hint of regret or sadness. It's as though the past two years meant nothing—I meant nothing. I drive away, leaving the man of my dreams standing alone in O'Malley's parking lot.

Ten minutes later, I'm home, parked in my designated spot in the lot behind my building. I turn the engine off but am unable to unfasten my seatbelt and get out of the car. Instead, I stare, eyes fixated on the full moon illuminating the parking lot and adjacent alley.

What have I done? Did I really end my relationship with David? Panic ping-pongs throughout my head. Knowing the power of the moon's pull, I wonder if that's what set me off. Was I momentarily crazed? Or did I finally say what ultimately had to be said? My head begins to throb, and my hands instinctively leave the steering wheel, allowing my thumbs to rhythmically massage my temples.

Finally, I exit the car and make my way inside and up the flight of stairs to my second-floor apartment. After turning my key in the knob, I walk through the dark doorway and switch on the light. My 1960s garden apartment, decorated in muted shades of gray and beige, appears different tonight. While I haven't made any changes to this space in the past year or so, somehow it feels odd, unfamiliar, foreign ... maybe even cold.

Ping.

I pull my phone from my purse and see there's a text from David.

David: *You OK?*

So now he's concerned. He certainly didn't show any when I left O'Malley's. He barely appeared to give a damn. And a text? If he cared, he would have called. Knowing David, he only wants to ease his conscience. Still holding my phone, I walk across the room and throw my purse on the sofa, then toss my coat next to it before I quickly type a terse response.

Without a second thought, I hit Send. Truly disgusted with this man *who was my world for two years*, I go to the kitchen, connect my phone to the charger plugged into an outlet above the kitchen counter, pour myself a glass of white wine, and take a carton of Talenti Sea Salt Caramel gelato from the freezer. After guzzling the pinot gris and scarfing down half of the ice cream container, I leave the glass and half-eaten carton on the counter as I head toward the bedroom.

I disrobe as soon as I enter this room, tossing my clothing carelessly into a pile on the floor. Stark naked, I crawl under the sheets of my queen bed and pull the pristine white comforter over my head. I take a big breath, then exhale loudly, perhaps in an attempt to expel tonight's revelation. But during this process, I smell David's cologne. Damn him! He spent last night at my apartment, and his scent still lingers on my sheets. Indignant, I begin to rip off the top sheet, then the fitted sheet and pillowcases, propelling them into the hallway through the open bedroom door.

Now alone, naked, and lying between my mattress cover and my down comforter, I take the pillow next to me and begin to punch it, releasing my pent-up fury. Two years! I gave up *everything* to be with him. I stopped seeing friends and trying to reconnect with my family—all because of him! After a while, my fingers release the pillow and I collapse into the fetal position.

When my body finally quiets, my emotions begin to shift. Slowly, sensations begin to rise within, resembling rippling waves.

Fury, regret, self-doubt, fear, hurt, betrayal … they arrive one after another, transitioning from a flowing surf to an overwhelming tsunami. *But I don't do emotions.* That's not who I am. I've always prided myself on having self-control, poise, grace. Yet I possess none of these qualities right now.

Confused with this onslaught of foreign feelings, I detect an internal combustion ignite inside me, and my body begins to heave up and down. It becomes hard to breathe as I gasp for air, seemingly unable to fill my lungs with oxygen. This terrifies me, as I've never reacted this way to anything before. What the hell is happening? Then the most gut-wrenching realization occurs: it's not David I'm irate with—it's me.

Get your shit together! David doesn't deserve you. He only cares about himself. In fact, he's incapable of love. He doesn't have it in him. He is a shallow, empty shell of a human being.

I deserve more.

Tears return, at first in small streams. But then their velocity rises and the flood gates open wide. I am one fucking hot mess … and I have no idea what to do to stop it.

CHAPTER 2

Itoss and turn all night, unable to escape the fact that I broke up with David. But that's not the worst of it. It's only the tip of the iceberg. My world's ended, not merely my romance, but *my world*.

I'd sacrificed so much for him. Actually, let me rephrase. I consciously chose to give up who I was and what mattered to me, without an ounce of regret, because I thought David was *the one*. But in reality, all we were was a convenient *thing*. Some*thing* with little promise, no true commitment, and zero future. How could I have misread him this entire time? My jaw tightens as I acknowledge the undeniable truth and the assumption I'd made.

Yet—and here is the hardest part for me to swallow—David didn't promise me anything, nor did he insinuate there would be more. And he was clear from day one about his daughter. He did not want her to know about us. He laid steadfast ground rules from the beginning; however, I chose to reshape the boundaries and create my own blueprint for how I wanted the relationship to be. Where he placed hard limits, I softened the straight lines into curves. I knocked down the brick walls he had carefully laid, and I envisioned clear windows where he installed opaque block glass. I broke every rule I'd written when it came to men.

The truth is, it was only me who envisioned a deeper bond between us. David did not deceive or manipulate me. He was clear about what he wanted. *I* made *us* something we were not. I wore rose-colored glasses, pretending he was my knight in shining armor preparing to sweep me off my feet onto his white steed and head into the sunset for a beautiful forever. But David never rode a horse, wore a coat of mail, or claimed any intention to rescue me. I created this fairy tale on my own.

Curled up, I duck under the comforter, avoiding both the morning sunlight streaming through the window and the inevitable fact that I must get up and go to work. I force myself to glance at the clock. It's seven o'clock. *Shit.* While Miles is pretty relaxed about us taking time off when needed, I am scheduled to give a huge presentation to the team on Monday. I can't skip work today.

Reluctantly, I crawl out of bed, grab the robe hanging on the hook inside of my closet, and shuffle out of my bedroom toward the kitchen, stepping over the pile of discarded sheets. I pour water into the back of the coffee maker, add grinds, then press the On button. Afterward, I pick up my sheets as well as my clothes from last night and put them in the hamper.

The last thing I want to do is go to work, but as I head to shower, I resign myself to the fact that there are no options. Looking into the mirror above the sink confirms I'm a mess. While I consider myself plain and somewhat simple looking, others have called me cute, sweet, pretty. But none of these terms apply this morning. My puffy, bloodshot eyes and sallow skin make me look like shit. Hopefully, some makeup and lots of coffee will help me pull myself together so no one will suspect anything.

Only after turning on the shower faucet do I remember texting David. I was so pissed last night, I didn't check it for typos, something I usually do. Oh well, does it matter?

Twenty-five minutes later, after emerging from my bedroom dressed in fitted khaki pants and a navy blouse, I take my travel mug from the counter and fill it with coffee. Being there's no time for breakfast, I throw a granola bar and my fully charged cell phone into my purse. After putting on my coat, I sling my purse over my shoulder, grab the travel mug, and leave.

Once inside of my car, I take a moment to check my phone for messages. There's only one text—from David. Trying to recall exactly what I said last night, I reluctantly open the message.

David: *I'm sorry you feel that way. Should I find any of your belongings at my place, I will put them in a box and leave them outside of your apartment.*

Sorry I feel that way? But then I begin to remember a bit of what I wrote. My heart sinks into my stomach as I scroll back and read my exact words.

Me: *You fucking asshole. You want to know if I am OK? What do you think??? How could you have done this to me? You said you loved me … I gave you everything … and this is what I get in return … go to hell!*

There's a sudden distaste in my mouth. That is so not who I am, nor is it how I want David to remember me. Mortified, I attempt to block this text from my mind, knowing there is nothing I can do to erase it. Emotionally numb, I navigate the route to work. Before I know it, I'm walking into Genesis's building. Quickly, I dash for the elevator before the doors close. But in an instant, I've time-traveled back two years as I see the back of a tall man with reddish-blond hair and a slim build wearing a conservative suit. I momentarily freeze before taking a step back then turning my body away from the closing doors. *Was that David?* My legs weaken, but I catch myself, preventing a fall. I turn toward the building's front door. Regaining control of my limbs, I begin to run, first out of the building and then to my car, unlocking it twenty feet away so I can quickly make a getaway and return to the safety of my apartment, where I never have to see David.

Ten minutes later, I'm curled into the fetal position on my sofa, shaking under an old crocheted throw blanket.

Stay here. Stay safe.

From out of nowhere, a voice speaks to me. Jolted by this unknown female talking inside of my head, I sit up and look around, wondering if someone else is in the room with me. But there's no one. The words came from *inside of me*.

Who said this and what does it mean? Am I supposed to stay inside my apartment? Will that keep me safe? It makes no sense. But the woman's soft and reassuring words reverberate in my brain. Unsure of the meaning behind this message, all I know is that for now, here, I am safe.

***

I must have dozed off. No wonder—I barely slept last night. I'm still on the couch in my apartment, terrified to leave and return to work because I cannot trust myself to keep my emotions in check if I see David. So, for now, I must remain here all by myself. Alone.

Alone is such an accurate word. For that is what I truly am. My life had come down to two things: my relationship, or whatever that actually was, and my job. I'd let everything else fall behind.

In most situations like this, the woman would reach out to her best friend. They'd get together for a few glasses of wine, call the guy all sorts of names, and then toast to meeting better men in the future. But I don't have a best friend. I don't have any friends, except for the couple friends David and I shared and a few acquaintances at work.

Yet I have no one to blame but myself. I'm the one who let friendships fall by the wayside once I started dating David. At first, I'd meet close girlfriends for lunch or dinner. This slowly dwindled down to once-a-month coffee, until finally, I'd cancelled on them so many times they stopped calling.

And my family, well, that's another story. Let's be real. I never belonged. Growing up in Upper Darby with five years between sibling number seven and me, I was pretty much on my own all of the time. Then my mother died from cancer when I was fifteen, leaving me alone with my father, who took his consolation from Johnny Walker. At that time, all of my brothers and sisters were either in college or married with families of their own. Their thoughts were on everything but me.

I received a Presidential Scholarship to Villanova, and once I started college, I pretty much distanced myself from my entire family. After all, Dad, who deep down meant well, had enough of his own problems. Plus, my brothers and sisters were so caught up in their own family dramas that there was little attention left for me. I guess I took this as an opportunity to become independent, learning to rely on no one except for myself. That served me well for many years. But then I met David, and I let my guard down. I became weak, dependent, needy.

Pausing, I try to remember the woman I was before, the one who confidently thrived and excelled. Priding myself on my successes, I lived by a disciplined work ethic, along with a strict diet and regimented exercise routine. These behaviors kept things under control, allowed me to be happy.

But once David came into my life, my job began to hold less importance. So did working out and eating healthy. My priorities shifted, and as a result, my rigid work hours and meticulous lifestyle slackened. I never allowed my output to suffer, but I know my heart no longer belonged to my career—I had given it to David.

My thoughts return to the present, and I'm reminded I must let someone at work know I won't be coming in today. Reluctantly, I uncoil from my protected position on the sofa and retrieve my laptop, which is plugged in and charging on my desk to the right, by the window facing Haverford Avenue. I bite my lip as I begin to compose an email to Miles. After a few moments of contemplating a BS excuse, I quickly type that I've caught a stomach bug and cannot possibly come into the office but promise to email Monday's Power-Point by the end of the day. Done. Problem solved—at least for now.

Shutting the laptop, I begin to wonder how I can pull myself together in the next three days. I'll remain home, where that voice told me it is safe. Working remotely on the presentation is the simple solution. Then Monday, I'll have a game plan and be ready to return to Genesis, fully prepared for the meeting. Perhaps that is what the voice was trying to tell me. Stay home and safe, only until Monday. Then everything will be fine.

CHAPTER 3

Dressed in my perfectly fitting brand-new black skirt, a crisp white button-down shirt, and stunning taupe pumps from Nordstrom, I begin my presentation. In a fluid motion, my left thumb clicks the remote, advancing the PowerPoint as I explain the complex graphs as well as the rationale behind the recommendations I'm proposing for our newest product launch. The charts are carefully color-coordinated, clearly illustrating the data behind my assumptions. The room's captive, heads nod. But it's Miles's reaction I wait for. As the presentation continues, a smile emerges on his face. His expression definitely reflects I'm nailing it. I'm back. This is the Ali Doyle who left a policy-driven corporate firm to work at Genesis, the company where passion, commitment, and teamwork matter.

But then I sense a shift in the room as the door slowly opens. I ignore the intrusion and continue with my proposal for the product launch. But when I catch the scent, *his* scent, I turn to face the doorway. However, it's unnecessary to look. I know who's there.

"Ali, I've asked David to join us today. It's important we make sure we're in total compliance with legal before we release our new product," Miles says, oblivious to what he's done, the lion he's allowed into my den.

My eyes lock on to the intruder. Venom rises from my core, through my chest, up my esophagus, and into my mouth. Feeling the urge to vomit, I reflexively swallow, hoping to force the bile-like fluid back into my stomach.

No doubt David senses my rage. But he doesn't look at me. Instead, he smiles at several of my coworkers before taking a seat next to Miles. Then David has the nerve to lean over and whisper something to my boss while I'm speaking. I shrink with his lack of acknowledgment. If he doesn't see me, do I exist?

Instantly, my voice quivers, and my body begins to shake. My team members, who only minutes ago were nodding in support, are now looking at one another, perplexed, as if trying to discern what has come over me. Miles's previously proud face becomes startled, perhaps unsure of who is presenting before him. I go to advance the PowerPoint, but nothing happens. I rush to the laptop sitting on the front table and furiously start pushing buttons. In an attempt to help, one of the younger analysts leaves his seat and offers assistance, but instead of being appreciative of his efforts, I snap, declaring, "I've got this!"

More startled looks. This time it's Miles who intervenes.

"Let's take a break, everyone. Obviously, we've got a technology glitch. How about we reconvene in fifteen?"

Rather than using this opportunity to compose myself and regroup, I run out of the conference room and into my office, loudly slamming the door behind me. Being that all of the offices have windows, I quickly crawl under my desk in an attempt to hide from anyone walking by. Five minutes pass, then ten. I'm not sure if I'll ever come out.

There's a knock. I ignore it. But then I hear the door open and someone walk inside. This person sits down in the chair across from my desk. I remain where I am, not saying a word.

"Ali, I have no idea what the hell happened in there, but we need to talk."

I gulp, loudly, clearly revealing there is indeed a human scrunched underneath the desk, hiding from her boss.

"I'm not upset. I want to help," Miles says, his voice softening considerably.

Peering from under the safety of my desk, I first see one knee, then another. Having left his seat to join me on the hardwood floor, my boss is now two feet away from me.

In a quiet, calming tone he says, "I didn't realize things had ended between you and David. I'm sorry. If I had known, I would have warned you that he needed to be at the meeting."

Humiliated, I accept I have two choices. I can continue to shroud myself beneath this desk, pretending my boss is not sitting on the floor trying to reason with me, or I can acknowledge I messed up by allowing my personal life to interfere with my job and be honest with this man.

I choose the latter.

Slowly, I push myself up, using my swivel chair as an anchor. After easing onto this seat, my stare transitions from the floor to the desk then to Miles, who has now also returned to sitting in a chair. He's right—he's not angry. But he is visibly concerned. His dark, bushy eyebrows furrow, and the corners of his mouth are pursed.

"Miles, I don't know what to say," I stammer. "What just happened … well, I'm ashamed." I break my visual connection with my boss to focus solely on the floor. A big lump forms in my throat, and my eyes well up with tears.

"You've obviously been through a lot," Miles says. His words exude warmth as his bearded face softens.

"But I totally made an ass of myself … in front of the whole team … and David," I snivel, regretting the last two words as soon as they escape my lips. Suddenly, my head begins to throb.

"People understand. They're your friends, not merely your coworkers, and they want to support you."

"But will they take me seriously again? That was so unprofessional." My fingertips push into my temples, hoping to ease the pain as I try to prevent a total meltdown.

Miles sighs. "Ali, you need some time to work this out. This breakup is affecting you more than you may think it is. Go home. Get some rest and sort through everything. Then, when you're ready, you can come back." Miles's voice remains kind, but I feel as if I'm receiving a directive, not a suggestion.

"You want me to stay home? Not come to work?" My voice cracks as the words exit my mouth. I can no longer prevent the tears.

"I think it is for the best. And I want you to talk with someone. I have the number of a therapist who should be able to help you." He hands me a folded piece of paper.

I wipe my wet cheeks with my fingertips before taking the slip of paper from Miles. I say nothing as I read the name written in capital letters above a phone number: HENRIETTA ROWLEY.

"Who is she?" I finally ask as I refold the paper and place it on top of my desk, physically distancing myself from the contact information for the therapist.

"Henrietta is an old friend. She's a psychologist, and a good one at that. Henrietta has a great deal of experience, and I believe she can provide you with the support you need right now. Madeline went to her years ago," he adds, perhaps hoping I'll be more apt to call knowing his wife had worked with her.

As I contemplate whether or not to take his recommendation, there's a knock on the door. Before either Miles or I can say or do anything, the door opens. David walks in.

"Miles, when you have a moment, I'd like to speak with you," David says in a nonchalant manner, once again ignoring me and the fact that he is barging into *my* office after ruining *my* presentation.

Within moments, my body fills with the unbridled heat of hatred, ready to erupt. The intensity magnifies to a point where I am no longer capable of containing myself.

"How dare you!" My words crackle as my right hand juts out, and I wave my pointer finger in his direction. "You have no right to be here. Leave ... at once."

Both men seem shocked with my outburst, but it is not David's reaction that worries me—it's Miles's. I look in his direction. He's sitting there, head in his hands. Miles sighs loudly. It's at that exact moment I know I've totally lost it, not only my temper, but more importantly the support of my boss and possibly my job. Slowly, I crumble back in my chair, pull my knees into my chest, and begin to sob.

Beep! Beep! Beep! Startled, I sit up straight then turn and stare at the alarm clock sitting on my nightstand. My hand instinctively hits the top, stopping the screeching sound.

Unaware of where I am, I look around, slowly taking in my surroundings. I'm in my bedroom, not my office. What's going on? What about the presentation? And Miles and David?

My body softens into the mattress beneath me. It was only a dream. I'm safe. Nothing bad has happened. No one at work knows anything. They all think I was sick on Friday.

Relieved, I sigh as I begin to massage my forehead, as if trying to erase the memories lingering from this nightmare. As my brain begins to awaken, it registers that today is Monday, the day of my presentation.

I hesitate, curling tightly into a ball before attempting to get out of bed. But what if my dream actually happens? It's not unreasonable to believe Miles would want David at the presentation.

There could be legal concerns that need to be addressed. And if he were to come, how would I respond? Would people know we were no longer together? Could I maintain control of my emotions?

While I haven't been super public about our relationship, my coworkers are aware that David and I have been together for some time. Whenever David came to Genesis's headquarters, he often stopped by my office to say hello. And it *is* possible that David could be at the presentation today. My throat tightens at the thought. Waves of nausea crash inside my body. Instantly, I grab my midsection. In less than two minutes, I dash to the bathroom, landing on all fours before vomiting into the toilet. When I'm finally done retching every last ounce of fluid from my stomach into the bowl, I slowly crawl up and make my way to the sink.

I stand crookedly, leaning one hip into the Formica countertop as I stare into the mirror. The woman I see cannot be me, for she appears as a stranger, lost and unsure of who she is or what she wants. After trying to decipher some sort of message from the expression on her tormented freckled face, I accept the fact she is indeed me and that I have absolutely no idea of what to do next. Conscious of the irreparable schism existing between my personal and professional lives, I must decide whether my career takes precedence or if my emotions rule. Do I choose the high road, step into the shower, eat my oatmeal, and listen to NPR on the radio as I drive to work, or do I succumb, hide, and wave the white flag, claiming that the risk of losing all control if I see David is too much for me to handle?

At this exact moment, I remember the voice: *Stay here. Stay safe.* It quickly becomes apparent that I am not equipped to see David at today's meeting. Because if he shows up, I am incapable of predicting my reaction. And if there is one thing I know about myself, it's that I must be in control at all times. My behavior on

Thursday night at O'Malley's and then the text response afterward proves that currently, I am not in control of my actions. Besides, both the nightmare and my retching at the thought of seeing David at the meeting absolutely confirm my suspicion. I cannot go to work.

And as bad as that dream was, I am fully cognizant the reality could be worse. I stare into the mirror, looking for a solution. Finally, it comes to me. I'll tell Miles I still have a nasty stomach bug and ask if he'll make the presentation on my behalf. After all, I did get sick, so it's not a total lie. Relief fuels my body as I let out a big sigh.

As the stress slowly seeps out of me, I leave the bathroom and pick up the phone lying on my nightstand. After writing a concise text to Miles, I hit Send. My eyes remain glued to the phone. Will my boss believe I'm ill, or will he suspect something else?

Five minutes later, Miles responds, offering assurance that he will take care of the presentation, directing me only to get well. Get well … what an odd term, yet it seems to be the perfect phrase for this situation. But how do I *get well*? It implies one is sick. Am I?

Logical by nature, I sit down on my bed, propping the pillow against the headboard as I lean back and ponder this question. I'm no stranger to mental unwellness—my father definitely suffered from it for many years. I wonder if I could be mentally unwell. Instantaneously, Matchbox Twenty's song, "Unwell," pops into my head, and those memorized lyrics reverberate loudly.

As the song replays in my mind, I find myself sinking deeper and deeper, identifying fully with the words, as if the song were written for me.

CHAPTER 4

With a red marker tightly gripped in my right hand, I scrawl a large *X* over the seventh block on the calendar that hangs inside of the kitchen cabinet. Above the grid of dates, there is a picture of a rustic wooden plank dining table. On top of the table are two heart-shaped mugs of hot chocolate and marshmallows as well as a vase of red roses and a dish of candy hearts with the inscription "BE MINE."

It's been fifteen days since David and I broke up. I sigh after I count the accumulated crosses, yet they help me grasp the length of my isolation.

Being here by myself is fine. Actually, I like the comfort of knowing all decisions are now mine—what to watch on TV, whether or not to open the blinds, how warm to set the thermostat. I don't need to be considerate of anyone and worry that their needs are unmet. Now I'm in control.

Two days ago, one of the wives from our couple friends reached out to me, wanting to know how I was. I guess she heard David and I broke up. Her text was sweet, but her and her husband's friendship came with David, so I assume their loyalties will remain with him.

I'm also receiving emails from people at work. They ask how I'm feeling, if I've been to the doctor, and whether or not they can drop off food. My answers are short and sincere: *Thank you, but I am fine. I hope to be back to work soon.*

But do I? Will I? Can I? I have not been to Genesis for two entire weeks, and this morning, Human Resources sent me an email requesting I receive a physician's signature regarding my extended illness.

While no doubt this is a sickness of sorts, I certainly have not seen a doctor about it. And besides, my only doctor is my gynecologist. And what, exactly, would I tell her? That I broke up with my grown-up "boyfriend" after I realized he wasn't going to marry me? And could I please have a note saying I am sick because I am terrified that if I come in contact with him, I will be reduced to a bumbling mess and uncontrollably lose myself in the pain and anguish from the fact that I gave up two years of my life for *him*, and in return, he left me with NOTHING!

It's come down to a simple choice: I either find a doctor who will sign off on my "illness," I return to work on my own, or I resign. Unable to deal with the situation, I continue to avoid the inevitable.

There are some upsides to living in seclusion. Being isolated from the world, I no longer need to deal with surprises or interruptions. Plus, for the first time in forever, I don't have to consider what David wants. Now I can cook shrimp without concern for his shellfish allergy. And I no longer have to wear a sweatshirt or light coat inside because he likes the temperature at sixty-five degrees. The bottom line is self-quarantining allows me to do whatever *I please*.

But the most important reason to remain in my apartment is that I won't need to see David. He dropped off a box of my clothes and personal items I had at his house, mainly a bathrobe, sweat pants, and some other casual clothes. There were also several of "the essentials," like tampons, a hairbrush, a toothbrush, and makeup remover.

The box with a Pottery Barn label, most likely from the new bar glasses he bought last month, was sitting outside of my entryway. It was labeled "Allison" in crisp, precise lettering. David had texted me after he placed it there, behind the holly bushes out front. I waited a full hour until I went downstairs to retrieve my belongings. But before I ventured outside, I scanned the area from my front window to make sure his car was nowhere in sight.

My phone rings. Before answering, I look at the incoming call. It's Eddie, the delivery guy from Whole Foods.

"Hi, Eddie. I'll buzz you in. Please put the bags by the stairs," I say, though he knows the drill. It's mostly the same guy who drops off my preordered groceries. I move to the front window and watch Eddie emerge from a white van sporting the store's name on its side. As soon as he approaches the door, I run to the intercom panel and hit Enter, unlocking the door into the entranceway. I then go back to the window, waiting for him to return to the van and drive away. I'm conscious to add a nice tip when I give them my credit card number. I think that's why Eddie carefully places everything exactly where instructed. I kind of like this new system. Besides, I might run into David at Whole Foods.

Looking at my watch, I'm fairly certain my neighbors will not be at home, allowing me to retrieve my groceries undisturbed. There are the Thompsons on the first floor. Both are accountants who work incredibly long hours, especially this time of year. And the man who has the apartment upstairs travels during the week, so I hardly see him.

I walk out of my apartment door and peer down the stairs. As predicted, Eddie has neatly placed three bags of groceries next to the bottom stair. Quickly, I run to the landing, grab my groceries, and then dart upstairs, back to my apartment. After shutting the door and turning the bolt, I gently pull the door several times to confirm it's locked.

It only takes a few minutes to put the groceries away. As I place the perishables in the refrigerator, I am sure to clean out any items that no longer look edible, like the bunch of radishes I bought because they were an online special last Tuesday. I toss the withered bunch in the trash. Noticing the can is nearly full, I decide to wait till tomorrow to take it out back to the dumpster. That is, after everyone has left for work. There's a door at the bottom of the stairs, opposite of the entryway, that leads to the back parking lot where the building's trash container is located. I can practically toss my garbage into the dumpster without taking more than a step outside.

Fifteen days alone in my apartment … it kind of reminds me of that huge snowstorm, back in the nineties, when school was closed for two weeks. Mom, Dad, my one brother, and I were the only ones at home. Yet, while we were housebound the entire time, I wasn't truly alone like I am now. I had meals with my family, and Mom would constantly check in and see how I was doing. She'd offer to braid my waist-long hair, suggest we paint our nails, or surprise me with a mug of tea. But I didn't mind the solitude. In fact, I had no trouble keeping myself occupied reading, writing in my journal, and drawing on my sketch pad. I guess I've always been comfortable on my own. Perhaps I prefer it.

No doubt there are definite benefits to my self-imposed social distancing. I've discovered I can easily order whatever I need online. All that's required is to go to the website and choose what I want. It's simple.

And whenever I feel alone and in need of others, I look out my front window. In fact, yesterday I placed one of the dining chairs by the large bay window, allowing me to have coffee and watch all of the action on Haverford Avenue. There's so much going on out there. Kids pass by on bikes. People walk their dogs. This steady flow of activity seems to connect me to the outside world. So I'm not *really* alone. I'm only intentionally staying away from work—well, from everything—right now. I guess I'm listening to what the voice told me to do. It's actually romantic in a strange way, casting me as a fairy tale princess in a castle's tower, safely tucked away from any looming harm.

I thought I'd miss people. But I don't. Besides those at work, who is there to miss? I don't see my family, and I lost most of my friends when I started dating David.

Whenever I think about work, I get the worst feeling in the pit of my stomach. Miles has been incredibly understanding, but how long can I continue this charade with him? Plus, there's that deadline with Human Resources. The sad truth is, I cannot return to Genesis as long as David remains as legal counsel. I've thought long and hard about this. And as much as I appreciate all Miles has done for me, unless I can remote indefinitely, I must resign and find a job I can do from here, because I can't leave this apartment, at least not now.

And since David doesn't live that far away from me, it's realistic I could bump into him anywhere. The thought of seeing him across the aisle in the grocery store, where he's adding almond milk or kombucha to his cart, paralyzes me. Or what if I was filling up my car with gas and he pulled up at the tank across from me? My throat tightens and my shoulders creep closer to my ears at this idea.

Stop thinking of him. He doesn't matter anymore. But then my mind returns to Miles. I look at my wooden desk next to the window. The desk cost more than I wanted to spend, but David convinced me that it would fit perfectly in my apartment and would provide adequate storage for my paperwork. Damn it ... there I go again, the *D* word ... stop!

There's a pile of unopened mail on the left side of this desk. I need to attend to all of the paperwork I've been avoiding, but first, I must respond to HR and to Miles.

Conscious that if I leave Genesis, I may not have income for a while. I've calculated my monthly expenses. Fortunately, I have a sufficient cushion, allowing me to easily go without employment for six to eight months. Yet that's not who I am. I need something to keep me busy, occupied, productive, worthy.

On a whim, or more likely in an attempt to once again avoid dealing with the inevitable and contacting my boss, I decide to explore opportunities where I could work from home. Ignoring the pile of papers, what I should be focusing on, I begin to search online for open positions. With ease, I immerse myself, eyes glued to the screen as I click away and read about various positions.

Of course, the beauty of remoting is there are then no geographic limits to where the company is located. I become entrenched in this new world of working from home, ignoring the clock and my rumbling stomach.

It's only when the room begins to darken from the setting sun that I become fully cognizant of how long I've been at this. Yet I've learned a lot from this time online and found some possibilities. I didn't realize how marketable I am. As a software engineer, I can easily design from home and then Zoom or Skype my way through meetings with coworkers in other locations.

Before I sign off for the day, I send three inquiries, all for positions similar to my current one at Genesis. One is based in Cincinnati, another in Seattle, and the third in Minneapolis. I can't imagine actually living in any of these cities. As strange as it may seem, I'm not sure I'd want to leave the Philadelphia area. Sure, there's no reason to stay—no family, no friends, no David. But it's what I know. It's home.

As I check for unread messages, I once again see the email from HR. Though it's not, it appears illuminated, calling my immediate attention.

No longer able to avoid the inevitable, I accept that I must resign from Genesis. Tears streaming down my face, I reluctantly compose an email to Miles, the man who offered me an incredible opportunity and then took me under his wing. I thank him profusely for giving me the chance to work for him at Genesis, but I skip the real reason as to why I am leaving. Unable to admit I've permitted fear to win and take precedence over my career, I instead write I'm trying to find myself, explore options, and that kind of bullshit. After rereading it five times, I wipe away the tears before I send these paragraphs of lies to a man whom I hold in the highest regard. But it's done. I've taken the final step.

Now I am truly safe.

CHAPTER 5

Peering out my front window, everything looks white. Tree limbs bend toward the ground, appearing as if they're about to snap. Plows make their way down Haverford Avenue, loudly scraping the road as they add to the height of the mounds of snow lining the street.

The weather station reported an accumulation of close to eighteen inches. But that's not the number I'm focusing on—it's twenty-seven, the number of X's on my calendar, landing me at February 19. Today is two days after Presidents' Day, when I was supposed to return from Costa Rica flaunting a gorgeous diamond ring on the third finger of my left hand. But that clearly didn't happen.

Recently there's been a shift occurring within me. It's now apparent I've been deceiving myself, assuming I could remain quarantined, alone, and be fine with it. Well, apparently I'm not. There seems to be more to my self-isolation than I was willing to admit …

***

Ten days ago, my serene solo existence ended in the most abrupt manner. Miles, no doubt concerned about me and my unexpected resignation, stopped by unannounced.

When I heard the buzzer, I jumped. Why would someone ring my doorbell? I hadn't ordered anything. Looking outside the front window, I observed a middle-aged man standing on the cement pad outside of the building's entrance. It was Miles, and I was staring down at his balding head.

Damn, he'd come to see me. Remorse and regret flooded my body as I shamefully contemplated pretending I wasn't home so I could avoid speaking with him. But the bell rang again, and in a moment of weakness, I pushed the button on the console, granting Miles permission to come upstairs.

For the first time in over three weeks, I was going to have a face-to-face conversation, and the thought of human interaction terrified me. Yet Miles had been so good to me, and he was like the father figure I wished I had. How could I deny this man? Didn't I owe some sort of explanation to my boss … my friend?

I heard the heavy thuds of his shoes, most likely the beige Timberland boots he wears in the winter, strike the wooden stairs. I had no idea how ominous this noise was of what was about to transpire. Suddenly silence, only to be replaced by three knocks. Against my better judgment, I unbolted the door, casting my eyes downward as I gently pushed it open.

Regret instantly oozed throughout my body. I'd never lied to Miles before. Could I continue this charade? Or would I finally be honest and let him know what was going on? But how could I possibly explain?

While I internally debated with my guilt-ridden monkey brain, I acknowledged that a real person was standing across from me, saying nothing, perhaps waiting for me to make the first move. But when I finally permitted myself to meet his eyes, looking at the man whom I've respected since first meeting him, I witnessed confusion, not the sympathy I had hoped for.

I'm not sure what he expected to find—me, curled up into the fetal position, not having bathed for days, with empty pizza boxes all over the counter? Unless physically incapable, my apartment would always be pristine and perfectly organized. That's who I am. In fact, my "emotional snafu" had only sharpened my need to clean, perhaps obsessively, as I've scrubbed every inch of this place.

"I heard about you and David," Miles said, as he offered me a lopsided half smile. Men are not good with these conversations.

"Yes, it's over," I said in a slightly dejected manner. But as the words exited my lips, my mouth began to quiver. While I'd accepted this relationship had ended, I had yet to declare it aloud to another, except, of course, to David. But that had been seventeen days earlier.

What happened next, well, I guess the best description would be to say I totally lost my shit. As horrible as the breakup night and following weekend were, this scene at my front door took the cake. My shoulders caved forward as my entire body began to rock. Then came tears—waterworks, actually—followed by the guttural noises resembling a wounded animal, not a woman's broken soul. No, this sound clearly announced pure agony and gut-wrenching sorrow. Before I knew it, Miles pulled me close to him, hugged me, and stroked my hair, like a father would. While I know this is totally taboo in today's environment, I needed human touch.

And I implicitly trust Miles.

I have no idea how long we stayed that way. All I remember is the unexpected emotional release that occurred. After I quieted down, Miles moved his hands to my shoulders, took a step back, and said, "Ali, how about I come inside and we talk, OK?"

Incapable of speaking, I slowly nodded my head in agreement. Walking backward, I then sat down at the dining table. Miles followed my lead, pulling out a chair right next to me.

"Do you want to tell me about it?" That's all he asked. He didn't probe, declare David didn't deserve me, or infer it wasn't that bad. He merely offered to listen. Without internally debating the pros and cons of bearing my innermost thoughts to my boss, or rather my former boss—I had resigned, after all—I let go and shared what had happened at O'Malley's, David's response, and my realization that I couldn't step foot into Genesis again. I admitted no longer knowing who I was or what I wanted and that the thought of seeing David terrified me.

But then it got real ... I confessed there was no one left to go to. I told Miles how I'd ignored my friends and stopped reaching out to my family once I met David. Finally, I insisted I was the only one who could fix this mess. No one could do it but me.

"Ali, there are many options for help," Miles said as he sat up straighter and folded his hands on the dark walnut table. "I know some good counselors. In fact, my wife sees one occasionally, and I think you'd like him. He's helped her resolve some family issues she's struggled with." Déjà vu ... immediately I remembered in my dream Miles gave me a slip of paper with a counselor's name, but it was a woman.

"I don't know if I could talk to anyone. I'm kind of private, you know, grew up fending for myself," I said, rejecting his kind offer.

"Well, you're talking to me now, aren't you?" Pause. Small smile. I breathed and shook my head yes.

So our conversation continued. Miles spent most of the afternoon seated at my dining table, listening and offering support, as I finally did exactly what I'd avoided for the past two weeks. I cried, admitted my part in misconstruing the relationship, and again voiced concerns about my fear of running into David.

"Ali, are you afraid of seeing David, or is there something more that's kept you here, locked in your apartment?" Miles asked, his chin propped in his hand, as he rested his elbow on the table.

"It's David," I quickly responded without thinking about the question. But then, I inhaled deeply and considered whether that was the truth. Was I afraid of David, or was it more?

"What do you mean?" I asked Miles, my eyes searching his, hoping that if I looked closely enough, he'd give me the answer.

"Well, you acknowledged you were a different person before David. I remember that woman." Miles grinned before continuing. "Not that who you were with David was bad, but you did change after you met him."

I unconsciously bit my lower lip as I considered his point.

"You became less sure of yourself. Let's just say your light didn't shine as brightly as it had before." After that statement, Miles paused, perhaps preventing himself from revealing more.

My head hung as I connected the dots. I had not only lost two years of my life, but I had also lost part of myself to David. But if I was no longer the same person I was when we met, then who was I? And how could I return to my former self?

We talked some more, but after a while, Miles looked at his watch, then apologized, saying he must be going. He and Madeline were meeting some friends for dinner.

As I walked him to the door, I realized we hadn't spoken about work or how awkwardly I left things.

"I'm sorry about the email telling you I was leaving Genesis," I humbly said. My body slackened as I admitted what had weighed heavily on my mind. I'd lied to Miles. He deserved better.

"I know you are," Miles said, scratching his beard. "What if I didn't accept that resignation yet? Let me think about some projects you could do at home while you get your life back together, OK?"

I hugged him, tears streaming down my face. "Thank you." That was all I could utter as I clung to Miles, knowing it would be some time until I had physical contact with another human being.

"Ali, I wish you would get some professional help. I'm going to email you the name and contact info for Madeline's therapist. And I'll be in touch after I figure out what you can do from home and how we will make this happen," Miles said as he put on his coat then opened the door. "But, in the meantime, I want you to think about that question I asked earlier. If it's not solely seeing David again that has you so unglued, what exactly is the real cause behind this retreat?" he asked, making a grand sweep with his hand, as if encompassing my entire apartment, the walls that kept me confined and separated from humanity.

I forced a brief smile as I said goodbye, thanking him for being such a good friend—actually my only friend. After he left, I securely bolted the door then sat down on my couch, wrapping the throw tightly around me as I began to think about what had just transpired. Why was I retreating, fleeing every known aspect of my life? What terrified me to the point of forgoing living for the safety of isolation?

Yet I had no answers. The more I questioned, the further down the rabbit hole I fell.

***

Miles's visit ten days ago forced me to take my head out of the sand. Since then, I've felt stuck, in a constant cycle of searching for some unobtainable answer. As I desperately dig for a root cause to my fears, it becomes apparent there's none to be found.

While before I feigned being OK, that is no longer the case. I admit I'm lost, uncertain, scared shitless. My world has become dark. Perhaps it always was. Maybe this entire time I've been pretending, creating a false reality of who I was and what I wanted.

The sad truth is, I don't know who I am. And I'm damned and determined to discover what, if anything, is left of my former self, who I was before David. I rehearse past conversations, hoping to find hidden clues, but none arise. I mentally review my actions, wondering if this might allow me insight, yet it's futile. And I analyze former decisions, questioning whether they were made by Allison, David's significant other, or Ali.

But no matter how hard I try, I am unable to piece together my true self. My days are spent going through the motions, reminding me of *Groundhog Day*. I get up, have breakfast, read the news, make my bed, get changed from pajamas to sweats, pull my hair back in a ponytail, and then curl up on the sofa and surf the channels for some sort of feel-good television show. At one o'clock, I have yogurt or leftovers from the prior night's meal. Then, around six, I begin to scan the fridge to decide what I am going to make for dinner. I barely sleep, spending the majority of the early-morning hours staring at the ceiling from my bed, shifting positions on my mattress, hoping I'll find comfort when I close my eyes. But that rarely occurs, as I'm barely rewarded with short spurts of slumber.

Ten days have passed since I've entered "phase two," a term I attached to this contemplative, inward searching stage of my illness. Phase one was denial, a sense I was fine as long as I kept my distance from everyone. But Miles changed all of that when he made me see it wasn't breaking up with David that caused me to hide—it was something much deeper.

CHAPTER 6

I've spent ten more days ruminating about the true meaning behind this sequestered state, and despite employing every technique I can think of, I cannot determine what's keeping me locked inside this apartment, secluded from reality. I actually wondered if it were all in my head, so earlier this morning, I decided it was time to venture outside and take a walk. After all, the sun was shining brightly this unusually warm late February morning.

After I finished breakfast and caught up on the news, I put on my puffy coat, walked out of my apartment, and descended the stairs into the communal lobby. Confident about heading outside, I actually caught a glimpse of a glow on my face as I passed the mirror in the lobby's entranceway. In fact, I swear I saw a bit of my old self.

Yet, as I was about to exit the apartment building, my body froze. It physically became impossible to make my way out the door. I tried. But as soon as I pushed open the heavy door and the cool, crisp air hit my face, every ounce of determination I had mustered left my body, propelling me back inside, up the steps, and into my safe haven.

And now I sit at my kitchen counter, wondering how everything got so fucked up. It was one thing when I *chose* to stay inside. But now, knowing I *cannot leave*, well, that is an entirely different story.

The past twenty days of self-contemplation have led me no closer to my truth. If anything, I'm more uncertain of what happened to me. *Am I going crazy? Do I need professional help?* I open the laptop sitting at the counter's edge and search for the email Miles sent regarding Madeline's therapist. After finding it, I reach for my phone then begin to dial the number. But I quickly cancel the call. I'm not ready. Where would I begin? And how would we meet? I'm unable to leave this apartment, as proven by this morning's disaster, and I doubt he makes house calls. No, there has to be a better way.

Recognizing I cannot do this alone and that I need help, I return to my laptop and begin googling, hoping to find some online resources. Surprisingly, there are many. But what I also find are suggested books, podcasts, and websites designed to help individuals like me—recluses.

Overwhelmed by the number of options, I slump onto the kitchen counter, cradling my head in the crook of my elbow. Do I call an online counseling center, hoping I can be connected with someone who knows what they're doing, or do I choose another route, finding my own mentors through other means?

Wary of an unknown individual giving me guidance, I decide to look at self-help sites, choosing those with the most recommendations.

After thirty minutes online, it becomes apparent how easy this is. I retrieve a notebook from the second drawer in my desk and begin to make notations of websites, practices, books, and gurus in the industry. Fully emersed, I'm intrigued with the wealth of information. After several hours, I rub my forehead, which is beginning to throb.

When I finally close my laptop, I'm shocked to see that it's already 8:15. I haven't eaten for close to seven hours and am now suddenly famished. But the fridge is empty, and unless I want to resort to peanut butter and jelly or fried eggs, which I don't, I must default to takeout. I call my go-to place and order Phở Bò Viên—pho with meatballs.

While waiting for the delivery driver to arrive, I pour a glass of white wine from a bottle in the back of the fridge that I'd been saving to share with David. As I sit at the kitchen counter and sip the sauvignon blanc, I begin to review what I'd written in my notebook. Reading over my notes, I'm amazed with the repeating themes: control, surrender, trust. These are the exact issues I've been struggling with.

Then, suddenly, my attention shifts to the cabinet door with the calendar hanging inside. I walk over to the cabinet, open it, and stare at the calendar. Today is February 29. I had no idea it was a leap year.

Leap.

I hear the voice again, the one that told me to stay safe. And now it's telling me to leap? Figuring it is only my mind playing tricks on me, I ignore it and return to the kitchen counter.

Thirty-five minutes later, I'm drinking a second glass of wine and eating a delicious container of steaming pho. Still reviewing the information from today's research, I'm confused as to what information is valid and what will prove futile. But maybe I *should leap*, take a chance, and pick something, anything, to move myself forward. After rereading my scribbles, I decide to download a book. But there are so many, where do I start?

As I rest my head in the palm of my hand, my eye catches a gift my hairdresser had given me last Christmas. I stare at this unopened green-and-yellow box filled with inspirational cards. According to her, these messages encourage you to look inward and discover positive ways of being. I certainly could use a dose of inspiration. So I retrieve the box and return to the table. *"Power Thought Cards"* is the title, and "Louise Hay" is written below. That name sounds familiar. Checking the pad of notes next to me, I see I'd written down several of the books that Louise Hay wrote.

Slowly, I open the colorful box and begin to examine the cheery plasticized cards inside. Each has a "pick-me-up" saying. After perusing a good third of the cards, I return them to their box, admitting this author knows a thing or two about getting better.

Kindle in hand, I search for books by Louise Hay. Surprised with how prolific she is, I download *The Power Is Within You*, as the write-up promises this book will assist the reader in overcoming emotional barriers. Sounds good to me, because I certainly don't know how to knock down these walls on my own.

Within minutes, I'm reading her book, totally absorbed in this entirely new genre—one that in the past I've dismissed, laughed at. Yet this might be the exact lifeline I've been hoping for.

Three hours later, mentally exhausted from the mind-expanding ideas I've read, I highlight the last passage:

"Trust is what we learn when we want to overcome our fears. It's called "taking a leap of faith" and trusting in the Power within that's connected to Universal Intelligence."

There is that word again: *leap.* Will trusting myself help me from being so afraid of losing control? Do I have that power within?

Lost in this thought, I leave the empty pho container on the counter as I shuffle to my bedroom and crawl under the sheets. Instead of staring at the ceiling above and squirming around for a comfortable position, my eyes shut, and before I'm able to begin processing today's events, I'm fast asleep.

***

I awaken to the sounds of birds chirping outside. Could spring be arriving so soon? Leaning over to the nightstand, I pick up my phone. Today is March 1.

For some unknown reason, this morning seems to proceed differently than most. I can't explain it, as my actions and routine remain the same. I drink my two cups of coffee, eat my yogurt with berries, and read the news online. But then, instead of retreating to the couch and turning on the television, my eyes move to the treadmill. I cannot remember the last time I ran on it. Before David, I was religious about running. It was a daily ritual. Not only did it help keep my body in shape, but it also calmed my mind, helped me focus. But after David came into my life, running, like so many other things, lost its importance.

Slowly, I rise from my chair and move toward the ignored piece of exercise equipment located to the left of the front window. For the past two years, its only function has been to hold delicates drying after a wash cycle. Looking closely, I see there's dust deep within the crevices of the control panel. I contemplate whether or not running would be a good idea, considering the farthest I've walked in the past month and a half has been up and down the stairs.

Yet something tells me otherwise. Then, with a new sense of conviction, I march into the bedroom, shed my robe and pajamas, and pull on running tights, a jog bra, my favorite Villanova T-shirt, and socks. After retrieving my running shoes from the back of the hall closet, I slide my feet into them, carefully tying double knots. Without hesitation, I step up onto the treadmill and turn it on, gradually increasing the speed and steadying myself by tightly gripping the side bars. My legs begin to move, somewhat awkwardly at first, but then with a more defined rhythm, determined to keep up with the speed of the tread.

Increasing the pace doesn't hurt my lungs or my legs, so I raise the incline to 1 percent and continue to add speed, coaxing my legs to turn over at the higher speed. Before I know it, I'm gliding. Beads of sweat begin to form on my forehead, slowly dripping down onto my shirt, making splatters on the moving tread. But it's not the physical sensation I notice the most. It's the internal release, a freedom of sorts propelling me forward, faster, farther. Damn, I like this. It's at this exact moment I begin to remember a tiny glimpse of who Ali is, rather who I was before David.

CHAPTER 7

Every muscle in my legs throbs. It's as though this creaky body belongs to a seventy-five-year-old, not a thirty-two-year-old. Oh yeah, the treadmill … I probably overdid it. But it felt so good.

Several minutes later, teeth brushed, face washed, and hair pulled up in a clip, I grab my robe and head toward the kitchen. After turning on the coffee pot, I retrieve my laptop and scan the incoming mail for daily news reports.

While I've begun each day with this exact routine since quarantining myself, I wonder if today might be different. Fully aware it's March 2, the beginning of a new week and a new month, I make the conscious decision to begin my reemergence. Inspired by what I read the other evening, I contemplate ways of making today special, unlike every other day in self-isolation. Louise Hay recommends creating affirmations to help manifest goals. Perhaps proclaiming something aloud will make this transition easier for me.

"I am ready and able to return to work." My voice bellows, strong and determined. But the only living thing that can witness my declaration is the lone plant on the desk by the window. Regardless, my ears absorb the vibration, so that counts for something.

After finishing my breakfast, sunny-side up eggs over a piece of toast, I decide to try again. Maybe March is the month I'm meant to reemerge. After all, it's the time of rebirth.

I check the weather report, noting the forecast is not as nice as the last time I attempted to go outside. So I add a fleece under my puffy coat, put on a woolen hat and gloves, and then begin the descent to the lobby.

Inhaling deeply, I turn the knob of the apartment building, push open the door, and hesitantly place my right foot on the worn rubber mat that lays on top of the cement step leading to the walkway. I pause and look around. There is no one in sight. Slowly, I move my left leg forward, then my right, out of the safe apartment building. My right arm continues to hold the door open, allowing access back into the building at a moment's notice.

For several minutes, I remain motionless. Unsure of my next move, I know that if I want to proceed, I must let go of the door handle. Yet, as much as I want, I cannot release the knob. But, instead of becoming dejected at my thwarted attempt to go outside, I decide to celebrate what I am able to do. It isn't much, but it is more than before. A baby step.

As I stand frozen in the doorway, two women and an older gentleman stroll down the sidewalk in front of the apartment building. The gentleman holds a pink leash with a large golden retriever on the other end. The women are walking smaller dogs. One has a curly poodle mix, and the other holds two leashes connected to Yorkshire terriers. The trio sees me and smiles. Clinging to the doorknob, I attempt my best happy face and nod in their direction. I watch them, walking and talking together, a simple action so easy for them but incredibly difficult for me. The dogs seem to enjoy one another's company. Parading down the sidewalk, heads held high, they stop occasionally to sniff at clumps of grass.

Letting out a big sigh, I wonder what is so freaking hard about me taking twenty steps to the sidewalk so that I, too, can go for a walk, be outside, and perhaps have a conversation with another human being. Overwhelmed with the realization that this is truly messed up, way beyond what I can admit, I turn around and retreat inside, up to my cloistered apartment.

One step forward, two backward. Wishing I could do more, I wave the white flag, admitting defeat as I plop down on the sofa. Curled into a tight ball with my head buried in my hands, I feel my eyes well up with tears. This is much more serious than I was willing to admit. Should I call the therapist? But there's the issue with actually going to see him. At a loss of what to do to get myself "well," I allow time to cry it out and let my emotions flow.

After releasing what is likely layers of unexpressed sorrow, I take my Kindle from the table next to me and open to the bookmark in *The Power Is Within You*. I continue reading:

"So, it really doesn't matter what anybody else did to you or what they taught you in the past. Today is a new day. You are now in charge. Now is the moment in which you are creating the future in your life and your world. It really doesn't matter what I say either, because only you can do the work. Only you can change the way you think and feel and act. I'm just saying that you can. You definitely can because you have a Higher Power within you that can break you free from these patterns if you allow it."

Is the power within me? It sounds so simple, but if this is true, then I am the only one who can get myself out of this, not a therapist, though he could provide guidance and speed up the process. If I could only leave this apartment, but I can't, at least not right now.

For some unknown reason, I have an urge to look outside. Listening to my intuition, I rise, walk to the window, and press my forehead against the cold glass, peering onto Haverford Avenue. I watch as the older man and his two female companions return, heading back in the opposite direction.

The man, who looks to be in his seventies, has a weathered face and sports a heavy beige winter coat. Thick white hair peeks out from beneath the rim of his navy tweed cap. His dog, no doubt a female from her light pink leash and collar, proudly walks in a slow and controlled manner. The dog looks fairly young, yet she doesn't pull her owner. Instead, she keeps a steady pace with the three smaller dogs.

The two women with him appear to be close to his age. The lady on his left is short and seems to be a bit pudgy under her thick puffy coat. But it is her radiant expression that catches my attention. From my window, which is about twenty yards from the sidewalk, I detect a sparkle in her eyes, perhaps mimicking her frosted pixie haircut. She has a bounce to her step. Likewise, her dog, a fluffy midsize poodle mix, gingerly prances next to the golden retriever.

The third in the group, who's tethered to two small gray-and-beige dogs, is much taller than her friend, closer to the gentleman's height. Her hair's short and chic, a beautiful shade of light gray. This lady wears a knee-length Burberry-looking coat covering slim black pants.

Gracefully striding in mid-heeled black boots, I'd expect to see her on a street in the Upper East Side of Manhattan, not on a sidewalk in Narberth, Pennsylvania. A side of me appreciates her sense of fashion—a trait I certainly lack.

Something about this trio fascinates me. As I watch them converse, the short lady giggles when the gentleman points to something across the street. But the elegant woman only smiles demurely as she shakes her head. What are they talking about? Feeling left out in an odd sort of way, I turn away from the window, resigned to the fact I'll never know their stories, what their dogs' names are, or why they are walking together. Is one of the women married to the man? Are they related?

Distracted by a ping from my laptop, I leave my post at the window to see if I've received anything remotely exciting. Perhaps there's a sale at one of my go-to online stores, or maybe there's a news alert. Instead, I find an email from Miles. The subject line reads "Proposed Project," exactly what I've been waiting for. Without hesitation, I click it open, praying Miles is truly offering me an opportunity to work from home.

Ali,

I hope you are doing well. Since we last spoke, I've spent a great deal of time considering possible ways you could support Genesis's operations through a remote working relationship. I've thought of several options, and after discussing these ideas with the administrative team, I've come up with the following proposal.

One of the areas in which our company has fallen short is in our ability to analyze the profitability of the various software offerings. The truth is, we've grown so quickly and focused more on product development than earnings. While this is not a project I would typically give to my top engineer, I do believe that with your experience, you could offer a distinct perspective.

In essence, I would like for you to develop a complete analysis determining whether or not we are putting our resources (time, money, and effort) into our most profitable product lines. I am not going to suggest a procedure for you to conduct this research. Instead, I will rely upon your knowledge, innovation, and enthusiasm to complete this project.

Please plan to meet with me at 9:00 on Wednesday, April 1, to share your findings.

Additionally, I trust you will also be returning to work on this date.

Best,
Miles

This email is a dream come true, until the final paragraph. April 1 is less than a month away. While it will be more than ample time to complete this task, will I be ready to go back to work in four weeks?

Later that night, as I lie awake in bed rehashing the content of Miles's email, my thoughts leave my boss's request and return to the scene from the window. I cannot stop thinking about these three individuals. The looks on their faces, their mannerisms, and the way in which they interacted with one another intrigue me. Even how they walked down the sidewalk was fascinating. I begin to imagine what their life stories truly are. Except this time, I take the liberty to fill in the blanks, creating real-life biographies for these mystery Dog Walkers …

Johnny Matthews and his golden retriever, Maggie, live in a small Victorian home three blocks from my apartment. He is a widower. His wife died five years ago. Shortly afterward, his grown-up kids decided he needed companionship, so they bought him a puppy and Johnny named her Maggie.

Johnny and Maggie are inseparable. He takes her in the car whenever he does errands, and he always brings her with him to visit his kids, all of whom live out of state. While Maggie cannot replace Ellen, his sweet wife whom he lost to cancer, this golden retriever does her best to fill the void in Johnny's heart. Johnny, a retired dentist, and Maggie spend their days walking in the park, puttering around the house, and watching sports on TV. At night, Johnny enjoys a nice cocktail and a frozen dinner while Maggie loyally sits by his side. After Ellen passed, many widows tried to snag Johnny. But his love for his former wife was so strong he could never open his heart to another woman ... of course, except for Maggie.

No one knows why Jackie Sherman, who lives two doors down from Johnny, chose to remain single. Speculation is she was having too much fun and refused to settle down. However, at age forty, she chose to adopt a young child from Brazil. The backstory begins with a trip she took to São Paulo where she met a gorgeous, wealthy man, the first person she considered marrying. However, before they could take their relationship to the next level, he mysteriously disappeared, leaving behind two things: a large bank account in Jackie's name and a daughter named Sylvia. Naturally, Jackie felt compelled to care for the girl. After promptly adopting her, Jackie and Sylvia returned to Philadelphia where Jackie provided her daughter with endless love and the finest education.

Fast-forward thirty-five years ... Sylvia, her husband, and two daughters now live in Miami, and Jackie continues to enjoy life to the fullest, comfortably supported with money left to her by this mystery man. Jackie and Sylvia visit each other frequently. During one of Sylvia's trips to Philadelphia, she bought her mom the most adorable miniature goldendoodle. She feared her mom was lonely and thought a dog would be a great companion. Jackie named the puppy Penny, and it's been a true love story since.

Like Johnny, Eleanor Jepson also lost her spouse, but to a heart attack, seven years ago. At the time, they lived in a penthouse apartment in Rittenhouse Square. Eleanor would spend her days shopping on Walnut Street, with visits to exclusive salons for hair and nail appointments. She and her husband, Philip, dined at the finest restaurants and enjoyed the symphony. However, several years after her husband died, Eleanor decided that city life no longer suited her, so she sold her apartment and bought another at the Corinthian in Bala Cynwyd. She also added two dogs, sibling Yorkshire terriers named Louie and Lucy, to her new way of life. Since Eleanor and Philip never had children, Louie and Lucy became the light of Eleanor's eye. While Eleanor continues to spend time downtown, Jackie, her best friend from growing up in Chestnut Hill, lives nearby in Narberth, and they've made it a habit to walk their dogs daily.

One day, Jackie invited her neighbor, Johnny, to join them on their dog walk. Not only did Eleanor and Jackie enjoy sharing their walks with a delightful gentleman, but also Louie, Lucy, and Penny adored Maggie.

And then my mind goes blank as I drift off to sleep.

CHAPTER 8

I wake up oddly refreshed. Then I remember the story—the one I made up last night about the Dog Walkers. Grinning, I replay the particulars for each character, lingering in bed a bit longer than normal.

After a hearty breakfast, curiosity rules my thoughts as I rack my brain to remember the exact time they walked by yesterday. I think it may have been around ten. Midmorning, I leave the dining table and transition to the window. Seated on the chair that I had placed there earlier, I wait in anticipation to see if Johnny, Jackie, and Eleanor walk by with their pets, Maggie, Penny, Louie, and Lucy.

While wondering whether or not the Dog Walkers will appear, I'm drawn to the tiny green leaves sprouting from the ground. Daffodils! As a little girl, I was captivated by these flowers. I loved how quickly they'd pop up from nowhere. Mom would call them "harbingers of spring." I sigh, recalling her round cheeks and light blonde hair. But what I remember most about Mom is the bubble-gum-pink lipstick she insisted on wearing every time she left the house. It's been seventeen years since she passed, a lifetime ago.

Returning to the present, I notice a hint of pink starting to appear on the branches of a maple tree outside of the building. Spring is here and things are starting to change all around me. But when will a shift occur inside of me? A heaviness forms in my chest as I'm reminded of how "unwell" I am. Yet I continue to focus on the sidewalk, waiting.

Although my Walkers are nowhere to be seen, many others travel up and down this route. There's a visible unevenness to the cement squares, caused by the rising roots from the large oak trees hovering above. But that doesn't seem to bother anyone. Actually, I can't believe how busy Haverford Avenue is. There are people walking by themselves, with dogs, with others. Morning must be prime time around here. In a fifteen-minute span, I witness a multitude of faces parading up and down the avenue, some pausing to greet friends, others strutting straight ahead, never glancing at those they pass.

The similarity between dogs and their owners becomes obvious. In fact, I begin to giggle when I see two middle-aged men walk a little pug wearing a doggie jean jacket. Damn, this is freaking hilarious. How could I have missed all of this action happening right outside of my apartment? Then I remember—I'd been at work, doing my job, being a productive, normal human being. Once again, I'm forced to acknowledge something's still wrong with me and needs to be fixed.

I pause, appreciative of the world that exists outside these four walls. It kills me that I am unable to join in. Leaving this place should not be this difficult. Why am I so afraid?

My fall down the oh-so-familiar rabbit hole, the one I journey to multiple times each day, is interrupted when the Dog Walkers appear, their four dogs proudly leading the way. Suddenly everything seems lighter with their presence. I lean closer to the window, laughing a bit when I notice how Maggie's eight times the size of the two smallest dogs. But she takes a back seat of sorts and follows them, sniffing tree trunks and signposts.

Mesmerized, I remain poised at the window as I closely observe their interactions. Jackie's talking and laughing while her two companions shake their heads, as if this is a familiar story, one frequently told by their cheery friend. The dogs also have their unique exchanges. It's as if Louie and Lucy are the dominant duo, followed by Maggie and then Penny. The tiny gray-and-tan Yorkshires prance in an aloof manner, perhaps a bit like Eleanor, as they lead the way. Maggie certainly doesn't seem to mind. Perhaps she's happy to be outside with Johnny and her dog friends. And Penny, well, she appears the most cautious of all of the dogs. Which cracks me up as her owner, Jackie, seems anything but timid.

But then my Dog Walkers pass out of sight. Reluctantly, I leave my post and return to the kitchen to refill my coffee cup. After sitting down at the dining table, I sip the warm brew and reread Miles's email. Knowing an official response is expected, I close my eyes and consider his request. The project should be manageable, something I'm sure Miles knows. It's the second part, that I present the recommendation to him and return to work, that's concerning. And he chose April Fool's Day—how ironic.

Taking a tie from my wrist, I pull my hair back into a ponytail as I consider my options. There are only two. Either I accept his proposal and figure out a way to *get well*, or I decline, acknowledging I am "unfixable." Biting down on my lip, a habit I started in college when faced with a difficult assignment, I see the method behind Miles's actions. He must think I am capable of doing this, or otherwise, he wouldn't have given me this timeline. So he believes in me, but do I? Can I trust in myself?

Knowing that refusing this proposal is pretty much a nail in the coffin of my confinement, accepting this challenge, well, that is a step forward toward my freedom.

It's then I remember the *Power Thought Cards* now sitting on the counter by the coffee maker. Slowly, I walk toward this box, take out the cards, and blindly draw one.

I claim my own powers, and I lovingly create my own reality.

This is exactly what the book was saying: I and only I have the power to change the way I feel and act. Knowing there are few coincidences in life, I decide this *Power Thought Card* might be a signal of sorts. Without allowing a moment to change my mind, I go to the desk, sit down, and begin to type my response.

Miles,

Thank you for this opportunity. I promise I won't disappoint you. I look forward to sharing the report with you on April 1. And I will be prepared to return to work at that time.

Best,
Ali

There, it's done. I hit Send then say a silent prayer I won't later regret this decision. Yet the idea of giving up on myself, well, that is unacceptable. While I am far from knowing exactly who I am, I am sure of one thing ... I am not a quitter, never was, and never will be.

Opening a new document in Excel, I dive in, creating a spreadsheet to lay out the necessary steps for completing this project. Labeling columns and rows, my fingers skillfully move as I organize my schedule for the next month. Forty minutes later, I hit Print. Standing to stretch, I yawn as I bend over to retrieve the document from the printer located on a small table to the right of the desk. After finding thumbtacks in the top desk drawer, I meticulously pin my spreadsheet on the bulletin board hanging above the printer. Color coded and clearly labeled, this schedule will keep me focused and on track.

My mind then shifts to the second term of this assignment, that I return to work by April 1. It was easy to create the necessary benchmarks in order to complete the project on time. However, how will I know if *I* am on track to go back to Genesis? Where are those reference points? Can I create a similar document to guide me toward becoming well?

Conscious no such program exists, I force myself to consider what I must do between now and then, so I am capable of driving to work, entering the building, going up the elevator, and then walking into headquarters without losing my shit.

While my brain is able to rehearse these necessary steps, I become stuck as to what happens once the presentation's over. I can pretty much plan for the first part. But after that, I have no control of what will come my way as well as how I will respond if presented with a difficult situation, like seeing David.

Acknowledging Rome wasn't built in one day, I take a breath and express gratitude for having done so much in one morning. I may have to accept that I won't know the answers to how life will look once I return to Genesis. What will my response be when I see David, and how will I handle coworkers who pry a bit, curious as to why I was away for so long? Will I become defensive, or will I smile sweetly and give some clever answer? Slowly, as I consider possible options, a calmness comes over me, as if to suggest all will be fine. I guess Louise Hay was right. In order to heal, I must have faith that I can handle whatever comes my way.

Thud! I turn toward the front window in time to notice a bird bounce off the glass. I rush over to see if it's OK. Luckily, it's alive, sitting on the grass below, appearing to be only stunned. Within moments, it shakes its head before flying away. Am I like this bird, unconsciously floating around, clueless to life happening around me, and about to crash into the nearest window?

As this thought flashes across my mind, I see another Dog Walker. She's a woman, somewhere around my age. With her is a medium-sized mixed-breed dog resembling a small German shepherd, but with floppier ears. I observe the woman stop, give some type of command, then pull something out of her pocket. Immediately her dog turns and sits, facing his owner. In response, she moves her hand toward his mouth and gives him some sort of treat. The dog gobbles down the reward, and then the two continue ahead. How do you train a dog? Growing up, we didn't have pets because my father was allergic.

Yet, since I was a child, dogs have fascinated me. I lean forward, my forehead pressing firmly into the cool glass. Then I see another Walker approach with two huskies. The man, who appears to be in his late thirties, has an auburn beard and looks totally jacked underneath his flannel shirt and jeans. But it's his dogs that intrigue me. One is black and white, while the other, slightly smaller, is a beautiful silver and white. The larger of the two walks in a majestic manner, but the smaller dog seems a bit submissive in her actions.

Then, in a few moments, all of that changes as the big husky squats, looks around as if embarrassed, and then does his business before regaining his composure and returning to the other dog's side, apparently ready to continue his walk. The owner turns his head in both directions as if deciding whether or not to pick up his dog's mess. Reluctantly, the man pulls a plastic grocery bag from his back jean pocket, bends down, and cleans up the poop, just as a family with yet another dog walks in this direction. Knotting the bag before holding it by the end in his left fingertips, as if it were infectious, he easily controls both dogs' leashes in his other hand. I find myself laughing as they move out of my field of vision. Here is a lumberjack of a man who looks absolutely ridiculous holding a bag of dog poop, far away from his body, as if this is the grossest thing in the world.

But then my attention shifts to the family. In addition to the parents, there's a little girl with curly black hair and a younger boy, whose dark hair is neatly trimmed. They look like an iconic all-American family, accentuated with a perfectly matching puppy. Unsure of the breed, this dog is mostly black and white, but with a touch of gray and brown. His fur looks soft, and he energetically runs in circles, tangling his leash in between the kids' legs.

After the family passes my building, heading west on Haverford, I realize I've been mesmerized by these Dog Walkers for close to twenty minutes. Conscious of the parade of people and dogs outside, where I apparently am incapable of being, I suddenly find it not so easy to breathe.

I've got to get myself together.

I look at my watch. It's a quarter till noon. Then I glance at the bulletin board, noting nothing more needs to happen today, for my project at least. For me, well, I need a miracle to meet the real deadline … the one where I walk into Genesis and return to work.

CHAPTER 9

Later that night, after I've brushed my teeth, washed my face, and applied face cream, I crawl into bed and turn out the light. Instinctively I reach for the remote, as I've started to doze off watching episodes of *Seinfeld*, *Friends*, or *How I Met Your Mother*. But as I begin to scroll through the cable guide, I change my mind and turn the TV off. I have a better idea. Why not tune into *The Dog Walkers*, my own story? After all, today there were new characters introduced into this drama, or is it a comedy? Slowly, I rehash my time at the front window, remembering who I saw, what they were wearing, and how they acted. Then, I focus on the dogs … their shapes, colors, and mannerisms. Closing my eyes, I allow my imagination to flow, and before I know it, I'm drifting into a serene state as I create details to my characters, the ones who could be my friends, someday, if I am ever able to go outside.

Jeremy and Will have been partners for three years. Jeremy is an architect at a firm in Old City, while Will practices optometry at Wills Eye Hospital downtown. Of course, the name coincidence is a running joke with their friends. This couple recently bought an old stone two-story home three blocks off of Montgomery Avenue. While both loved living downtown in Old City, they decided to renovate this home, viewing it as a fun project for the two of them to invest in. Jeremy loved the challenge of keeping the integrity of the original house while infusing it with a modern flair. Will, who admittedly lacks the foresight his partner has, had great appreciation for how the dilapidated structure transformed into a magnificent home. Jeremy and Will officially moved in last month. At first, they were a bit concerned whether or not Jasper, their pug, the one I saw in the jean jacket, would enjoy life in the suburbs. But Jasper, like his owners, has adjusted beautifully.

***

Jennifer Mattern, a single thirty-three-year-old originally from Conshohocken, manages a fitness center on City Line Avenue. Only open for two years, this innovative gym is constantly packed, especially before and after work hours. It has the most up-to-date equipment and offers a host of classes. Sure, stay-at-home moms fill the midmorning yoga and mat Pilates classes, but the majority of clients exercise around their work schedules. Prior to taking this position, Jennifer was a trainer at a studio in Haverford. However, she wanted more responsibility and steady hours, so she applied for this head position and was hired last July. Then, in September, she adopted Roxie, a classic mutt she rescued from the Humane Society. Jennifer and Roxie quickly bonded. In fact, Roxie goes to work with Jennifer, remaining in her back office while Jennifer interacts with clients or employees. The shelter told Jennifer that Roxie's former owner was a heroin user who abandoned her. Jennifer's unsure of Roxie's actual age, but when she first took Roxie to the vet, the veterinarian thought the dog was about a year old. While in pretty good shape, Roxie appeared a bit malnourished and was sometimes skittish around strangers. No wonder, after all Roxie had been through.

After finding a new job and adopting a dog, Jennifer, who had been living with a college friend in a duplex in East Falls, moved to a one-bedroom apartment off of Wynnwood Avenue, close to the train station. She loves living by herself. Her friends ask her if she's lonely, but she's not. She's got Roxie to keep her company.

***

Lucas Watts, the bearded guy who almost didn't pick up the dog poop, loves dogs and grew up with German shepherds. At age nineteen, he enlisted in the Marines and served two tours in Afghanistan. Now he's thirty-nine and no longer in the armed forces, having left the Marines in 2015. Presently, Lucas is a head foreman for an upscale Mainline contractor. Oh, and he moonlights as an Uber driver, because the extra money is too good to pass up.

After returning to civilian life, he moved into a small home on Conway Avenue in Narberth, which was formerly his grandfather's. Lucas was the only grandchild, so his mother's father left the house to him. Lucas always regretted he was in the Middle East when his granddaddy passed. They had such a close bond and had written each other weekly. He vividly remembers his mom calling him to let him know what had happened. Unable to return for the funeral practically destroyed him. Yet he was there in spirit.

Shortly after moving into this new home, he was searching Craigslist when he found an ad for two husky puppies, a male and female from the same litter. Something told him they were meant to be with him, so without hesitation, he responded. Four days later, he had two yapping puppies crated in his new living room. He named the boy Walter, after his grandfather, and the female Lydia, for his grandmother. He knew it was a bit strange, but it gave him comfort as it allowed him a sort of reunion with the generation that had passed.

***

The Andersons are originally from Chicago. They moved here last June, after Alexis's final day in first grade at their local elementary school in Buffalo Grove. Tom Anderson, rather Dr. Tom Anderson, had recently accepted a position in Obstetrics at Lankenau. Unsure where they ultimately wanted to live, Tom and his wife, Jada, chose to rent a home in Merion Station, allowing Alexis to go to Cynwyd Elementary School for second grade while they decided where they would ultimately settle. Her little brother, Isaiah, doesn't begin kindergarten until this upcoming fall. While Isaiah was too young to fight the move, Alexis became inconsolable when her parents shared they were going to be living near Philadelphia. The six-year-old cried relentlessly about leaving her girlfriends. Pennsylvania seemed so far away. Her dramatics earned her a puppy, as her parents convinced themselves it would make the move easier for Alexis. So, as soon as they settled into their large house on Avon Road, they bought the Australian shepherd puppy whom Alexis named Chloe. Now the Anderson family is fully immersed in the suburban Philadelphia life. In fact, Tom and Jada made an offer on the house they are renting. And Chloe, well, she loves her new family. Jada walks her to the bus stop in the mornings and afternoons, and the kids and Mom take a big walk every day, two on weekend days.

***

I wake up before the alarm sounds, energized and with a smile on my face. Entranced by my backstories for the Dog Walkers, I lightheartedly pop out of bed. Within five minutes, I am in front of the coffee maker, watching the French roast stream into the glass pot. Unable to think about anything but the Dog Walkers,

I wonder if there's any truth to my assumptions. Have I correctly predicted any details of their lives? When the coffee maker stops dripping, I fill my mug and then sit down at the kitchen counter, enjoying the warm brew.

Look.

It's the voice again. Unsure of what to do or where to look, I get up from the stool and walk over to the window. It's early. None of the Dog Walkers should be out. They pass by later, after I've eaten breakfast and caught up on the news.

As I sit down on the chair and lean my cheek against the glass, I realize the window's not so cold. How unusual … it's probably due to the warmer than normal weather, nothing more. The sun shines brightly as I observe the squirrels playfully scurrying throughout the tree limbs. Then out of the corner of my eye, I see a man with a dog. He's unfamiliar, not one of the normal Dog Walkers whose schedules I'm beginning to notice. Since he's wearing a hoodie, it's difficult to determine his age or what he looks like. But he's medium height, and I can see wisps of dark hair escaping the confines of his hooded sweatshirt. Tethered to him is a beautiful black lab. I'm unsure whether the dog's male or female, yet I'd guess male based on the green leash and collar as well as its stature. While not that big, this dog appears strong and has a broad head.

Peering through the window, as much as I try, I can't make out what this guy looks like. His pace is slow and steady. His shuffling feet momentarily stop when he turns his head toward my window for a few moments. But from what I can see, he's not looking my way. It's as though he's lost deep in thought, perhaps carrying the world on his shoulders. The only clue I can decipher regarding his identity is the "LEHIGH" printed on the front of his sweatshirt. But it doesn't mean he went to that college. Maybe a sibling attended, or a girlfriend.

The lab pulls his owner, forcing him to continue down the sidewalk. As the front view transitions to the back, I can't help but become aware of how well his jeans fit and the broadness of his shoulders beneath his baggy sweatshirt. Something twinges inside me. It's a feeling I haven't had for a while. This sensation pulsates throughout my body. Why won't he turn around and come back this way?

Then he's gone. Vanished. Out of my view. My upbeat attitude leaves with him as I find myself, once again, alone at this window, watching others live a life I am incapable of experiencing. Damn it! What is wrong with me?

My throat begins to tighten and my shoulders cave forward. Then the trembling starts, and before I know it, I'm slowly crumbling to the floor beneath the windowsill, spilling drops of coffee on my robe. I cannot continue this way. But I don't know how to make it stop.

CHAPTER 10

Cupping my chin in my left hand, I stare at my keyboard, hoping letters will magically emerge on my laptop's screen to form a miraculous message, telling me exactly what I must do to fix myself. But the screen remains blank. Of course, I must figure this out by myself.

While daylight savings began ten days ago and yesterday the world celebrated Saint Patrick's Day, I am frozen in time, no closer to returning to work on April Fool's Day. Yet I'm able to focus on my assignment. Analyzing data and formulating preliminary recommendations for Miles provides comfort in a strange way. Working with numbers has always made me happy. Numbers are concrete, manageable, understandable, and reliable. There are no misinterpretations from faulty assumptions, ulterior motives, or intentional deceptions, like there are with people.

I stand up from my desk to look out the front window. Entranced by spring's landscape, I see that the entire world is about to bloom—everything, that is, except for me. Like a flower bud that remains closed tight or a chick that is incapable of hatching from its shell, I'm stalled, unable to leave this apartment.

However, a small part of me remains hopeful. Reading has helped. I've devoured seven books in the past fourteen days. While each author offers a unique perspective, their themes appear to overlap. I guess it all boils down to trusting and letting go, concepts

I may intellectually understand but have no clue how to put into practice. Perhaps I need more time.

Besides voraciously reading and regularly running on the treadmill, I've been diligently watching the Dog Walkers. In fact, I've established a mental map documenting their routines. Once I realized each Dog Walker has a particular pattern, it became simple to chart who was going to show up when. While some are religious with their habits, others, like the Andersons, are more apt to mix things up, venture out at different times. Yet I'm pretty good at predicting when this family will walk by. It seems to mostly depend on Isaiah.

However, it's Johnny, Jackie, and Eleanor I enjoy the most. I can trust that every morning they'll show up outside of my window, first heading west, then returning east. As they travel down the tree-lined street, a calmness comes over me, as if what is supposed to occur has happened.

My daily schedule during this phase two has become routine. After breakfast, I clean up the dishes then move to my desk, becoming completely immersed in my assignment. Automatically, I seem to stop right around the time the trio makes their first pass. While they are walking, I do a few chores, like change the laundry or take something out of the freezer to defrost. Sometimes I'll dust or vacuum, a small break while I wait for them to return.

It's only after they make their final pass that I return to work. Then I break for lunch around one and do a few things here and there, intermittently watching the midday Dog Walkers before I sit back down at my desk.

Around six, I close my laptop, change into running clothes, and climb on the treadmill. While running, I gaze out the window, observing the evening Dog Walkers. Most are familiar, like Will and Jeremy with their pug or Lucas with his huskies. Occasionally there are new faces. This intrigues me, and I later create backstories to these new Walkers, people I have yet to meet but imagine knowing well.

Evenings are as predictable as the days. I make a simple dinner, pour myself a glass of wine, then read. Usually I climb into bed around ten, allowing an hour of television before the timer automatically turns it off.

While not ideal, my schedule fits my needs—at least it does for now, until I figure out a phase three. But I'm eating well, exercising, working, expanding my mind. In general, my life has become more balanced. Except, of course, I'm unable to leave my apartment.

***

I emit a loud exhale, shoulders sliding down my back to their natural position. The report is nearly complete. Only a few tweaks are needed before it's ready. While Miles requested specific outcomes, I've broadened the scope and added additional components to this presentation. Doing so better demonstrates the current profitability of our product lines. This is something the old Ali would have done … before I met David and became Allison.

I sit up straighter, acknowledging that slowly I may be returning to who I was. My jaw loosens at this thought as I return my gaze to the laptop screen. Yet I keep an eye on my watch. Jackie, Eleanor, and Johnny are soon due. My mind drifts into the land of the Dog Walkers as my brain struggles to focus on work. But I can't help but wonder about him, the unnamed Dog Walker who hasn't returned. I know nothing about this guy, except he's probably pretty amazing looking under his big sweatshirt and he could have some connection to Lehigh University.

When I hear a thud against the window, my heart drops as I realize another bird has hit the glass. I race to the window and look below, happily confirming there's no dead bird on the walkway or in the shrubs. I say a silent thank-you to God for letting the bird survive. Sometimes I question whether anything higher exists. David was an atheist and constantly rolled his eyes at my Catholic upbringing. Yet, now, after all I've read these past few weeks, I believe there may be more than solely this life, perhaps something greater than I was brought up to believe. Like so much lately, I just don't know.

As I stand watch by the front window, waiting for my trio to appear, my mind returns to the stranger, the one with no name. Who is this man? A flame begins to flicker, and warmth slowly spreads throughout my core. I desperately want to see him again, know his story, understand why he's only come by once. Or has he walked by more frequently, and I'm the one who missed him?

The whole thing doesn't make sense. Was that a random walk-by? Does he even live here? He could have been visiting his parents, a friend, anyone for that matter. As I try to put together this mysterious puzzle, I sense my energy rising, as if I'm supposed to fill in the missing pieces. Leaning against the glass, I gaze toward the green-tinged branches hanging over the sidewalk and allow my imagination to run wild, creating a backstory for this man without a name.

Stephen Blackwell works for the government, the CIA to be exact. Stationed in Washington, DC, he returns to the Philadelphia suburbs, specifically Narberth, once a month to visit his mother who lives by herself in the house he grew up in.

It's a simple home: white-painted siding, black shutters, a small fenced-in backyard where his mother, Jan, grows tomatoes, green beans, zucchini, and asparagus in a raised flower bed she bought at the local garden store. Her ten-year-old lab, Mia, keeps Jan company. But his mom is fine with being alone. It's been that way since Stephen left for Lehigh, close to twenty years ago. The fact is, it was always only the two of them. Stephen's dad was never a part of his life. Jan and he only had a brief relationship. In fact, this man didn't know he had a son.

After graduating with a degree in mechanical engineering, Stephen was offered a job at Lockheed Martin in Bethesda, Maryland. He worked there for eight years, quickly advancing through his department. But it became apparent he wanted more, yet he wasn't sure what more meant. It was at this time that he was contacted by an Agent Green, Sam Green, about meeting to discuss a possible position. Immediately, Stephen knew this would be a major shift, not only professionally, but also personally. While secrecy was important at Lockheed Martin, working for the CIA would be a totally different ball game. He'd learned a great deal from his current job, but what could he offer the country's highest intelligence agency? Why did they recruit him?

One thing led to another, and now Stephen's finishing his seventh year at Langley. He spends some of his time traveling to known and unknown locations, but the majority of his days are spent at the CIA's headquarters.

Yet, once a month, he returns to Narberth to visit his mother. They're tight. She's all he has. While Stephen's been in several long-term relationships, none of them have been meaningful, at least to him. The endings were undoubtedly painful, promises of friendships that never transpired. That's why he now avoids commitment. It's easier to keep things simple, at the purely physical level. Doing so prevents others from getting hurt and him from feeling guilty.

Two years ago, while at a friend's house for a cookout, Stephen met Burton. Actually, he met Burton and his seven siblings … and mom. Apparently, his friend's wife was also a dog breeder. All of the most recent litter's puppies were claimed except for one.

While technically the runt of the litter, this little guy looked vibrant and strong. And, he had a huge personality.

Stephen left that cookout with a new roommate ... an eight-week-old black lab. At first, he was conflicted about having a puppy and second-guessed his decision. His travel schedule was so unpredictable, and he didn't want to leave a dog in a kennel. The next morning, he told his neighbor, Brett, about his predicament, as Brett had a female chocolate lab. In no time, Brett convinced Stephen that adding a dog to his life was the right move. Plus, he agreed to take Burton whenever Stephen traveled.

While a part of Stephen debates whether it was fair to adopt Burton, considering his haphazard lifestyle, he's found comfort in the fact that his dog has two families. Watching the neighbor's daughters' faces light up whenever they see Burton helps Stephen be at peace with this somewhat unusual arrangement. They even walk him during the day when Stephen's at work. It's become a win-win situation for everyone.

This "runt" with soft floppy ears and big paws grew to eighty pounds and wedged his way into Stephen's heart. In fact, this dog opened up a side of Stephen he didn't know existed. Finally, someone else's needs trumped his own. Stephen learned about unconditional love from a black lab pup, one he had no intention of bringing into his life. It happened out of the blue when he went to that cookout. Yet on that day he made a promise to Burton. Stephen swore he'd be there for him, no matter what. Yes, his job would require that he travel, but he'd always come home.

I smile, somewhat relieved to finally have a backstory for this mystery man. Then, when I least expect it, the voice reappears.

Surrender.

As she whispers these words, the individual letters pop into my mind, appearing as flashing lights on a movie theater marquee.

What do I need to surrender to? As I try to figure out this message, I lean into the window, the smooth glass cooling my face. I've let go of so much—my relationship, going to work, the outside world. What else is left to surrender?

I watch as a robin lands on the branch directly in front of the window. The bird stares in at me, tilting its little head to the side, as if it is trying to say something. I stand up and begin to pace around the living area. What does all of this mean? Even the damn bird is looking at me as if I'm supposed to have the answers. Surrender? I squeeze my eyes tightly, hoping for some insight.

Then suddenly the meaning becomes apparent. Could I be clinging to the need to control everything around me? Have I been trying to manage my surroundings, through isolation, because I'm terrified of who I really am and how I might behave? Does this explain my compulsion to invent backstories for the Dog Walkers, to create a sense of knowing when I actually have no idea?

But this thought causes waves of conflict. Being in control is not bad. For years, it's allowed me to be successful. In fact, I pride myself on how I strictly navigate my behavior, emotions, and future. Controlling myself and my surroundings is what's kept me stable, in the game, at my best. Or has it?

Deep in contemplation, I transition to the sofa and pull my knees to my chest. How does someone let go of control? It's not like I can release everything I've always clung to.

Subconsciously, my fists tighten and my jaw clenches as this concept creates havoc within. After a bit of time, my body softens, and I sink deeper into the sofa. Sensing a stronger connection to my inner self, I ponder if I actually have control over anything. After all, if I return to work, I cannot prevent myself from seeing David, nor can I ensure how I'd react in his presence. The truth is, I am unable to guarantee anything outside of these four walls. Because if

I leave, I become vulnerable, allowing others to see me for who I am … Ali Doyle, a thirty-two-year-old woman filled with flaws, fears, and doubts. My throat tightens as I acknowledge this truth.

I continue to explore the voice's message. *What if* I trusted in myself and believed it's OK not knowing all of the answers, having the perfect response, or consistently maintaining my composure? Then, could I begin to loosen my grip on life? If I felt safe, not only inside this apartment, but also in my own skin, could I surrender and have faith in the unknown? And if I am not yet ready to trust myself, can I trust that the Universe has my back?

Goosebumps form on my forearms, sending shivers down my spine. It's at this exact moment I know I am getting closer to walking out of this apartment and returning to life.

CHAPTER 11

After carefully spreading my English muffin with raspberry jam, I take the plate and a fresh mug of coffee to the kitchen counter and sit down to eat my breakfast. As the savory jam meets my tongue, I begin to rehash my aha moment from yesterday.

I guess I've been a control freak for most of my life. It probably began when I was in high school. After my mom died, Dad certainly couldn't watch out for me, so I took it upon myself to make all of my decisions. Unlike most of my friends, I had my act together at an early age. I excelled in college and professionally, probably because my actions were precisely planned and I seemed to make the correct choices. As a result, my career flourished, and I pretty much accomplished every goal I set. I guess that is one of the reasons Miles hired me.

But then I met David. And it all changed—I changed. I take a big bite of the English muffin. As I connect the dots to this "how I became a control freak" analysis, my heart races when I realize the one thing I never had control over was my relationship with David. Instead, I tried to please him, hoping to earn his love in return. I assumed that if I allowed David to call all the shots and didn't question what he wanted, then he'd always be there for me. But that didn't happen, and in the process, I allowed fear to rule. In the end, I felt as though I was never enough.

And then, as the months passed without any permanent commitment in sight, the fear of abandonment escalated. Yet, instead of seeing the situation for what it was, I only held on tighter, creating scenarios that were not reality … like the idea that he would propose in Costa Rica. I guess painting these "happy ever afters" made me feel in control.

As I take the empty plate over to the sink, I realize I've never been in control … of myself, my relationships, or my environment. This entire time I've been fooling myself, thinking my hard work and safe choices would keep me comfortable, secure, and loved. But that's not living … it's merely refusing to trust and let go.

Perhaps it was my fear of looking weak and vulnerable that pushed me to excel when I was younger, before I met David. And it's that exact threat that's been keeping me here, in this apartment, preventing me from coming and going, interacting with others, experiencing happiness and joy. I rinse my dish and place it inside of the dishwasher before I refill my mug.

Returning to the counter with a fresh cup of coffee, I clearly own that fear has been ruling my every move. It's then I sense a bit of liberation as my breaths even out and my heart rate slows. Finally, I know the answer to Miles's question. It wasn't seeing David that kept me in isolation; it was the fear of not being in control of anything that paralyzed me. And if what I've been reading is true, then the only way to break fear's spell is to trust—in myself and in something bigger. As I exhale, it seems as if I am floating, finally believing freedom is possible.

In the midst of this wondrously surreal understanding of who I am and what's been holding me captive, I spy movement outside. Instinctively, I run over to my window onto humanity and see my favorite Dog Walkers. But something's wrong … there's only Jackie and Eleanor. Where's Johnny?

I look closely through the window, attempting to figure out what's going on. I home in on the women's faces. Jackie, who is usually jovial, seems solemn as she walks Maggie and Penny. Her mouth remains in a straight line, not its usual impish grin. And Eleanor, well, she seems to be scrunching her forehead while talking with Jackie. No, this is not normal. Then, before I can determine what's wrong, they pass by.

I wait, unable to leave my post. Finally, after twenty minutes, they return. I lift the window open, hoping to catch a bit of their conversation. Luckily, there's no wind and I have exceptional hearing, so I'm able to figure out what they're saying.

"Maybe by the time we get back there will be some news," Jackie says in a dejected tone. It seems like a piece of her deflates as she speaks.

"It didn't sound good," Eleanor says, momentarily stopping to pet Maggie.

As the women take a break in front of my window, I can now clearly see that Jackie's holding a tissue in her hand, which she uses to dab her eyes.

But then they turn their backs toward me, and I am no longer able to decipher their conversation. Before long, they are gone.

For the rest of the day, I can only think about Johnny. Is he sick? He must be. And from the way it sounded, he might be in the hospital. Is Jackie taking care of Maggie?

There's a pit in my stomach I can't shake. Something is definitely wrong. My concern grows deeper, as my mind imagines the unimaginable. Something horrible has happened to Johnny.

CHAPTER 12

Sleep is impossible. As I lie awake in bed, sheets and comforter tossed all about, I cannot stop thinking about Johnny ... and Maggie. Is he going to be OK? And if not, what will happen to Maggie if Johnny is unable to take care for her?

Immediately, I envision the golden retriever, standing tall and majestic, her gorgeous well-brushed light blonde hair blowing in the wind. She wears a happy look, energetic and full of life. But then a dark shadow appears, shifting this golden's demeanor. Her eyes, once sparkling, lose their glimmer and slowly become sad and forlorn. A lone tear begins to drip as her head drops. She then lies down, curling up in a ball ... all alone.

All alone? No ... not Maggie. I know what that's like, and I cannot let that happen to her. My heart races violently as I jolt out of bed. While only a bit after four, I switch on the lights, take my robe from its hook on the closet door, and then go to the kitchen.

Coffee ... that will help me think. I fill the glass pot with water then dump it into the back of the coffee maker. After adding the French roast grounds, I hit On and stand there, impatiently waiting for it to brew.

I'm torn. A part of me worries something's terribly wrong with Johnny. Yet I'm equally concerned about Maggie.

My mind goes in all sorts of directions, creating twists and turns to these stories about people I don't know. Common sense tells me I'm making something out of nothing, but my gut says something different.

I take a mug from the cabinet, fill it with the freshly brewed coffee, grab my laptop from the desk, and then sit down at the counter. The liquid fuel trickles down my throat, warming my entire body. If only there were a way for me to google Johnny. But that's not his name; it's only what I've called this man while playing an invented game meant to keep me from feeling lonely.

It's as though a heavy weight bears down on my chest, hitting me with the fact that I've *made up* all of these stories, creating friends out of strangers. During this self-quarantined state, my only interactions with others—besides Miles—have been in my head, with people who don't know I exist.

Yet acknowledging my disorder does not erase what is happening with this man and his dog. Clearly, something is wrong. Though I am a complete outsider, I want to help, sensing a connection in some odd way. Setting the mug on the side table, I rest my head in my hands, considering whether or not I can actually do anything.

Thirty minutes later, I'm no closer to an answer. The only thing I can think of is asking Jackie and Eleanor, I mean the two women, what happened to their friend. But if I do, they'll know I've been watching them. That will make me look like a psycho. Who does that kind of shit?

Two hours later, as the sun begins to rise, I have yet to come up with a better solution. So I have a choice: I either walk away from this and resolve myself to the fact that I can do nothing, or I take a risk and somehow find a way to ask what happened to the man who goes with the golden retriever.

If I'm going to go out on a limb and try to communicate with these ladies, some nourishment may be helpful. I retrieve a small pan from the lower cabinet and place it on the burner. After turning on the flame, I grab the butter dish and two eggs from the fridge, toss in a small slab of butter into the pan, then crack open the eggs, carefully adding each. I put a slice of whole wheat bread into the toaster, and within a few minutes, eggs sizzle and the toast pops up, signaling breakfast is almost ready.

Plate in hand along with a refilled mug of coffee, I sit down at the table and slowly begin to eat. Obviously, I can't fling open the window and yell out to these two strangers, asking where their friend is. They'll think I'm crazy. I have to come up with a better strategy.

Perhaps it would be more natural if I were outside, close to the sidewalk, and then a normal conversation could occur. But that would require something I haven't been able to do … walk out the building's front door then make my way toward the street. However, it's been a while since I've tried. Maybe I can do it this time, because now there's a reason.

I look down and see that my plate is empty. I've consumed my entire breakfast without consciously tasting the food. Instead, I've only focused on how to ask Eleanor and Jackie about Johnny's disappearance.

After rinsing the dishes, I place them in the dishwasher then grab my mug and head toward my bathroom to shower. If I plan to venture outside, I better look my best.

Twenty-five minutes later, now clean and resembling a real human being, I decide to do a test-drive before I actually need to be outside to greet the two Dog Walkers when they pass by.

After putting on a warm coat, knowing it must be cold outside as it's only seven o'clock, I lock the door behind me and head down the stairs into the building's foyer. My hand grips the knob of the heavy door. Slowly, I push it open.

Cool air hits my face, while the sunlight simultaneously offers an unanticipated warmth. I tell myself to keep moving as my right foot steps onto the entry mat, followed by my left. My right hand remains on the knob, clinging to my security blanket. Yet, for me to move forward, I must surrender and release my hold. So I let go.

Instead of panic, something different surfaces. Unsure of how to describe this new sensation, the best word I can conjure is *curious*. Cautiously, I take one step forward, followed by several more until I am halfway between the street and the door. Birds tweet overhead in the pale blue sky, overpowering the voices coming from the sidewalk. The cement path feels cold and hard under my feet. Slowly, I bend down, brushing my fingertips against the cool blades of baby grass to the side of the walkway. My nose begins to twitch from the smell of pollen in the air.

Suddenly I stop in my tracks, unable to go farther. Unsure if my senses are on overload or if it is something else, I accept my progress and refrain from criticizing myself. If I can do this again later this morning, when the Dog Walkers are scheduled to arrive, I'll be able to ask about the missing man. I don't have to be *on* the sidewalk to talk to them.

Content with this plan, I turn and head back to the building. Yes, my pace is quicker returning than it was getting to this midway point, but who cares? I did it, and that's what matters.

Once upstairs, I pause outside of the locked apartment door. Staring at the dark-stained wood with the brass "2A" nailed into it, I examine the opposite side of my white door, the one that's kept me safe but isolated. The solid door looks to be in good shape, especially when considering the age of this garden apartment building. Yes, it definitely hosts a few dents, which have been repaired and stained throughout the years. But it does its job, remains strong.

No doubt I, too, have my fair share of bruises, some from David and others who have hurt me. But most are self-inflicted, results of self-criticism, self-doubt, and the need to prove I am enough. It's right then, as I'm fixated on the door's surface and how it parallels my existence, that I realize how silly this all has been. While I first thought I was hiding from David, the truth is, I had lost myself in that relationship, and when it ended, I wasn't sure what was left of me. So I remained small and turned off my light while the rest of the world carried on. I desperately clung to whatever I could to keep myself safe. It was easier to do this than to face my fears, realize it was OK to show my emotions to others, and become vulnerable. I was unable to admit control had become more important than anything else. But I was so wrong. I never had control … it's fear who's had control of me. And now, as I attempt to face my fears and regain what I so freely gave away, I'm struggling, desperately hoping to reclaim my lost pieces, the ones I can no longer remember.

I place the key into the lock then let myself into the apartment. Somehow it looks different. I've been away for less than ten minutes, but something's changed. Intellectually, I know everything's remained untouched. That's when it hits me … perhaps the shift is occurring inside me.

CHAPTER 13

A s I continue to wait for the Dog Walkers to appear, I move to the floor and sit crossed-legged on a batik cushion I ordered on Amazon, trying to center myself. But it's no use. Clearly, I am struggling.

I began meditating last week. It's one of the practices I've incorporated into my schedule. But this morning, my monkey mind's all over the place. All I can think about is making it to the sidewalk to speak with the women. I look at my watch. While I was partially successful earlier this morning, the true test will be in two hours.

Accepting today's meditation attempt is going nowhere, I get up from the floor. Too nervous to sit down and work, I resort to cleaning. Within no time, my apartment is spotless. Yet something's not right, so I decide to rearrange a few things. I begin by moving the sofa. After all, it's been against the wall for the entire time I've lived here. What if I were to reposition it, place it parallel to the dining table? Then I switch the TV, along with the stand beneath it, to where my desk currently is. After shifting these pieces of furniture, I take a step back.

"Much better," I say aloud. I wonder what else I can change.

I begin moving items from here to there. Ten minutes later, I survey my altered environment, and I like what I see. It's cozy, much warmer than before. But I don't stop. I rearrange picture frames, removing those that no longer seem relevant. This may open space for something new, though I'm not sure what. I take the ugly crocheted throw, the one David gave me that's been draped over the sofa, and toss it in the garbage can under the sink.

Scanning the apartment to see if there are any other remnants of David, I spy a ceramic dish we bought in Cape May as well as a framed picture of me he took during an arts festival downtown. Without a second thought, I toss both into the garbage can. A weight immediately disappears from my shoulders. On a whim, I go to my laptop to access Sonos. I haven't played music for weeks, months actually. I choose a playlist titled "Confidence Boost." Its uplifting beat seems to ignite a surge of energy within. Smiling, I rearrange items on the kitchen counter, discarding those things that no longer feel right. Then, as soon as I'm satisfied with how the kitchen and living area look, I continue this process in my bedroom and bathroom.

Before I know it, it's nearly ten. Eleanor and Jackie are soon due to walk by. It's time for me to stop what I'm doing so I can take the necessary steps to go outside and, hopefully, speak to these women.

Five minutes later, I'm standing on the walkway, exactly where I was earlier today, halfway between my apartment building and the sidewalk. I'm amazed with the vibrant sensations … the smell of spring in the air, the sound of people, and the gentle breeze blowing against my face. For years, I've failed to notice my surroundings. Instead, I only focused on getting from point A to point B, as quickly as possible.

While I'm taking in this beautiful spring day, I see the two women and four dogs approaching. But instead of reaching out to greet them, I'm unable to move, practically cemented to the walkway. As confident as I was earlier today, I am now questioning why I am here and what I will say. The courage I felt earlier leaks from my veins and is replaced with a paralyzing fear. I can't open my mouth to ask about Johnny. Instead, I stand there, eyes cast downward, as if I am ignoring the Dog Walkers, the ones who I've so anxiously waited for.

They pass by.

Hanging my head in defeat, I feel the heaviness return. I thought I was ready, but I guess I'm not.

As I'm about to retreat, disgusted with myself for being too weak to ask the two older women about their missing friend, Jennifer and Roxie appear. I look at my watch, noting how odd it is for them to be out at this time. Roxie comes charging toward me. Jennifer follows, visibly embarrassed.

I kneel down to Roxie's level and greet the dog with open arms. Roxie immediately accepts my invitation by jumping up on me, licking my face with her warm tongue. It feels so good to have contact with a warm-blooded being.

"I am so sorry," Jennifer says as she bends down to regain control of Roxie's leash. "I didn't realize I wasn't holding tightly to the leash," she adds as she pulls her dog off of me.

"No worries," I say, as I stand up. "She's adorable. What's her name?" I ask, a part of me wondering if I possibly guessed correctly.

"This is Hope. She's two years old. I adopted her this past fall from a local shelter," the woman says as she affectionately strokes the top of Hope's head.

"What breed is Hope?" I'm pretty sure I know the answer, kind of like I nailed the detail about her being adopted from an animal rescue.

"Who knows," she says, smiling as she rolls her eyes. "I think she's part shepherd with some beagle and possibly lab." With that, the woman runs her free hand through her long, auburn hair.

Realizing I don't know her true name, I smile and offer mine. "I'm Ali," I say. "I live in this building." I motion to the garden apartments behind me.

"Lisa." She reaches out her hand as she introduces herself, following up with, "How long have you lived here? I walk by most days, but I've never seen you before."

I pause, reminded of how invisible I've become. But I don't miss a beat.

"It's been almost four years—no five," I say, amazed with how quickly time has passed.

"It's a beautiful neighborhood," Lisa says. "My younger sister and I live three blocks away." Lisa gingerly points her finger east, toward Montgomery Avenue.

"It must be nice to live with your sister," I say, wondering what that would be like, yet knowing I'd never have that opportunity.

"Yes, well, she's having some problems, and she kind of needs me to stay with her. Before this fall, I lived downtown, in a great studio in Fishtown." Her smile disappears.

"Moving to the suburbs is definitely a transition," I say, though I do not know from experience.

"I don't miss living in the city. It's my sister ... she's not in a good place. She deals with a lot of depression issues. Spending so much time with her kinda brings me down." Lisa takes a big breath. "That's why I adopted Hope." Her mood instantly lightens when she talks about her dog.

"Now I know how she got her name," I say as I take a few steps forward, bend down, and pet the soft fur on the top of Hope's head.

"Yep, you've got it." Lisa's smile beams. "Well, I've got to be going. Nice talking to you," she says as she waves goodbye and she and Hope head back to the sidewalk.

I can't believe I had a normal conversation with an absolute stranger. No, I take that back. She isn't a stranger ... I'd seen her, multiple times ... and her dog. But I only observed a version of her. Now I've met the real woman—Lisa, not Jennifer, who has a dog named Hope. The story of Jennifer and Roxie fades away, replaced with the real version, the one I just experienced, not the story created in my head.

As I begin to wonder about Lisa's sister, Jackie and Eleanor—I mean the two women I was waiting for before I lost my nerve—reappear. They're making their second pass before they head home.

Approach.

Without questioning this inner voice, the one that sounds so different from the critical tone that's forever lived inside my head, I listen and begin to move toward the two women and four dogs.

When they see me approach, they slow down, smile, then continue to walk by. Knowing it is now or never, I force myself to make three additional steps forward. Then, hesitantly, I say, "Excuse me ... I was ... wondering something."

Somewhat startled, the women stop though their dogs continue to pull.

"Sit," the taller woman commands, and all four obey. She and her companion pause and give me their full attention.

"You see, I live in that apartment building," I say, pointing behind me, "and I frequently see you walk by." I force a smile, so I don't appear creepy. Then I continue, "But yesterday, I noticed the gentleman wasn't with you, but his dog was." I look at Maggie and my heart sinks. "And you both appeared so sad."

The taller woman looks at her friend. The shorter woman nods, then a tear falls down her cheek as she says, "Mike, the man you're referring to, had a stroke two days ago. Mike and I live in the same building but on separate floors, so I heard the ambulance's siren. It was about nine at night. I had just turned on my favorite television show, *Magnum PI*, but then I became distracted by the commotion going on outside. When I looked out my window, that's when I saw there was an ambulance and three paramedics headed into our building." More tears begin to fall. She takes a moment to calm herself.

"It seems Mike fell, from the stroke. He was wearing a life alert necklace … his kids insisted on it … and he was able to pull it, notifying the system that there was a problem."

"Is he OK?" I ask, choking back tears of my own, for a man whom I didn't know but felt like I did.

The taller woman shakes her head while the shorter lady begins to cry aloud.

"No, he passed this morning," the taller lady says, her face contorting as if to contain her own emotions.

"I am so sorry," I say, as I take two steps closer to the mourning friends. Trite as it may sound, I mean it with my whole heart.

"Thank you," the smaller lady says, then sniffles.

"I'm Ali," I say, extending my hand, first to the taller women who is closer to me, and then to her friend, who is now completely unraveling. Sensing a handshake is so not appropriate, I instinctively move closer and place my hand on the shoulder of this tiny stranger whom I'm only now meeting. Upon feeling my touch, she moves toward me, dissolving in my arms.

"I'm sorry." She looks embarrassed as she pulls back. "I'm Susie, and this is my friend, Gail." She sniffs and blots her cheeks with a tissue before continuing. "We're sisters-in-law, widowed sisters-in-law." Gail lovingly places her free hand on Susie's back.

This all makes so much sense. It explains their closeness as well as their lack of resemblance.

"What's going to happen to Mike's dog?" I automatically exhale as I ask the dreaded question. I move closer to Maggie, then get on my knees and gently stroke her head. She responds with a little whimper, as if she knows what we are discussing.

Susie is the first to answer. "We both adore Josie. She's an amazing dog, but I can't take her. We can't have two large dogs where we live, and Joy, who is a mini goldendoodle, qualifies as a large dog because she is over twenty-five pounds." Susie looks affectionately at Joy.

"Yes, Susie's correct. Both of our buildings have a strict pet policy. Will and Grace are each under ten pounds, which is allowed. But I don't know what we're going to do with Josie," Gail says as she emits a loud sigh. "Mike has a daughter who lives in Arizona. But her son is allergic to dogs."

"And Josie's only three, so she has many years ahead of her. I'm guessing we can take her to the Golden Retriever Rescue. I've heard they're pretty good with placing dogs," Susie says, yet her inflection drops, cuing to me she's not so sure about what she's saying.

I gaze at this beautiful creature serenely sitting next to me. Her name is Josie, not Maggie. Actually, I think I like Josie better. It suits her. Her pink tongue hangs slightly out of her mouth, and her tail wags as I continue to pet her. She seems to like it when I scratch behind her ears. Josie's eyes begin to sparkle. Staring straight at me, she lets out a little whine, as if she's asking me to consider ... if it wouldn't be too much of an imposition ... could she possibly come and live with me?

Without thinking, the words fly out of my mouth: "I'll take her."

Both women turn to look at each other then return their gaze to me.

"I'm serious. We're allowed to have dogs in my building. I've seen my neighbors with them, plus I remember reading the by-laws when I first signed the lease," I say in a rapid-fire manner. "And I've always wanted a dog ... and Josie's trained ... and so beautiful ... plus, she needs a home."

I watch as Susie and Gail communicate without words.

Finally, Susie says, "But we don't know you. More importantly, you do not know us, or Mike." She eyes me as if trying to determine whether or not I have an unforeseen motive to my offer.

"You're right … you don't know me … but, well, I sort of know you," I stammer, wondering if I should try to explain. But if I want to help Josie, I must. "You see, I've been watching you … from my window … and I loved how you all interacted. You looked so happy, free, at peace." I stop, conscious I've shared too much.

"From your window?" Susie asks as her jaw drops and eyebrows lift.

Then Gail chimes in, "Don't you work, Ali?" Her tone is cautious yet caring.

Caught in a web, not of lies, but rather a delicate weave made from threads of fear and uncertainty, I rub the center of my forehead, as if searching for an answer deep within. None comes, so I do the only thing I can. I tell my truth.

"Yes, I have a job … at least I think I do. For now, I'm working remotely, while I, um, while I get myself together." My voice fades a bit as I admit the last three words. Fighting the urge to look away in order to avoid witnessing these women's uneasy faces, I take a breath before continuing. "This past January, I ended a two-year relationship with a man whom I believed was the one. But he wasn't. I thought we were going to get married, but then he clearly let me know that was not in the cards. I don't know what happened. Sure, I was upset about the breakup, but then I slowly realized it was much more than that."

Susie steps toward me and, without saying anything, puts her free hand on my arm in a loving, motherly fashion. She peers into my eyes, as if encouraging me to continue.

"David, my ex, is the legal counsel for our company ... Genesis ... a software firm nearby. I knew going back to work meant we'd have to interact at some point. It wasn't seeing him that terrified me; it was me losing it, becoming emotional, embarrassing myself." But then I pause, deciding to get real with these women. "But the deeper issue is I discovered how much I've tried to control my life. However, this hasn't served me well, not in the least." I sigh, internally debating if I should have shared all of this.

I finish my story. "But I'm going back to work April 1. I promised my boss." My eyes well as Gail moves next to me, tenderly putting an arm around my shoulders. The dogs are all sitting down, as if they know their walk is temporarily halted.

Feeling the comforting touch of two women who are clearly holding space for me to share my story, I continue, revealing how I'd isolated myself since this past January. I told them of my days alone in my apartment and how I'd taken to watching the Dog Walkers, so I'd have some kind of connection to the outside world. However, I avoid discussing the stories I created about each person, pretending I knew him or her and they were my friends. That's too pathetic for me to admit.

"... and, when I saw you with the golden and he, rather Mike, wasn't there, well, I became concerned. I had to reach out to you." Tears stream down my cheeks as I declare my truth.

"Honey," Susie says, "you realize what happened, don't you?"

I look at her, unsure as to the meaning of her words.

"It took you caring about another to leave your apartment." Sweet, simple, and yet right on target.

"I didn't think of it that way ... I knew something was wrong, and I wanted to help."

"That's what Susie means," Gail says, an encouraging look appears on her face. "Your fear of not being in control of your emotions kept you inside, but because of your innate compassion—an emotion you could not contain—you had to come out, not for yourself, but to check if we were all OK."

Susie nods.

I gulp twice as I digest what is being said. Yes, today has been unlike any other day. After barely sleeping, I arose and was determined to find out about Johnny—who is now properly named Mike. And in the process, I made it outside, twice—the first time as a dress rehearsal, and the next as the real thing. I'd also rearranged my apartment, purging it of anything reminding me of David and my former life. And, on top of that, I met and spoke with Lisa, one of the other Dog Walkers, whom I had been referring to as Jennifer. But the biggest achievement of today is I embraced the courage to reach out to Gail and Susie and ask about their missing friend. Then I offered to take Josie. My brain is about to explode as it's had more activity in the past five hours than in the last two months.

"This is a breakthrough!" Susie says, her spunky self I'd witnessed before returning. "Seriously, it's huge." Susie's eyes light up, which I take as an encouraging sign.

My body relaxes, as I wipe the tears from my cheek. Reflexively, I shake my head yes, acknowledging the significance of my actions. Then, before I know it, I'm in Susie's arms, and she's rubbing my back in small circles, like my mom would do when I was little.

But then Gail asks, in a solemn tone, "Ali, are you serious about taking Josie?"

This time I don't respond automatically. Instead, I take a moment and think. While my apartment is not big, it is large enough for a dog. After all, Josie's trained, so I won't need a crate or a dog gate. I bet she'd like to sleep on my bed. Momentarily, I imagine this furry friend nestled against my legs, sensing how nice it would be waking up with Josie next to me. Plus, taking in Josie would solidify my return to the real world, as I could no longer hermit myself inside. Was I ready? I'd made so much progress in less than a day, but could I continue at this pace?

"You know you'd have to walk her several times a day," Gail says, as Susie scowls at her friend. "Well, she will," Gail says to Susie in an older sister fashion.

"Yes, you're right," I say, acknowledging her comment is justified.

"Do you think you can?" Susie asks, in a pleading manner.

Biting my lip, I seriously consider what is being asked. If I say yes to taking Josie, I cannot change my mind. Living with me would be a major change for the dog. She's already lost her owner. *If* I commit to her, I must keep her. She can't handle more disruption. But this requires I abandon my quarantine state and return to the land of the living.

I decide the answer lies not within me, but with Josie. So I turn to the golden retriever, search deep into her eyes, and offer her the sweetest smile I can muster. As if on cue, she arises and slowly walks over to me, lies down, and then rolls onto her back, offering her belly for me to rub.

Out of the corner of my eye, I see Gail and Susie look at each other, their faces bright with joy.

"I guess that's a yes," I say, as I gently rub Josie's belly.

CHAPTER 14

Right, left, right, left, right, left … my legs turn over quickly as I pump my arms to the beat of Moby's "Go" playing through my headphones. Yet my thoughts are on anything but running. I'm about to become the proud owner of a three-year-old golden retriever named Josie. Today at two, Gail and Susie will bring Josie and all of her belongings to me. At first I offered to drive to Susie's apartment to pick up Josie. But my two new friends thought it's best if I proceed slowly. Besides, I haven't driven my car for over two months.

Of course, they're right. I've made so much progress, and the last thing I want to do is go backward from pushing myself too hard. One step at a time.

When I think about yesterday's apartment overhaul, it's as if I was getting rid of the old and making space for something new in my life … Josie. Now, as I look at the layout, I wonder if there will be enough room for her. Will she have a dog bed? What else will she require?

It's then I glance at the treadmill's panel, only to see I've run five and a quarter miles. Unsure how this happened so quickly, I lower the speed and walk for a bit. After I've cooled down, I turn the tread off and move to the floor.

While stretching my hamstrings, I survey the living area. There's clearly enough room for a large dog bed in the far corner.

I move into the kitchen, considering possible spots for Josie's dog bowls. She'll have two, one for food and another for water ... plus a large bag of dog food. I find a spot for the bowls but wonder where there will be enough storage space for her food.

Perhaps the cabinet under the sink? Looking inside, it appears to be adequate if I move the cleaning supplies to the side. So I do, creating an open area for Josie's food supply.

As much as I love the idea of Josie on my bed, I also like my white comforter and would prefer to keep it that color, free of paw prints and dog hair. Then I remember the old set of sheets I'd kept in case I wanted to do a painting project and needed something to protect my furniture. I dig into the back of the bathroom linen closet and find the purple top sheet, open it up, and cover my pristine comforter. There ... all set.

Now all I have to do is wait. Gail said they'd text me when they arrive. I look at my watch and see I have four and a half hours until they're due. While my work assignment is on its way to being complete, there's certainly plenty left to do.

I sit down at my desk, which is now at its new location. I'm so used to looking out the window. I turn my head in both directions. Actually, I think I like it better this way. It's easy to see out the window when I look right, and if I turn left, then I have a clear view of the kitchen.

This will work nicely.

Three hours later, my stomach begins to rumble. Lunchtime. I save my work before heading to the kitchen. There's leftover bacon in the fridge and a ripe tomato sitting on the counter, waiting to be used. After toasting two slices of whole wheat bread, I carefully spread mayonnaise on both halves before piling on the lettuce, sliced tomato, and bacon. I press firmly on the top piece of bread, gently smooshing the insides together. Mayo begins to ooze out of the sandwich. Wiping off the excess, I lick my fingers, savoring the mixture of bacon fat, tomato juices, and mayo.

After devouring my sandwich, I make myself a cup of tea and break off a piece of dark chocolate from one of the bars I keep in the top kitchen drawer. The smooth, rich chocolate lingers on my tongue, reminding me of the sweetness of life.

Knowing I have close to an hour before Susie, Gail, and Josie are scheduled to arrive, I return to my desk and delve into the final element of my assignment: creating the PowerPoint presentation. Miles didn't ask for this, but it's something I want to do. Plus, it will be beneficial when I ultimately share this information with our team. But will I be able to present to my coworkers? After all, my dream about this exact scenario is what ignited my seclusion.

Surprisingly, this thought doesn't seem to rattle me as it had in the past. Could I finally be ready? I allow time for this concept to disseminate throughout my body. After several moments, it's apparent the idea of returning to Genesis no longer paralyzes me with fear; it only causes slight butterflies.

With a new sense of confidence, I open up PowerPoint and dig in. Fifty minutes later, I've finished ten slides. I'll need another fifteen or so to make this project complete, but it's on its way … and so am I.

My phone pings. I practically jump out of my seat as I pick up my cell that's charging on my desk. It's from Gail. They're here.

Without hesitation, I grab my keys and run down the stairs and out of the door to greet them. Their faces, visible through the car's windows, show definite surprise at the speed with which I appear. To be honest, I'm a bit impressed myself. I didn't pause at any of the usual checkpoints I'd created during my ritualistic attempts to venture outside.

The door of Susie's VW wagon opens as she energetically pops out. Gail exits the passenger side in a more graceful, dignified manner.

"Are you ready?" Susie asks, opening the car door behind her. But then I realize she's talking to Josie, not me.

Josie comes bounding out of the car, the end of her pink leash in her mouth, as if she doesn't want it dragging behind her. I get down on the grass, noting it's somewhat wet from the morning's dew, and open my arms. She runs to me, and I embrace her. This could almost qualify for a scene in a Disney movie, only this time, the dog isn't returning home; she's finding a new one. As I bury my face in Josie's warm fur, I thank God for sending her to me.

"I have a few bags of Josie's things, along with her dog bed," Susie calls as she opens the hatchback.

Then Gail and Susie bring Josie's belongings from the car. Gail carries two Wegmans reusable grocery bags while Susie manages the large dog bed. I grab Josie's leash then offer to carry one of the bags.

"We've brought all of her toys and dog bowls. There's also a brush, an extra leash, and her favorite treats in this bag," Gail says. "The dog food bag is still in the car. It's a bit large, and I might need some help lifting it," Gail adds as we walk toward the building. "I have no idea how Mike carried it from his car to his apartment." Her face momentarily becomes solemn.

Up the stairs we all go, then into my home, now Josie's home … our home.

"I love this place," Susie says as soon as she enters.

Gail smiles after I catch her surveying my living space, eyes darting up and down as if inspecting the site. Perhaps she noticed its tidiness and cleanliness. I suspect Gail keeps a neat and orderly house. I'm not so sure it's a priority for Susie, I think, suppressing a chuckle.

"Where would you like this?" Susie asks, holding Josie's bed, which is at least half her size.

"How about we put it right under the window, to the right of the treadmill?" I suggest as Susie plops the bed down, dog hair flying everywhere.

"Um, Josie sheds a bit," she says, in an apologetic manner. "In fact, I need to vacuum as soon as I get home. Since she's been staying with me, my apartment's been covered in dog hair." Her hand flies to her mouth, looking a bit embarrassed, as if her admittance of the massive amounts of dog hair may cause me to second-guess my decision.

"Well, I expect her to," I say, as I start laughing. "And as it becomes warmer, she's sure to shed more." Luckily, I invested in a top-notch vacuum cleaner last spring. Now it will come in handy.

While Gail and I head back to the car to retrieve the large bag of dog food, Susie remains with Josie. When we return, we see Susie sitting on the floor, next to Josie, crying.

"Are you OK?" I ask, concerned about my new friend.

"Oh, honey, I'm fine. You caught me saying goodbye to Josie. I was telling her how lucky she is to have you and that you'll take excellent care of her. I'm going … to miss … her." More tears fall down her face. "I know, I only had her for two days, but she kind of grows on you … so gentle and loving. Plus, we walked together every day for almost three years." Susie wipes her eyes then gives the golden a sweet little kiss on her nose.

"Susie, it's not like you won't see Josie again. She's become a part of your family, with all the walks and everything," I say as I move toward her. Kneeling down next to her, I realize how tiny this woman is. The top of her head comes to the bottom of my chin.

"What if we walk together, at least until I return to work, then maybe on the weekends?" The words come out of my mouth before I can stop them. Yet they're spoken, so I cannot take them back.

"Really?" Susie asks. "You'd be willing to walk with two old ladies and their dogs?" she adds.

"Are you kidding?" I teasingly poke her in the arm. "I'd love that. Plus, it might actually be good for me, you know, to help ..." As much as I'd like to say what's in my heart, I'm hesitant to finish the sentence because I don't like admitting the truth ... that I'm still somewhat afraid of venturing outside.

Gail jumps in, perhaps picking up on my mood dip. "We would love that, wouldn't we, Susie?" Gail says as she takes a seat on the sofa, facing the two of us who are still on the floor next to Josie.

"Since you walk your dogs by here every day, I could join you, that is, if you're OK with it."

"Oh, Ali, that would be perfect!" Susie's energy has returned. "Though Josie towers over our dogs, they love her ... she's *their* family too."

"Then it's settled," Gail says with a tone of finality. "In fact, it's probably time for us to get going," she adds, giving Susie a nod.

Susie picks up on Gail's not-so-subtle cue and quickly stands.

"Yes, you and Josie need to get acquainted," she says. Her tone's upbeat and her eyes gleam. "But we'll see you tomorrow morning, around ten o'clock, right?" she asks, as if double-checking my commitment.

"Yes, we'll be downstairs waiting for you," I say, hoping to provide assurance to these women who are entrusting me with their deceased friend's dog.

"And if you need anything or have any questions, please call us," Gail adds. "In one of the bags is a purple binder with Josie's certifications, medical history, everything you'll need. She goes to The

Mainline Animal Clinic off of Montgomery Avenue, but of course, you may take her wherever you wish. I checked, and her shots are up to date. In fact, it seems like she had her annual appointment this February, so she should be good for a while."

Thank goodness for Gail. I hadn't thought about a vet.

"I appreciate you organizing everything for me," I say as I give Gail a quick hug. While I can guess she's not a natural hugger, she appears open to my embrace. Then I move toward Susie.

"She will be good for you," Susie whispers in my ear. "You need her, and she needs you."

Susie pulls my upper body down so she can kiss my forehead. Before leaving, both women pet Josie one last time.

"See you tomorrow, Josie," Susie yells as they make their way down the stairs. I stand at my door and wave as my two new, real friends leave, trusting me with Mike's dog.

After locking the door, I turn and see Josie's already settled in her dog bed. Khaki with a cream fleece inside, this is one big bed. It takes up more space than I imagined it would.

I go to the bag and pull out the purple binder, quickly reviewing its contents. When I come to the notes from her February visit, I see she weighed in at sixty-eight pounds. While not as large as some goldens I've seen, she certainly isn't small. I replace the binder in the bag, knowing I'll unpack the contents at a later time.

"Come on, Josie," I say to my new housemate, "let me show you the place." I wave my arm in a "come here" motion. Immediately, Josie rises and follows me, her tail wagging. Impressed, I give her the full three-minute tour of my apartment. I explain how I have a special purple sheet for her to sleep on. I then take her into the kitchen, pull her dog bowl out of the bag, fill it with cool water, and place it on the floor in a spot I figured is safe from me tripping over it. Josie goes to her bowl and, without hesitation, begins to lap the water, droplets falling all around.

Newbie mistake, I think to myself as I retrieve an old towel from the linen closet and place it under the water bowl. I pat her head.

"It's not your fault that you dribble," I say and laugh aloud, "I guess it's tricky to lap water with your tongue without dropping a bit." Josie looks at me, tilts her head, and smiles.

"Josie, you and I are going to get along fabulously," I say as I run my hand down her back. Josie responds by licking my face. Her cool wet tongue tickles. Yet I don't mind. Something inside me expands, growing warmer and filling me with gratitude. I think I've found my heart. It's been gone for some time, but now, I believe it's back.

CHAPTER 15

Two hours later, Josie begins to whine. I check my watch. It's only five o'clock. Susie told me Josie doesn't eat dinner until six or six thirty. Maybe she's testing me, like kids do with babysitters. So I ignore the dog and return to work.

But Josie's insistent, and her whimpers increase in frequency.

"Josie, you have another hour till dinnertime," I say in my sweetest tone.

But then it hits me—she's probably not hungry. She might need to go to out. I hadn't thought this one through. Sure, I'm walking with Susie and Gail tomorrow, but I can't expect the dog to hold it until then. I shake my head, amazed with my ignorance about dogs and their needs. It's plain and simple. I have to take her outside for a short walk. Otherwise, well, I won't go there.

Searching inside the Wegmans bags, which I have yet to unpack, I find her pink leash and the roll of dog bags inside. Immediately, Josie starts to prance in a circle, relieved I finally figured out her signal.

I hook the leash to her collar, grab my coat, and put my keys and the roll of bags in my pocket before we head out the door. Unlike earlier when I ran down the stairs to greet Susie and Gail, this time, I walk in a deliberate, somewhat cautious manner. I've never walked a dog. But I've watched the Dog Walkers and how they do it.

When we get to the front door, I hesitate. However, Josie yanks me forward, pulling straight ahead. It's as if she's helping me out of the building, preventing me from turning around and retreating inside. She continues to jerk me toward the sidewalk. Once there, she moves to the grass and relieves herself. This one does not require a baggie pickup.

"Are you good, Josie? Ready to go back inside?" I ask in a hopeful tone.

But apparently, she's not, as she continues down the sidewalk, in the direction she's used to heading on her walks. I've never seen her pull Mike this way, or Susie for that matter. It's as if she knows that I'm younger, stronger, and more capable of handling an active dog.

She keeps jerking the leash, so reluctantly, I continue walking. We go twenty yards to the large oak tree next to a fire hydrant, exactly where the view from my window ends. But Josie doesn't stop. Instead, she keeps charging forward, seemingly unconcerned about me and my fears. Finally, Josie pauses, sniffing the grass next to a lamppost. It's there that she squats and does what requires a bag. Carefully, I unwind the roll and tear off a purple bag, fumbling with the opening. Damn, this is difficult. Finally, the plastic bag separates. I place my hand inside of it then lean over to clean up after *my dog*. Josie sits and watches as I pick up her mess.

If it were up to Josie, we'd keep walking. But I'm far past my comfort zone, so I sweetly cajole her back with the promise of biscuits and an early dinner. Josie readily agrees. Apparently, goldens are easily swayed by food—something to remember.

Once we're both inside, we go through the foyer then out the back door to discard the smelly bag in the dumpster. As soon as we reenter the building, Josie charges up the steps, forcing me to run in order to keep up with her. After I unlock the apartment door and unleash Josie, she bolts inside and sits down by the kitchen counter, looks at me, and barks.

Oh, this must mean she wants a treat. I reach into the bag and find a box of doggie snacks. I offer one to her, and she gently takes it from my fingers.

"Good girl," I say in an approving tone, patting her head. Josie wags her tail and then goes over to her dog bead and lies down.

Now seems as good of a time as any to unpack Josie's belongings, so I spend the next fifteen minutes doing exactly that. First, I empty a kitchen drawer filled with extra plastic and paper bags. Realizing the enormous dog food bag is too big to fit under the sink, I neatly place the bags where I planned to put the dog food. Next, I carefully fill the newly emptied drawer with Josie's things. Not wanting to leave a box of dog treats on the counter, I find a colorful ceramic bowl that doesn't go with any of my other dishes and fill it with dog biscuits. Then, I go to my bedroom closet and retrieve a wicker basket filled with clothes for Goodwill. I put the Goodwill items in one of the paper bags I *just* placed under my sink, promptly returning it to the bedroom closet. Then I fill the empty basket with Josie's dog toys and place it near her bed, creating a designated "Josie area."

Somewhat proud of my ingenuity, I've found a place for everything, except for the huge bag of dog food. There's only one location big enough to house this gigantic bag, so I drag it to the coat closet. After catching a whiff of kibble, I retrieve a big clip from the top desk drawer and secure the opening of the bag. Hoping to prevent the dog food odor from permeating my coats, this is the best I can do until I can buy a Tupperware tub. But I resign myself to the fact that dog hair, water on the floor, and stinky dog smells are all part of having a dog.

I look over at Josie, who is resting on her bed, eyes shut. For the first time in what seems like forever, a wave of peace settles upon me. She seems happy here, with me. I guess I'm not so unwell. Perhaps I am getting better. One thing's for sure, caring for another is pretty incredible. It keeps me from focusing on all of my shit.

After thirty minutes or so, I decide to feed Josie. There's a red solo cup inside of the food bag, so I fill it to the brim, toss the kibble into Josie's food bowl, and call for her. Immediately she's at my feet, looking at me, not her dinner that's right beneath her on the floor. What's wrong? Isn't she hungry?

"Don't you want to eat, Josie?" I ask, but she only sits there, staring at me, as if she's waiting in anticipation of something.

I wonder if there's some command Mike used, to let her know it was OK for her to begin her meal.

"Eat," I say … nothing.

"Dinnertime."

But these are not the magic words.

Quickly, I grab my phone and call Susie.

"Susie, Josie won't eat her dinner. I put her bowl in front of her, but she only stares at me, almost like she's waiting for permission. Did Mike say or do anything special to get her to eat?"

All I hear is laughing. Finally, Susie says, "Honey, first you hide her bowl of food behind your back, and then you call her, saying, 'come and get it.' That's when Josie barks three times, the cue for you to put the dog bowl on the ground and say, 'ta da.' Mike loved playing that game with her." Her voice drops when she mentions Mike.

While I can't envision myself doing this, I thank Susie then remind her we'll see her tomorrow at ten.

"OK, Josie, let's give this a try. Come and get it." My voice sounds fake, somewhat contrived.

Josie lets out three quick "ruffs."

I feel my jaw drop as Josie seemingly responds to Susie's suggested phrase. It's then that I realize I'd forgotten to do the "ta da" part. Quickly, I say the phrase then place the dog bowl in front of Josie, who immediately dives in, tail wagging as she gulps down the dried kibble. This dog is pretty hilarious.

While Josie's eating, I go into my bedroom and change into running clothes. After filling a bottle with water, I hop on the treadmill and begin my run. When I look out the window, I notice that though it's six thirty, the sun has not set. I let out a big sigh and feel a smile emerge. I love daylight saving time.

Josie, who is now lying in her dog bed, puts her head on her paws and looks curiously at me. I'm wearing headphones and am running to the beat of Radiohead's "15 Step." Josie's eyes follow my feet, her head moving back and forth. I doubt she's seen anyone on a treadmill before. Watching her observe me makes me laugh. But then I think of Mike, and I realize I failed to ask Susie and Gail if there was going to be a funeral. I seemed more concerned about Josie than her owner. But would I go if there was a service? Wouldn't that be odd? No, taking Josie was my greatest gift to Mike, who will forever be Johnny in my heart.

The rest of Josie's and my first Saturday night together is pretty uneventful. After showering, I make myself a simple dinner. While cutting carrots for a salad, Josie comes to the sink, sits straight up, and gently nudges my calf with her nose. Hmmm, does she want a carrot?

Can dogs have them? Unsure, I grab my phone and google this question.

"Yes, carrots are allowed," I say as I hand her a small piece. "But no raisins or chocolate," I quickly add, in case she's listening. After inhaling the carrot, Josie comes back over, this time tapping me with her paw for another.

I succumb, but warn, "That's it, Josie."

Josie takes the carrot, this time chewing it more slowly. When she's done, she hangs her head before slowly returning to her bed. Damn, I think that dog understands me.

After my dinner of roasted chicken breast, sautéed asparagus, and salad, I pour myself a glass of white wine before turning on the TV and settling onto the sofa. While I begin to surf the channels, Josie comes over and puts her head on the sofa cushion. Her big eyes look at me pleadingly.

"Are you hungry, or do you want to go out?" I ask, confused because she already ate and she shouldn't need to go out yet. Josie shows no response regarding either of my questions.

I ignore my dog and return to the TV listings on the screen. It's the *plop* I hear before I feel the couch shift. I look to my right and Josie's nestling herself into my sofa, gently placing her head on my feet. While a part of me wants to cuddle with my new buddy, another side remembers how much this sofa cost. Opting for a compromise, I go to the hall closet and search the top shelf for the bright orange throw my secretary, Carole, had given me for my last birthday. I stuffed it in the back, knowing I could pull it out last minute if Carole came over.

"Josie, get up a sec," I say as I shoo her off of the couch.

After sweeping my hand across the cushions to wipe away any stray dog hair, I place the throw on Josie's half of the sofa. Immediately, Josie jumps back up then positions herself into a tight ball, this time laying her head on the covered armrest.

Happy with my new dog next to me on my now protected sofa, I, too, curl up and choose a movie. *Failure to Launch*, one of my all-time favorites, is the winner.

An hour and a half later, Tripp and Paula finally realize they are in love. As they kiss, the corners of my mouth curve upward and my heart flutters, even though I know how this movie ends. I look over at Josie; she's fallen asleep and looks content. The sight of her, here with me, invokes more joy than Paula and Tripp ending up together. I now have a purpose. I've saved Josie. Or could it be she who saved me?

Go outside.

The voice shakes me from my thoughts. Am I imagining things, or is this voice giving me another message?

Noting the time, I figure I better take Josie outside once again before it gets too late. Would I have done this had the voice not reminded me?

Surprisingly, it's easier than I expected to go out of the building at night. I guess the dark skies offer some sort of protection, like a cloak, keeping me covered, safe.

As we walk down the sidewalk, Josie takes her time, sniffing every tree and sign. But I don't mind. It seems like ages since I've smelled the night air. I notice the tips of my nose and fingers are cold, and I wish I'd put on a hat and gloves.

"Come on, Josie. Go to the bathroom," I say in an encouraging voice, wanting to go back inside where it's warm.

She walks a bit farther, stops, and sniffs, looking as though this might be it. I move ahead of her, attempting to coax her along. But then someone approaches from the opposite direction. I can't make out the face, but it's a man. And he's walking a dog. It appears to be a black lab.

This person comes closer, nods at me, but then walks by. However, his dog halts when it gets to Josie. They conduct the sniff test, checking out each other's rears in a dance-like fashion.

It's only then I hear his voice. "Come on, Rocco, let's go."

Could it be *him*, the one I've only seen once? Stephen ... who works for the CIA and comes here every month to visit his mom? While I watch this person and his dog continue their walk down the sidewalk, my frigid body turns warmer. The street is somewhat lit from lampposts. I squint, trying to discern anything about this man. It *could* be Stephen. And the dog certainly *looks* like a lab. Yet it's too dark to tell.

Deciding to follow him, I gently pull on Josie's leash, but she won't budge. Of course, now is when she decides to do her business. I wait impatiently. By the time she's finished, he's out of sight, gone. In the most innocent fashion, Josie turns and pulls me back toward my building. Two minutes later, I trudge up the stairs, filled with regret for not speaking to him. I was so close.

But the good news is, he's back. Unsure of what this means exactly, my mood lifts as I hang up my jacket and place Josie's leash on the side table.

"Thank you, Josie. If it weren't for you, I wouldn't have seen him." I lean down and embrace the golden retriever. Josie's large tongue licks my cheek. But instead of wiping off the dog slobber, I bury my head in her fur and hold her tightly. She is my angel, my savior. This dog is helping me heal.

CHAPTER 16

"How was your first night with Josie?" Gail asks as soon as she, Susie, and the dogs arrive outside of my apartment.

"It was great. Josie's amazing. I can't believe how easily she's adapting to living with me," I say as we all head down the sidewalk toward a nearby park, one they assured me is Josie's favorite.

I look at *my dog*. I like how that sounds. A part of me softens, noting how happy Josie is to be with Joy, Will, and Grace. Even though she towers over the smaller dogs, Josie seems to be aware of the size difference because she doesn't bump into them or invade their space. Their interaction is completely natural.

"And look at you—you're beaming," Susie says. Gail nods in agreement.

I take the compliment, recognizing how much I've progressed. "I told Josie she's my angel." Then I turn to see that without realizing it, we've walked four blocks. I'd been so distracted talking with my new friends that I hadn't noticed.

"She may be from a higher realm," Susie says as she looks questioningly into the sky. "I know she was for Mike."

"What do you mean?" I ask as we pause at the corner, waiting for traffic to pass so we can cross the street.

"Well, Mike had recently lost his wife, Betty. She died from some sort of cancer—I can never remember," Susie begins.

"Ovarian," Gail interjects.

"That's right." Susie touches Gail's shoulder for a moment, in a gesture of agreement. "Anyway, after Betty passed, well, Mike was a mess. He depended on her for everything ... to grocery shop, cook ... Betty never taught Mike how to do laundry or manage the household. He was clueless. She even took care of all of their finances."

"What did Mike do during the day? He was retired, right?" I ask.

"Mike loved building models ... airplanes, ships, you name it. He had an entire room filled with them." Susie pauses as she shuts her eyes and momentarily travels to another time. But then she returns. "His craftsmanship was amazing, truly gifted."

"But when Betty died, well, he lost his enthusiasm for everything," Gail adds.

"So he no longer was interested in constructing the models and didn't know how to care for himself ... kind of frozen ... like I was?" I ask.

Both women nod their heads in agreement.

"But it was more than that," Gail says. "Those damn casserole queens descended on him like flies on rice." She shakes her head disapprovingly. "Susie and I were his friends. Neither of us wanted more than that. He used to tell us about these women and ask us what to do. Mike didn't want to hurt anyone's feelings, but he had no interest in dating again."

"That's when I suggested he get a dog," Susie says. "He loved my Joy. So we found a breeder in Downingtown, and five weeks later he brought Josie home."

So that's how Josie and Mike came to be. This dog *is* an angel. She helped him, and now she's here for me.

"Tell me about yourselves. You're sisters-in-law, right?" I ask, wanting to better understand their relationship.

"Our late husbands were brothers," Gail says, then stops for a minute. She looks at Susie, as if to ask, "Do you want to tell her, or should I?"

Susie nods her head yes before speaking. "Fifteen years ago, my brother-in-law, Gail's husband, suddenly died of an aneurysm." I watch as Gail's eyes tear up a bit. "While Gail and I weren't that close at the time, we started to see more and more of one another," Susie continues.

"Walter and I didn't have any children, so when he passed, well, I was all alone," Gail says as she looks tenderly at Susie.

"It's true that sometimes tragedy brings people together, at least it did with us," Susie says. "Before long, we spent holidays together, even vacations."

"Susie and Henry's kids became like my own," Gail adds. "But then Henry died, and the kids moved away. It became solely the two of us."

Now Susie's face saddens. "Yes, we're an odd couple of sorts, but we've got each other." She looks up at Gail.

"You're both lucky," I say, admiring their kinship. "But how did you meet Mike?" I ask, wondering about the impetus to this trio's friendship.

"Mike and I were neighbors. We lived in the same apartment building. He was on the fifth floor, and I live on the third," Susie says, pausing a moment before continuing. "After Henry died, I didn't want to remain in our home. It was lovely, but it was too big, and besides, it housed too many painful memories. So I sold our home and decided to rent. Why tie up the capital?" Susie shrugs her shoulders.

"And you, Gail … where do you live?"

"Walter and I lived downtown, near Rittenhouse Square. How we loved being in the city …" Gail drifts momentarily, as if remembering a sweeter time. "There were fabulous restaurants within walking distance, the Academy of Arts was right down the street, and of course, there was shopping close by."

I nailed it, I think, amazed at how closely Gail's life resembles "Eleanor's."

"I continued living in our apartment for many years, but the city seemed to become colder, perhaps more dangerous. I'm not sure what it was; maybe it was merely me getting older. Regardless, I didn't feel comfortable anymore."

"I convinced her to move to the suburbs," Susie chimes in. "And now she loves it."

Gail chuckles in agreement. "Yes, you did. And it was the best thing, even though I fought you every second of the way," Gail teases her sister-in-law. "Susie found me an available townhouse, three blocks from her building. Actually, it's perfect for me."

"And then you bought Will and Grace?" I ask, wondering how they came into her life.

"That was not my idea," Gail says, raising her eyebrows. "Susie thought I shouldn't be alone. She worried I'd keep to myself too much once I moved from the city." Gail momentarily pauses, as if she regrets saying these last words in my presence. "And when Susie gets an idea in her head, it is difficult to dissuade her." Gail lets out a big sigh. "She saw an advertisement for a female Yorkshire terrier, but when she arrived to pick up the dog, they told her the brother was also available. Apparently, he was the only remaining puppy from the litter that had not yet been adopted."

"How could I take the sister and not him?" Susie butts in.

Gail only shakes her head then says, "So she took both."

Now I'm laughing to the point where I let out a small snort. "What a great story! And you called them Will and Grace after the TV show?"

Gail rolls her eyes before saying, "Susie named them."

"I did, couldn't help it. Love that program."

By now, all three of us are giggling.

It's then I remember Gail mentioning that Susie has kids. Wondering if they live nearby, I ask, "Susie, you have children, don't you?"

Immediately an awkward silence replaces our lighthearted conversation. Gail and Susie stare straight ahead. My chest sinks as I realize I've gone somewhere I should not.

"My kids and I don't talk much," Susie finally says. "After Henry died, they became furious with me that I sold the house. They wanted things to stay the same, honor the memories. But I couldn't. They didn't understand. My son said I was being selfish, and my daughter shut me out of her life ... and out of her kids' lives." This normally bubbly woman appears to age with this statement.

Gail tilts her head and raises her eyebrows at her sister-in-law.

"There's more." Susie takes in a big breath, avoiding Gail's glare. "I was sad, hated being alone. It was horrible. I didn't understand how Gail had done it for so many years. Let's say I found comfort probably earlier than I should have." With that, she stops talking. Gail then looks to me as if to gauge my reaction.

"Oh, Susie. You did nothing wrong. You were lonely." While I don't know what it's like to lose a spouse, I definitely understand how isolated and lost Susie must have felt.

"Wish my kids could see it that way." Gail gently places her free hand on her sister-in-law's shoulder. I watch as they exchange glances. No doubt these two are total opposites, but there's an unspoken bond.

The rest of our walk is filled with small talk. They ask me about my family, and I openly share how things went south after my mother passed. The women also inquire about my career. I tell them about Miles, how much I loved working at Genesis, and then briefly explain my at-home assignment.

"It's due April 1," I say, as if reminding myself of the deadline.

"Are you ready to go back to work?" Gail asks. Her eyes narrow and the tone of her voice seems to deepen.

"I hope so." I shrug as I say this. "So much has changed in the past twenty-four hours. Two days ago, I couldn't leave my apartment." I bite my lower lip, taking in the enormity of it all.

"Yet work's a different matter?" Gail asks, even though I suspect she knows the answer.

"Yes." I pause. "There's so much that could happen," I say as I hang my head a bit, remembering the calamity in my dream.

"But look at how far you've come," Susie, my cheerleader, says. With that, Josie turns her head back toward me and smiles. My God, this dog's angelic.

"Thanks," I mutter as we stop at another corner.

"No, seriously, you are getting better. And if it took adopting a dog to do so, who cares? The fact is things are turning around." Susie leans down to pet Josie. "You take care of Ali, OK, Josie? Just like you did with Mike."

Thirty minutes later, I say goodbye to Gail and Susie, promising to meet them tomorrow at the same time. As I unlock the door to the building, the sun shines on my face. I pause, soaking in the welcomed warmth. Yet there's another heat beginning to glow. But this one is internal. Though still a small flame, the light inside of me flickers, steadily growing stronger.

While I cannot predict what tomorrow will bring or whether or not I will be able to return to "normal," I am slowly healing; no longer am I unwell. Could I be entering phase three?

***

Later that evening before bed, I take Josie for her final walk. It's the same time as last night, but there's no Stephen, or whomever he is. As we make our way back upstairs, I reluctantly accept that my encounter with this man was merely a coincidence. I may never see him again. While this saddens me, I choose to reflect on all the good that's been happening. I've adopted a dog, gained two friends, and left my apartment multiple times. I'm starting to change, becoming stronger and more capable. Sure, I have further to go, but I am making progress. However, it's so much more than meeting people and adopting a dog ... I think I'm beginning to trust myself, the first step in letting go.

CHAPTER 17

As I make my way to the bathroom, I almost trip over Josie. Wherever I go, this dog's constantly next to me. It's as though she's my shadow. But I don't mind. And the more time we spend together, the easier it is to notice her subtle cues, such as how she paces by the sink if her water bowl needs to be refilled or the way she circles when she wants to play.

As the back-to-work deadline draws closer, I'm becoming more and more confident that the presentation and I will be ready. While a few slides must be tweaked, the PowerPoint is close to being finished. Now I must focus on me returning to work. But unlike minor adjustments easily made to a PowerPoint presentation, I'm confused how to fine-tune myself to ensure I'm as solid as my report.

As I begin to recalibrate the scale of one of the graphs depicting the projected increase in efficiency, I receive an email from Miles. It's the first one since he gave me this assignment. In pure Miles fashion, he's delegated then allowed me to do my thing. That's one of the traits I value most about my boss. I open the email.

Good morning, Ali,

I hope you're having a great day. Wanted to confirm we will be meeting at 9:00 next Wednesday (April 1) to discuss the project you've been assigned. I look forward to hearing your analysis and subsequent recommendations.

But mostly, it will be good to have you return to work. You've been missed. It's not been the same without you.

Miles

The last paragraph sticks with me. *I've been missed?* Throughout this entire time, I hadn't considered that anyone would notice my absence, let alone miss me. Do I truly matter to Miles and the others at Genesis? I think I do. Filled with gratitude, I compose a response:

Hi, Miles,

Thanks for checking in. The project is 99 percent completed. I look forward to sharing the results with you on April 1.

I pause. Should I include that I will be returning to work, or will he make that assumption? Deciding to make it crystal clear, I add,

It will be nice to be back to work. I've missed all of you.

Best,
Ali

Before sending, I read the email aloud to ensure it sounds appropriate. This habit has served me well and prevented some big "oops" from occurring. Of course, I failed to do this when I last texted David. Surprisingly, this thought does not evoke that familiar sensation of shame.

Instead I move my head back and forth as I shake off the memory. Several minutes later, Josie comes over and nudges my leg. It's not time for her walk. She then begins to lick my ankle.

Hmmm. "What are you trying to tell me, Josie?" I ask my dog, unsure if she's bored and wants attention or if there is a deeper meaning. I look closely into her eyes. That's when I see a tinge of sadness. Could Josie have understood what I'd said … that I would return to work?

While seemingly impossible, I decide to ask her—why not?

"Josie, does it upset you that I'm returning to work?"

Josie whimpers then lies down at my feet and puts her paw over her head.

Oh my God, this dog gets it. Whether it is intuition or an inane ability to comprehend what I am saying, I fully believe my dog, whom I haven't even had for a week, realizes she will be left alone when I go back to work.

I slide off my desk chair, positioning myself on the floor next to Josie. Slowly, I rub behind her ears, something she usually enjoys.

"I have to return to work. How else can I pay for your dog food?" I try to be funny, but do dogs even understand humor?

Yet Josie's mood doesn't lift. Instead, she lets out a deep moan.

My heart aches as I look at this beautiful golden retriever. She's probably used to being with someone all day. After all, Mike didn't work.

I sit up straighter as my gaze drifts toward the ceiling. If only Josie could come to work with me? But is this possible? I do have my own office, so she could stay there. And I'm sure everyone would love her.

"Josie, I think I have an idea." I return to my chair and begin typing a follow-up email to Miles.

Miles,

I have an unusual request. This past week, I adopted a three-year-old golden retriever named Josie. I did this after learning her owner, an older gentleman, had passed and his friends were unable to care for his dog.

Would it be possible for me to bring Josie to work? She'd stay in my office and wouldn't be a bother to anyone. I know I'm making an unconventional request, but Josie's had major changes in her life, and I'd hate for her to be alone all day in my apartment. I guess you could say I relate to her situation.

Please know I totally understand if this is not possible.

I look forward to seeing you on April 1.

Best,
Ali

Sent.

"Now let's see what Miles says." I stroke the top of Josie's head. She lets out a big sigh then rolls on her back and offers me her belly.

***

Three hours later, I save then print the document and accompanying PowerPoint. Finally, the project is done. Now the real work begins. Luckily, I have an entire week to prepare for my transition back to Genesis.

Taking a moment, I sit silently at my desk and mentally rehearse how I'd like next Wednesday to proceed.

I envision it being a sunny day and enjoying a leisurely drive to Genesis's headquarters. Soft meditative music plays on the Volvo's stereo system as Josie sits upright on the passenger seat, a big smile on her face. After finding the perfect parking spot, I confidently walk into the building, my tote in one hand and Josie's leash and bag in the other. When we enter the elevator, people fawn over Josie, declaring how beautiful she is.

I inhale and feel the energy vibrate through my body. Next, I imagine the elevator doors opening into Genesis's reception area. There's Monica, the receptionist, visibly happy to see me. She gets up from her desk to hug me before kneeling down to pet Josie. As Josie and I walk down the hallway to my office, coworkers wave, saying, "Good to see you, Ali," and "Welcome back! We've missed you."

When we finally get to my office, Josie instinctively knows what to do. She lies down and quietly plays with a stuffed squirrel. Carole, my secretary, pops her head in, sharing how things haven't been the same without me. Then, after Josie's settled, I tell my dog I will be back in a bit. That's when I go to Miles's office, exceed his expectations with my presentation, and regain his trust and support.

I heave out a big sigh as I practice visualizing my successful return to work, one of the strategies I've read about. I've also been saying affirmations each morning. Repeating "I am ready to return to work," "I will confidently walk into Genesis," and "I will remain composed when I see David" help to calm the jitters I thought were untamable. I'm beginning to believe it was me who created these fears, and only I possess the power to dismiss them.

Forty minutes later, I look for Josie. She's sleeping soundly on her bed. "Ready for our walk?" I ask, gently rubbing her back. "Susie and Gail will soon be coming by with Joy, Will, and Grace."

Upon hearing her buddies' names, Josie sits up, shakes her head, then walks to the small table by the door and retrieves her leash lying on top of the table.

"OK, let me grab my coat." I shake my head, amazed with this dog's intelligence.

Five minutes later, we're on the sidewalk waiting for Susie and Gail. It's then I see Lisa and her dog, Hope.

"Hey there," Lisa says as she approaches.

Immediately, Josie pulls toward Hope. The dogs greet each other in their familiar canine way as I walk over to Lisa.

"Hi, Lisa," I say, happy to see a familiar face. "Good to see you."

"It's nice to be out," Lisa says as she pushes her long auburn hair from her eyes. "Work's been crazy. I've only been able to walk Hope early in the morning then later at night. My sister has been taking her out in between. Actually, that's been good for both of them." Lisa's freckled face brightens as she shares this.

"What do you do?" I ask Lisa, wondering how close my prediction was that she managed an upscale fitness center.

"I'm a paralegal at a small law firm in Manayunk," she says. "This summer I'm taking the bar, so who knows, hopefully I'll be working there as a lawyer soon." Her green eyes shimmer when she says this. Something inside tells me her determination will make this a reality.

"It must be difficult to find the time to study, especially while working all day."

"Yep. My social life's taken a big hit." She laughs as her hand flies through the air. "But it's all good. I've wanted this for so long. And nothing comes free in life. There's a price for everything."

"I guess there is," I say as I consider the cost I've paid by hiding inside. That's when I get an idea. "Hey, I know you're busy, but are you free this Saturday to take the dogs for a walk and then afterward stop for coffee?"

"I'd love that," Lisa says. "I haven't met many people since I moved to this area. I have friends downtown, but sometimes it's a hassle to go there."

"I used to work in the city, so I know what you mean."

"Where do you work now?" Lisa asks. Her question catches me off guard. I don't want to share my entire story, yet I have to be honest.

"I work for a firm, Genesis, in Bala Cynwyd. But for the past two months, I've been working remotely from home. I return to the office next week."

"Wow, that's awesome. I'd love to work from home," Lisa says, not even questioning my reason for remoting.

"There are pros and cons." That's all I say as I shrug my shoulders, perhaps realizing the truth in this statement.

Then I see Gail and Susie coming down the sidewalk. "I'm going for a walk with my friends," I say as I point toward the older women approaching us. "You're welcome to join us," I offer.

"Thanks, but I have to head back home and get ready for work. We had a project that kept us there until nine last night, so our boss told us to take the morning off. But I'd love to walk this Saturday."

"Does nine work for you? Should we meet here?" I ask.

"Absolutely, and I know a great café nearby where we can get coffee and sit outside with the pups," Lisa says.

"Perfect. I'll see you Saturday then," I say, as I wave goodbye and head down the street to meet the two ladies.

***

Our walks with Susie, Gail, and their dogs are truly the highlight of my days. I love getting to know these two older women and hearing their stories. We have real conversations, sharing honest thoughts about current issues, emotions, and family. I've found that Gail and Susie think much younger than someone their ages might. Perhaps this explains why we get along so well.

During our time together, I've learned that before Gail knew Walter, she was a buyer for Saks Fifth Avenue. That most likely accounts for her impeccable style. Her husband, who she claims looked like Don Draper from *Mad Men*, swept her off her feet, proposing only five weeks after they met. It sounds like they had the perfect marriage.

Susie shared she was a kindergarten teacher, and I can totally see her in a classroom working with five-year-olds. After Henry died, she started volunteering at her old school, helping one of her former students who is now a kindergarten teacher in *her old classroom*. She also plays bridge and mah-jongg. Though from the sound of it, I think she enjoys the socializing more than the actual competition.

Unlike her sister-in-law, Gail is a loner by nature. She prefers to spend her time reading, going to Pilates, and riding her horse, which she keeps at a stable in Radnor. Recently, Gail became interested in horticulture and spends a great deal of time taking classes at Longwood Gardens. She's planning a perennial garden in the back-yard of her townhouse, meticulously mapping out plant placement to ensure a constantly blooming garden from spring through fall.

***

Later that evening, after the dinner dishes are in the dishwasher and Josie's had her final walk, I curl up in bed, inviting Josie to join me on her special sheet. I'm excited to start a new book that arrived today, *Rising Strong*, by Brené Brown. As I focus on her words, I appreciate how the author openly tells her story, presenting her thoughts in a clear and honest manner. But it's when I come to this paragraph that I find myself pausing to better digest her message:

> *"I want to be in the arena. I want to be brave with my life. And when we make the choice to dare greatly, we sign up to get our asses kicked. We can choose courage or we can choose comfort, but we can't have both. Not at the same time. Vulnerability is not winning or losing; it's having the courage to show up and be seen when we have no control over the outcome. Vulnerability is not weakness; it's our greatest measure of courage."*

I thought the word *vulnerable* had a weak connotation, like allowing your belly or Achilles' heel to be exposed. But what if Brené Brown is right? Could vulnerability be a sign of strength? If we permit ourselves to be seen for who we are and avoid hiding our thoughts and desires in an effort to remain safe, then are we actually being brave? If we show up as our authentic selves, without our protective armor, will we be accepted, even loved, as who we truly are?

I close the book after turning down the corner of this page. Questioning my foundational belief regarding vulnerability and courage, I have some rethinking to do. If I shifted perspectives and allowed my vulnerability to surface, might I find peace, even happiness? As I mull that thought over in my mind, my eyelids become heavy, and within moments, I fall asleep.

CHAPTER 18

I check my incoming mail. Nothing. A lump begins to form in my throat as I acknowledge that Miles has not responded to my request. But I know Miles, and if he thought me bringing Josie to work was a bad idea, he would have let me know immediately. Maybe he's checking to make sure no one's super allergic to dogs. Or perhaps he doesn't want to tell me no.

I walk into the kitchen to pour myself a cup of coffee. It's then I hear small pings against the front window. I turn and look outside, only to see it's begun to rain. It's been a particularly dry spring, and I wonder if Gail and Susie walk in the rain. But we're not meeting for a few hours, so hopefully it will stop by then. Pushing that thought from my mind, I decide to put in a few miles on the treadmill before showering.

As I begin running, I consider how my schedule will shift once I return to work. My morning runs seem to motivate me, and I want to continue this habit. But that means I'll need to get up earlier.

Wednesday is only five days away. Knowing that before leaving for work I must walk and feed Josie, run, shower, and have my own breakfast by 7:45, I decide to start setting my alarm for 5:30 a.m. Hopefully, my body will only need a few days to adjust to an earlier wake-up time.

There are definitely habits I don't want to revert to during phase three, my "life after quarantine." Gone are my afternoon visits to Starbucks when I rarely left with only a latte. Most days, I'd indulge in a cookie, chocolate-covered almonds, or some icing-covered treat. I certainly don't miss the four o'clock sugar crash.

As I begin the third mile, my mind shifts to other changes I want to adopt. The truth is, I've ignored my appearance these past weeks. I can't even remember the last time I blew my hair dry. From now on, I'm going to make an effort to look my best. That means paying attention to my hair, putting on makeup, and wearing something besides sweats or yoga pants.

My eyes travel to my hands, noting my ragged cuticles. I definitely need to give myself a manicure before Wednesday. Plus, a facial scrub and some extra moisturizing certainly couldn't hurt. I spend the rest of my run envisioning looking better, which will no doubt translate into feeling better.

When I hit five miles, I stop and walk for a bit before stretching out on the floor next to Josie. She licks the sweat from my legs. Her prickly tongue tickles, causing me to flinch a bit.

After taking a quick shower, I put on a touch of makeup and twist my hair in a clip, making an effort to loosen a few strands to frame my face. Instead of instinctively putting on yoga pants and a T-shirt, I dress in a pair of jeans and a white long sleeve shirt.

The weather app on my phone tells me it's now fifty-nine degrees with a slight breeze. As I look out of the window, I see the rain has stopped and rays of sun are beginning to shine, mirroring my exact emotions.

Calling for Josie, I grab a lightweight jacket and gather all the necessary items before we head outside. My golden must also sense the change in weather, as not only is there a bit of a spring in my step, but there's also one in Josie's.

Gail and Susie arrive five minutes later. Susie looks adorable in her yellow slicker, a flowered umbrella tucked under her arm.

Her sister-in-law, wearing a gorgeous Burberry jacket, seems unfazed by any impending rain.

"I think the weather's turning," Susie says in a hopeful, singsong fashion, "at least that's what AccuWeather reports." She opens the top of her coat, perhaps warm from the plasticized material.

"I think we'll be fine," Gail says as she winks in my direction. I can only imagine the conversation that ensued prior to them arriving.

We begin our normal route, catching up on what occurred since we were last together. It's then I realize these morning walks with my new friends will soon come to an end. Swallowing hard, I say, "I'm going to miss these walks when I go back to work."

"What day do you start?" Susie's eyes seem to pop with enthusiasm.

"Wednesday. At least that's the plan." I wish my reaction was as positive as Susie's.

Gail places her arm on top of my shoulder as she says, "Ali, you know it's time."

When I fail to respond, she stops walking. Susie and I follow suit. All four dogs sit down, waiting to be directed to continue their walk.

"Look at how much your life has changed since we met last week. While you've only had Josie for a few days, I see a significant difference in you," Gail says.

"You should have seen me a month ago," I joke. Yet I'm not kidding, not one bit.

"Honey, Gail means you're ready ... you have everything you need to return to work, return to *life*." Susie gently grazes her fingertips across my forehead in a concerned manner. "But it doesn't matter what we see ... it's you who has to believe it."

"Susie is correct. Trust yourself, Ali. I haven't known you for long, but I'm an excellent judge of character. And it appears you're quite self-critical," Gail adds, tilting her head for emphasis.

"Don't you see? Leaving that guy was the best thing you could have done." Susie's eyes glow, and I sense I'm about to get some motherly advice, something I haven't received in almost twenty years. "It kills us to watch you constantly beat yourself up. You are a rock star, Ali. You have all of the skills you need to be successful at work and happy in life. And you will meet the right man. But *you* have to stop judging yourself. Remember, no one is perfect."

"And perhaps the time you spent alone was necessary. Sometimes we have to hit rock bottom before we can begin the climb back up." Gail's tone suggests that she, too, has been in a similar position. Maybe she experienced this after her husband died.

"Plus, from what you've said, your boss sounds like a gem! Do you actually think he would have asked you to come back to work if he thought you weren't ready? He sure has a sense of humor … choosing April Fool's Day as the date for you to return." Susie starts to giggle as Gail shoots her a look.

"I appreciate the confidence you both have in me." I smile, looking at each of them. "Actually, I'm beginning to feel better about returning to work. Of course, I'm nervous about seeing David." Instinctively I roll my eyes.

"So what if you see him," Gail says with a sternness in her voice as she narrows her eyes. "Do you still love him?" she asks in her usual direct manner, her free hand on her hip. Josie looks up at me, as if also waiting to hear my answer.

I haven't thought about this. Do I? My eyes naturally fixate on a specific cloud above, allowing me to consciously contemplate this question.

Several moments later, I look at Gail and say, "No, I don't ... maybe all along I was only in love with the idea of being in love." I surprise myself with the words that come from my mouth. While I haven't thought about David lately, I never questioned whether or not I loved him. I assumed I did. But now, I'm not so sure.

"So, if you didn't truly love him, then it won't matter if you see him, will it?" Gail gives me a small smirk then signals to the dogs to get up so we may resume our walk. I remain silent, mulling this point as we amble down the uneven sidewalk toward the park.

Small talk ensues for the next twenty minutes as I avoid answering Gail's question. But when we make the turn and head back to Haverford Avenue, I garner the courage to ask, "So, all along, it's been my mind telling me that if I see him, I'll lose control and embarrass myself?"

I look at Gail, who only raises an eyebrow as if to say, "Yep."

"But why did it hit me so hard? What was the reason I stayed locked away for weeks?" If this was all in my head, then why did I feel like shit for two months? I'm totally confused.

"Sweetie, this wasn't about David ... it was all about you trusting you. He was only the trigger. When you realized you weren't going to get married, well, you had two options. You either stay in the relationship, knowing it was going nowhere, or you leave. Wisely, you chose the second route. But the price was you needed to sit with yourself to remember who you are and what mattered. You had to discover who Ali is."

Gail then adds, "And then, when you noticed the two of us walking Josie without Mike, you knew something was wrong. That's what gave you the courage to finally go outside. Your compassion compelled you to see if Josie was going to be alright."

Scratching my forehead, I try to grasp everything these wise women are telling me.

"So this entire time I haven't been hiding due to fear?"

"I don't think it was fear of seeing David," Gail says, her tone serious. "Perhaps it was time for you to make some changes in your life, deal with the issues you've pushed aside for years."

The concept is plain and simple. "And Miles understood ... and that's why he was OK with me working from home, but gave me a deadline, knowing it would be time for me to return?" I ask.

Susie nods her head up and down. "Miles knows you. He could see what you were facing."

And then I remember the question Miles asked me that night: *Ali, are you afraid of seeing David, or is there something more that's kept you here, locked in your apartment?* He knew it wasn't David; it was me, not trusting and believing in myself. Miles must have seen me as a deer in headlights. Able, but totally blinded and unsure which direction to go. Yet he had faith I'd figure it out.

"You may be right," I say to Susie, which causes her to beam. "To me, David represented security, safety. However, there was no adventure in the relationship. We had a nice time together, but it was routine, perhaps even a bit boring," I admit, a bit reluctantly.

"See ... you knew being with David was not in your best interest. But you needed to realize he wasn't going to propose, forcing you to end it. Otherwise, who knows how long it would have gone on. Yet it sounds like you lost a bit of yourself while you were with him. And that scared you, made you fearful of who you were on your own. That's why you locked yourself in your apartment. You were searching for you."

Zing. While Susie's words shouldn't sting, they do. Yet she's absolutely homed in on the main issue. I was not comfortable with me because I didn't know who I'd become. The past two months gave me the necessary time to pause and choose how I wanted to move forward—what parts I wanted to keep, and what I wanted to leave behind.

"Of course, there will be missing pieces to your puzzle," Gail says while she carefully looks both ways as we cross our final intersection before we get to my building. "And perhaps those pieces are gone forever."

As she makes this statement, my mind immediately goes to my mother. Is it possible leaving David triggered the pain I endured when my mom died? It sounds far-fetched, but in some strange way, it makes sense. When I lost my mom, I had to fully rely on myself, as she was my only source of protection. Fast-forward to meeting David … that was the first time I felt safe again. But because our relationship was based on faulty assumptions, there wasn't any true sense of security. I had invented it in my head.

Gail brings me back to the present. "Now you are able to view the big picture of who you are. The stories you have been clinging to have served their purpose. They've given you the necessary information, completed most of your puzzle. But these stories no longer serve you. You can finally let them go."

Her last sentence resonates with me. The words *let them go* etch into my brain.

As our conversation concludes, so does our walk. My building is now in sight, signaling my time with these amazing ladies is about to end. While today has proven to be insightful in terms of my personal healing, I return to the sad fact that soon I won't be able to join them on their daily walks.

"I can't begin to thank you for everything you've said today." I stop and turn to face both women. "I think I am ready to go back to work. But I'm definitely going to miss walking with you." The tone of my voice drops an octave. My eyes then move to the four dogs, and I realize this will impact Josie too.

"But we can walk on weekends," Susie jumps in. "We can schedule in advance."

"I'd love that." Smiling, I give Susie a gentle hug. "And so would Josie. After all, you're like family to her ... and me," I add.

"I know we'll see each other before Wednesday, but trust yourself, Ali. That's all you have to do." Gail catches me by surprise as she pulls me into her arms, holding me for several moments before she takes a step back.

How blessed I am to have found these two beautiful ladies and, of course, Josie. I watch as the sisters-in-law amble down the sidewalk. Will, Grace, and Joy lead them back to their homes. Susie and Gail are practically opposites, yet their bond is beautiful and unique.

Josie suddenly tugs at her leash, causing me to turn. She pulls toward a little girl. I recognize her from the Dog Walker family, the Andersons. But it's only the mom and daughter. The dad and son are nowhere in sight. The little girl runs to greet Josie.

"Sasha, please wait. The dog may not want you to touch her," the mom calls out while scooping up their puppy. The child ignores her mom's plea.

"It's OK," I tell the mom. "Josie is super gentle."

Sasha reaches Josie, leans down, and wraps both arms around the dog's neck. I watch the interaction with curiosity. Josie's tail wags and her eyes light up. My dog seems elated to have the little girl's undivided attention.

"What's your dog's name?" I ask Sasha, who is totally focused on Josie, ignoring her own puppy.

"Millie," she says in a polite enough tone, though she shows no interest in me; she's enraptured with Josie. "She's an Australian shepherd."

"I'm so sorry," her mom says as she gently tries to coax Sasha away from Josie, placing Millie on the ground.

"It's totally fine. We just got back from a walk," I say as I pet Millie who seems pretty timid. "And it's obvious Josie's loving the attention."

"Well, as long as you're OK with it," she says before adding, "I'm Kristie, and this is my daughter, Sasha."

"Nice to meet you," I say. "I'm Ali, and this is Josie."

"How old is she?" Kristie asks. Millie slowly approaches Josie. Josie pulls slightly out of Sasha's clutch to check out the pup.

"Josie's three, but I've only had her for a week," I admit, amazed with the fact that we've become so close in such a short time.

"Did you find her at a shelter?"

"No. Josie's owner, an older gentleman, suddenly passed away. She needed a home, and I guess I needed a dog." I sigh. The words seem so trite, yet that's exactly what happened.

"That's a beautiful story," Kristie says. "I'd love to chat, but I need to head home so we can pick up my son at preschool. Sasha should be at school too." She looks at her daughter with raised eyebrows. "But someone had a tummy ache and didn't want to go to school today."

I laugh, remembering claiming that same imaginary ailment. Mom would call those "mental health days." Ironic, isn't it. I've had two entire months of mental health days. "Well, it was nice to meet you," I say as I bend down to say goodbye to Millie.

Josie follows my lead and sniffs the puppy. Slowly, Millie becomes more responsive.

"This dog's so afraid of everything." Kristie laughs then shakes her head before prying Sasha from Josie. Taking her daughter's hand, the mom heaves out a big sigh as she heads toward the sidewalk.

"But she's so cute," I say, imagining what it's like to have a puppy. I bet it's loads of work. This makes me appreciate Josie even more.

***

That night, at around nine thirty, I decide to take Josie out before heading to bed. I'm exhausted, perhaps from digesting the enlightening conversation with Susie and Gail. Regardless, if I hope to begin waking up earlier to run and prepare myself for my new routine, I'll need to go to bed soon. But first, Josie must be walked.

Tonight seems warmer than the past few nights have been. I'm fine with only a light jacket. As Josie and I slowly make our way down the lit sidewalk, I wonder how I'll feel walking into the office and facing people I haven't seen since mid-January. What has Miles told them?

Do they think I was sick, or do they know the truth?

Josie pulls me forward. Yet I remain lost in my own world. But then her playful bark startles me. Jerking my head in her direction, I see she's with another dog. Where did it come from? The dog's big and seems to be black, with a red leash. Then I see *him*.

"Hi," he says.

"Hey." My eyes light up, though I doubt he can see them. I can barely make out the features of his face. Yet tonight he's not wearing a hoodie, so I have full view of his profile. "Nice night," I add, not wanting this interaction to end.

"Yeah, it is," he says, somewhat distracted. It's then that his wavy dark hair becomes visible. It appears to fall toward his eyes, which are blue … light blue … crystal blue, actually.

My heart begins to race. There's an uncomfortable pause, and I'm unsure what to say.

144

After a moment, he begins to walk away. "Have a nice evening." He then adds, "Come on, Rocco."

And with that, the black lab sniffs Josie once more, as if to say goodnight, then follows his owner down the street, away from me. Have I missed my one and only opportunity to know this man's true identity?

CHAPTER 19

"And then he left, walked out of sight."

"And out of your life?" Lisa teases as she takes a sip from her mug of coffee.

After finishing a six-mile loop that Lisa and Hope do every weekend, we are now seated outside of a coffee shop in downtown Narberth.

"He was never in my life in the first place," I quickly respond as I close my eyes and shake my head. "I didn't think I'd see him again, but then I did, and I was tongue-tied." I let out a huge sigh.

"You know, it's probably best you played it cool." Lisa leans closer to me in a sympathetic fashion.

"Really?" I've been out of the dating game so long, I no longer know the rules.

"Yes, guys like the chase—you know that, don't you?" Lisa laughs a bit as she takes a bite of a peanut butter cookie. She then feeds a tiny morsel of it to Hope.

"I guess. But there wasn't much of one with my last relationship," I say as my mind reverts to my first encounter with David in the elevator. "It all happened pretty quickly," I admit.

"How long were you together?" Lisa asks.

"For over two years. It ended this January."

"Was it a tough breakup?" Lisa asks as she rests her chin on the palm of her hand, fully attentive as if she truly wants to know what happened.

And so I begin to share the tale of David, his daughter, whom I never met, and our cancelled trip to Costa Rica, where I thought he'd propose.

"I read the situation all wrong," I say, staring into my coffee mug.

"Well, it's no wonder you got that impression," Lisa says as she waves her hand and rolls her eyes. "You spent over two years together, you're thirty-two, and he's thirty-nine. Plus, you had a professional relationship ... why wouldn't you assume he'd propose?"

It's comforting to hear Lisa confirm my exact thoughts. Maybe I wasn't overreacting. I was merely behaving like any woman would.

"Well, the whole thing set me back, made me doubt myself, and pretty much everything else," I say.

"What do you mean?"

"Well, the day after we broke up, I was pretty devastated. I wasn't exactly psyched to go to work, but I made myself get up and headed to the office. But then, as I was about to get into the elevator, I don't know if I had a flashback to how I first met David or if I only imagined he was in the elevator that morning, but I panicked and fled back to my car in the parking lot. After that, I was unable to return to work."

Lisa's eyes widen as she pulls her chair closer to mine, waiting for me to continue.

"One thing led to another, and before I knew it, I'd sequestered myself in my apartment. I knew I wouldn't have to face him again if I stayed home." I pause to take in a breath before continuing. "It wasn't so bad at first. I was amazed at how easily you can order everything you need. But then my boss, Miles, stopped by, unexpectedly."

"What did he say? What had you told him?" Lisa quickly interjects.

"I had said I was sick, but he knew it wasn't the case. Besides, David told him we broke up, so he put two and two together. Actually, it was Miles who made me question the real reason I was hiding. I thought it was because I didn't want to see my ex. But he helped me to discover it was so much more."

"What do you mean?"

"I had lost my own identity. Before I started to date David, I was determined, self-sufficient, incredibly focused, and productive. But a lot of that changed. I gave up so many of my needs in order to satisfy his. I guess I became dependent on him, relied on him for a sense of security. In the process, I lost a big part of myself. Recently, I've been trying to find those missing pieces, sort of put myself back together." My stomach clenches as I admit this. However, sharing what I've been through with another woman my age provides a sense of comfort.

"Well, I think it's pretty fucking amazing you figured all of this out by yourself, Ali. Not many women would. I know a few who would continue to blame the man instead of admitting there is ownership on both sides."

"Actually, it's pretty much all on me. David didn't ask for anything. I willfully gave myself to him." A lump forms in my throat as I declare this truth. "He never insinuated we'd get married either. From the beginning, he made it clear he didn't want me to become part of his daughter's life. That, in itself, should have spoken volumes."

"But now it's different, right? You're starting to remember who you are?" Lisa's eyes begin to dance in a somewhat devilish manner, suggesting she knows the answer to this question.

"I think so. At least I'd like to believe that's what's been happening. At first, I was in denial, most likely depressed. But then, I started to rebuild myself, ask questions, read books I used to think were for the helpless people who were desperately searching. But suddenly I became one of the seekers, and somehow, I found answers in those pages." I take a sip of coffee before continuing. "And, of course, there's Josie and how she ended up in my life," I say as I lean down to my dog sleeping by my feet and scratch behind her ears. She lets out a little moan then places her head on my feet. I then share the story of Mike's disappearance and how it propelled me out of the apartment and into Josie's life.

"I can't believe I've told you all of this," I say, somewhat embarrassed. I hope I haven't scared her away, made her think I'm batshit crazy.

"Are you kidding? Your story is amazing. Seriously, you've done some major work on yourself—discovered quite a bit, if you ask me."

"It's certainly been a journey. And now, this Wednesday I return to work. Of course, Miles chose April Fool's Day as my first day back." I laugh at the absurdity of it all.

"I think I like this Miles guy. You've got a great boss." Lisa finishes the last bite of her cookie as she tells me what I already know.

It's then I realize I've monopolized the entire conversation. All I know about Lisa is that she and Hope live three blocks from me and she recently moved from Fishtown in order to help take care of her sister who has depression issues. Oh, and she works at a law firm in Manayunk as a paralegal but is studying for the bar.

"So now you know pretty much my entire love life. What about you? Are you seeing anyone?"

Lisa looks up at me, her cheeks glowing brightly. "I think so," she begins, then stops. "I met Robbie on a train headed downtown," Lisa says as she takes several strands of hair and begins to twirl them in her fingertips. "It started as harmless flirting. I assumed he was chatting me up to pass the time, you know? But then, last week he asked me to go to a concert at the Electric Factory to see The xx. Afterward, we went out for drinks. He's pretty awesome." Lisa actually giggles as she continues to play with her hair.

"Are you going to see him again?" I ask, curious.

"Yes, we're having dinner tonight. I'm not sure where, but he said it was casual, but nice. I've been trying to figure out what to wear all day."

Clueless regarding fashion, I decline to offer clothing advice. But I can give encouragement. "He must like you. Two weekends in a row, well that says something. At least it says something to me."

Twenty minutes later, I'm more up to date with Lisa's life, and we place our empty mugs in a bin on a table inside then head back.

"Ali … " Lisa pauses in a slightly awkward manner.

"Yes?" I ask, sensing she needs permission to proceed.

"Would you mind if I shared your story with my sister? Her situation is different, but she's kinda frozen in time, if you know what I mean."

I nod, as I can definitely empathize. "Of course you can. If you think it will help."

"Thanks. Kimmy's been through a lot. Like you, she had a difficult ending to a long-term relationship. But they didn't break up. Luke, her boyfriend, was shot." With that, Lisa stops then turns to look at me. Her face suddenly appears ten years older as the lines in her forehead become more pronounced and slight wrinkles form at the corners of her eyes.

"Oh, Lisa, that's tragic. Kimmy has a *real reason* to isolate herself from life." Suddenly, a wave of suffocating shame envelops my body, causing me to look away, embarrassed with the deal I've made of my problems, which are incredibly insignificant compared to Kimmy's.

"Don't compare your situation to Kimmy's. What you felt was real. It's unhealthy to deny your emotions. Stuffing them inside will only cause damage to your body," Lisa says in an emphatic tone. "Seriously, that's why I'm working so hard to help Kimmy. She's not in a good place, but if she doesn't go through the process and instead ignores her feelings, well, they will only resurface later, causing her even greater pain. You're doing the work, processing things, and because of that, you're going to be fine—no, better than fine. You're going to be great." And with that pronouncement, Lisa takes my hand and gives it a squeeze.

"I hope so." In return, I offer her a half smile.

"Letting me share what you've been going through will be huge." Lisa pauses, somewhat hesitating before continuing. "Ali, would you be willing to talk with her? Perhaps if she met you, she'd feel inspired, see there's a light at the end of the tunnel, so to speak."

"Anything. If I can help in any way, I'm in." I look Lisa straight in the eyes as a way to emphasize my commitment.

We plan to walk again next Saturday, and Lisa promises to fill me in on her date. I wish her luck and again extend the offer to meet with her sister. Before Josie and I head inside, Josie nuzzles Hope a few times. I think my dog's enjoying making friends as much as I am.

As soon as we get home, I decide now is as good of a time as any to start some self-care. Looking in the back of the bathroom cabinet, I find a jar of Mayan clay, the label promising to tighten my pores and exfoliate dead skin cells. I read the directions, and in ten minutes, the mud-like substance tightens on top of my face. I then find my pedicure tools and promptly begin to soak my feet, softening the skin so I can then pumice the callouses away. Pondering several shades of polish, I choose a pale pink tone. Once I've washed off the hardened mask, I proceed to paint my toenails and then my fingernails. Afterward, I lie on the sofa and pick up Eckhart Tolle's *A New Earth*, allowing my nails to dry as I read about happiness:

"The primary cause of unhappiness is never the situation but your thoughts about it. Be aware of the thoughts you are thinking. Separate them from the situation, which is always neutral, which always is as it is. There is the situation or the fact, and here are my thoughts about it. Instead of making up stories, stay with the facts."

Eckhart Tolle confirms it's my thoughts that have held me hostage for weeks. It wasn't breaking up with David; it was my reaction to everything. Like Gail said yesterday during our walk, I need to let go of my stories because they no longer serve me. Instead, I must stay with the facts. Unable to put the book down, I continue reading.

Finally, my nails are dry, and I've finished half of the book. I look at my watch. It's five o'clock.

Wondering what I'll make for dinner, I go to the kitchen and look in the fridge, only to discover there's nothing inside. I could heat up a frozen pizza or order takeout, but that doesn't sound appealing. For some reason, I want to cook, prepare a proper and nutritious meal for myself.

"I'll be right back," I say to Josie as I grab my purse and jacket. Josie stands to follow me, no doubt thinking we're heading out for another walk. But we're not; it's me who is leaving, for the first time in months, to go to the grocery store.

"You stay here, Josie. I'll be back in no time, OK?" I say, leading Josie to her dog bed, motioning for her to lie down.

Reluctantly, she settles into the bed, giving me a look as if to say, "Fine, whatever."

This dog definitely has a sense of humor. I chuckle as I walk down the stairs and out the back door into the parking lot. I'm actually excited to pick out my own produce and discover what new products may be on the shelves. As I get into my car, which I have not driven for over two months, I sense a new freedom as I pull out of the lot. Instead of uncertainty, I note confidence, perhaps even optimism. It's then the sun appears from behind the clouds, rays hitting the windshield of the Volvo. Yes, the sun is glimmering, and finally, I am too. No more dimming my light. It's time. I'm ready to shine.

CHAPTER 20

I let out a big yawn, feeling refreshed after nine hours of solid sleep. Josie's head rests on my calves as she gently snores. Careful not to disturb her, I remain in bed and allow my mind to wander to the upcoming week.

The thought of returning to Genesis no longer causes panic. In fact, I'm kind of looking forward to seeing everyone. Well, almost everyone. But he won't be there, at least not this Wednesday. Miles wouldn't let that happen.

Speaking of Miles, he still hasn't responded about me bringing Josie to work. I lift my head from the pillow to gaze at my slumbering dog. Susie and Gail offered to take Josie with them on their daily walks, but she'd be home alone for most of the day. The thought of leaving her sequestered in this apartment saddens me. I've certainly been there, and I don't want Josie to experience what I have. Plus, she'd love coming with me to Genesis.

I put on workout clothes before taking Josie out and feeding her breakfast. As I'm about to hop on the treadmill, I look outside, noting how beautiful it is. The buds on the trees appear as if they're about to burst. Yellow daffodils are everywhere, causing me to question why I would choose a treadmill over the outdoors. I shift gears and decide to run outside.

Moments later, as I'm about to walk out of the door, Josie looks at me with those "I want to go" eyes.

Yet I'm a bit nervous about doing an entire run with her. It would be better to take her out for a mile or so at a time, so she can build her stamina.

"How about if I come back and get you after a few miles? We can run the last bit together, OK?"

Josie smiles and wags her tail. I think she likes the word *run*.

I chuckle at my dog's reaction as I head down the stairs and out the door, not once second-guessing leaving the building. Walking outside has become natural. The woman who is about to run to the nearby park is definitely not the same person who locked herself in her apartment, ordered out for all of her needs, and fell into a deep depression. I guess sometimes it does take a breakdown to have a breakthrough, and I sense that's exactly what happened.

Forty-five minutes later, I'm back, climbing up the stairs to get Josie. She's waiting at the door, leash in mouth, looking eager to join me.

Once we get to the sidewalk, I begin to jog. Josie follows. Then after a bit, she takes the lead, confidently forging ahead.

Slowly, I quicken my stride until I'm at a comfortable pace. It doesn't seem to be a challenge for Josie to keep up. I watch for signs that she's tired, but she appears to be a natural at running. It's amazing how quickly Josie's adapted to me. This must be so different from her life with Mike.

After fifteen minutes, I decide she's had enough for her first official run. Since Josie doesn't look tired, we keep walking.

As we head down the path, I'm in awe of the number of people out this morning. And no wonder—it's an amazing day. This is the warmest it's been all year. My forehead's beaded with sweat, and my long sleeve shirt's damp, clinging against my skin. Yet the sun's rays keep me warm and comfortable.

As I'm wondering whether or not Josie will be able to do a full run with me someday, Josie yanks me toward the grass to the right of the sidewalk. Frowning at her for her aggressive behavior, I then realize why she pulled so hard. She spotted a black lab and wants to say hello. But this is not any black lab—*it's Rocco.*

Slowly, my eyes follow his leash to Stephen, or whomever my mystery man is. When I look up at this gorgeous guy, I realize he's watching me. And he's got a big grin on his sweet yet sexy face. There's a boyishness to his look, but for some reason, I think he may be older than me.

"Hey," he says, but this time with a smile, not the distracted look he wore the other night.

"Hi," I say, feeling like a schoolgirl whose crush finally noticed her during science class. Yet this time I'm committed to keeping the conversation going, even if I'm a bit tongue-tied at first.

"What an amazing day," I say in my most upbeat voice. I know, it's lame resorting to the weather, but I'm not exactly skilled in small talk with hot guys.

"I know. Too good not to be outside," he says. His eyes continue to look into mine.

Wanting to know his real name, since referring to him as Stephen suddenly seems ridiculous, I introduce myself. "I'm Ali, Ali Doyle," I say. "I think we bumped into each other the other night," I casually add, though my intent is anything but casual.

"We did?" he asks, looking confused. "If so, I apologize. I had a lot going on. In fact, this past week has been a blur." Then he quickly shakes his head, his curls falling into his face as he says, "I'm sorry ... I'm Nate Cavanaugh." He reaches his hand out to me.

Not expecting to actually touch this man, I place my hand in his, instantly noting its warmth and smoothness. We hold on a bit longer than what I consider ordinary. My cheeks blush as I self-consciously remove my hand from his, pulling it back close by my side.

It seems as though Nate, too, noticed the tinge of awkwardness, as he switches topics and turns to his dog. "And this is Randolf Octavious, or Rocco for short." I remember him calling his dog by his name the other night, but I had no idea Rocco was short for something else.

"What's your dog's name?" Nate asks as he crouches next to the dogs, scratching both behind their ears.

"Josie, just Josie." I laugh realizing I don't even know her official name, the one on her certificate.

Nate and I proceed to discuss how labs and goldens always seem to gravitate to one another during walks. It's something I've noticed but didn't realize it was "a thing."

As we continue to chat, I learn Nate is a pediatric oncologist at CHOP—Children's Hospital of Pennsylvania. He's not a CIA agent who lives in DC and comes to suburban Philadelphia every month to visit his mom. And he's at least my age, as it takes a long time to become a pediatric oncologist.

"Your hours must be pretty tough," I say, wondering if that is why his mind was elsewhere the other night.

"This is my fifth year at CHOP, so I guess I'm used to the craziness by now. What do you do, Ali?" I like the way he says my name, pronouncing the *i* like a soft *e*.

"I'm a software engineer. I work at a small firm that specializes in telephone software," I say, which is the truth, only I haven't worked *there* for a while.

"I have to admit, I have absolutely no idea what a telephone software engineer does." He begins to laugh and shake his head, and I think to myself that his might be the cutest laugh I've ever heard.

"Well, it's not that exciting," I begin, "a bit boring, actually." Damn, I am a horrible flirter. However, I continue. "It mostly involves design, coding, things like that," I say in a nonchalant manner, trying to downplay my job.

But he doesn't let me. "No, seriously, that's pretty high-tech stuff. Impressive." Once again, his crystal blue eyes lock on to mine, causing me to slowly melt.

All this time, Rocco and Josie are sniffing, nuzzling, smelling nearby bushes—typical things dogs do.

"Which way are you headed?" Nate asks when the dogs begin to get a bit restless.

"Nowhere," I say, then clarify my answer. "I ran earlier this morning, then I wanted to see if Josie would like to try running a bit with me." Suddenly, I realize how sweaty I am. Do I smell? Is my hair a total mess? My God, I didn't even look in the mirror before I left this morning. At least I brushed my teeth. I sigh, conscious there's nothing I can do about it at this point.

"How old is Josie?" Nate asks, looking confused.

And then I realize how odd it sounds for someone to randomly take a grown dog running for the first time. Most people introduce the sport to them when they're puppies, gradually building up mileage.

"Josie's three, but I've only had her a bit over a week. Her owner died suddenly. And, well, she needed a home, and I wanted a dog, so it all kind of fell in place." I give him the short version, conscious I don't want to scare the guy by telling him I was watching the Dog Walkers and became concerned when my imaginary friend failed to show up one day.

"You two kind of found each other? Now that's pretty incredible." Once again, he gazes into my eyes, and I become lost in the intensity of his stare.

"I'm pretty lucky," I finally say as I move toward Josie and lean down to kiss her head.

"I'd say you're both lucky." Nate winks.

Dear God, did he really do that?

"So did she like running?" he asks in a curious tone.

"I think so. She had no trouble keeping up. Figured fifteen minutes was enough for her first time out."

"And I bet you're pretty fast." Nate's eyes travel to my legs, and a strange sensation envelops me.

"Not really." The words instinctively come from my mouth, but my total focus remains on him.

"So I guess home is that way," he says, pointing in the direction from which we came.

"Yes, it is. I live a bit over a mile down Haverford Avenue."

"That's near me. We're practically neighbors." He laughs while shaking his head. "How come I haven't seen you before? Besides the other night when I was so out of it."

"We must have different schedules. Plus, I didn't walk around the neighborhood much before Josie," I say. The truth is, before I sequestered myself, I was rarely home. And if I was, David was usually with me, and he wasn't one for taking strolls around the block. "Where do you live?" I ask, hoping I'm not being too bold.

"I live near Iona and Windsor."

I know exactly where that is. It's only a few blocks from my place, and I've driven by there multiple times.

"That is close by." All this time he was right in my backyard, and I didn't know it.

Twenty minutes later, we're standing outside my apartment, but I don't want my conversation with Nate to end. Looking at Josie, it appears she, too, is a bit smitten with Rocco.

"Hey, would it be strange if I asked you for your number?" Nate inquires as he takes his phone out of his back pocket. "I promise you, I'm not a stalker or anything."

Once again, he winks, causing my core to rumble. Telling myself to get it together and not do or say anything embarrassing, I give my number to Nate ... who is not Stephen ... nor does he work for the CIA ... but is a pediatric oncologist ... who lives only blocks from me.

As Josie and I turn and follow the walkway to the building's entrance, I can sense Nate's standing there, watching us. When I get to the door, I turn and see I was correct. He hasn't budged, and he's got an impish grin on his face, making me giggle. I unlock the door, then turn to wave. My heart flutters as he waves back.

"Josie, did you recognize Rocco?" I ask, my voice filled with renewed energy. I wonder if she intentionally pulled on her leash so Nate and I would have to talk. It reminds me of the scene from *101 Dalmatians* when Pongo entangles his leash with Perdita's, forcing Roger to collide with Anita. Josie wags her tail, blankly staring at me as if in full denial. Yet a part of me wonders.

It's past eleven, and I realize how thirsty and hungry I've become. So I decide to make pancakes. I can't remember the last time I allowed myself this indulgence. I take the box of mix from the cabinet, pour the contents into a ceramic bowl, add a tablespoon of oil, then crack open an egg, tossing it carefully into the bowl. After rigorously mixing the batter, I put a skillet on the burner and turn the flame on medium. Then, as I add a dollop of butter before pouring batter into the pan, my mind returns to earlier this morning, when I officially met Nate. How can this guy be so incredibly hot and sweet at the same time? And he's a doctor? There's no way he's interested in me.

Within minutes, bubbles appear in the batter, signaling it's time to flip. I take the spatula, slide it under the pancake, and carefully toss it, watching as it lands perfectly on the other side.

Four minutes later, I'm sitting at the counter, a pancake on my plate, and another one cooking in the skillet. Instead of adding syrup like most people do, I sprinkle granulated sugar over it before taking my first bite.

Mmmm. It's delicious. So is Nate. My mind replays this morning's exact conversation. He assumed I was a fast runner? Merely thinking about him makes me giddy, something I haven't experienced in years. I bask in this new sensation. But once I'm halfway through my second pancake, while my emotions may be light, my stomach certainly isn't. I don't think I can finish what's on my plate, so I give Josie the rest, suspecting she must be hungry after our run.

***

I spend the rest of the day organizing … I'm not sure what, as my apartment is in order. Yet I can't sit still. My phone pings. I jump. Could it be Nate texting me?

I literally run to my phone that's plugged in on the counter. Scrolling the screen, I see it's from Lisa, not Nate. Regardless, it's exciting. It's been a while since a friend texted.

Lisa: *Hey, want to grab a drink with my sister and me tonight? I know it's a Sunday, but when I told her about you, she said she'd like to get together. And that's the first she's wanted to go out in a long time. How about O'Malley's at 7:00? Do you know where it is?*

Do I know where it is? *Shit.* I toss the phone on the sofa in frustration. Of all of the places she could have picked, O'Malley's? What if David's there? But I want to see Lisa and meet her sister. I promised I'd talk with Kimmy, try to help. I shut my eyes tightly as if I'll find the answer behind the closed lids.

Several moments later, I hear the voice.

Accept.

That's it. Not "go, but ask to meet somewhere else." Knowing that if I have any chance of transitioning back to real life, I'll need to take chances, so I choose yes. I will go, and if I see him, at least I won't be alone.

Reluctantly, I pick up my phone from the sofa and reply that I'd love to meet them tonight … at seven … at O'Malley's.

CHAPTER 21

Pulling into the parking lot momentarily takes me back to January 23. But before I go down that rabbit hole, I quickly snap out of it, knowing tonight will be different. It's not dark and cold outside, and there's no black ice lurking between the parked cars. Plus, I'm not having dinner with David, who is sitting at *our* table with a manhattan in front of him as he glances down at his watch, wondering why I'm late.

No, it's late March, and the sun is only now beginning to set. And I'm meeting my new friend and her sister, not my boyfriend who is about to cancel our trip to Costa Rica.

O'Malley's is quiet when I enter. There are only a few patrons sitting around the U-shaped bar, most likely regulars. After all, it's a Sunday night. Aren't most normal people home with their families?

My eye catches an arm waving, forcing me to turn in that direction. Lisa and her sister are at a round table in the back corner, away from the other diners. As I walk toward them, I sigh in relief as it's clear *he* is nowhere in sight.

"Hi, Lisa," I say, then turn to the somewhat younger, brunette version of Lisa sitting to her right. "I'm Ali," I say, extending my hand.

"Kimmy." It takes a moment, but Kimmy tentatively places her hand in mine. Her touch is cool, and her fingers are small. I give her hand an encouraging squeeze.

"Have you had their margaritas?" Lisa asks, after opening the drink menu.

"Yes, they're delicious," I say, remembering how David and I would come here on Cinco de Mayo. I know, it's strange to celebrate a Mexican holiday at an Irish pub.

"Could we have a pitcher of margaritas?" Lisa asks a waitress as she approaches our table, tablet in hand. "Oh, and an order of nachos," Lisa assertively adds. "Chicken nachos?" she asks, looking directly at me.

"Sounds great," I say as the waitress turns to leave, but not before she looks at me twice, as if she recognizes me. This causes a slight shiver to run down my spine.

I shift my attention to Kimmy. "It's great to meet you," I say, hoping to pull her into a conversation.

"Thanks," she mumbles, then casts her eyes down to the dark hardwood floor.

"Ali, Kimmy also runs, a lot," Lisa says, as she smiles at her younger sister.

This causes Kimmy to perk up a bit. "Yes, it's my favorite thing to do. That, and read," she shyly reveals.

"I love to do both of those too," I say, happy to learn Lisa's sister and I have some things in common. That will certainly make tonight go more smoothly, as I was a bit unsure how drinks and dinner with Kimmy would be.

"In fact," Lisa begins, "Kimmy is considering running the Philadelphia Marathon this November. If she does, it will be her tenth marathon." Lisa beams as she shares this fact.

"I haven't decided yet," Kimmy replies. "I'd like to, but November, well, it's so far away." The volume of her voice drops as she ends her sentence.

"Well, I've never run one," I admit. "But it's been on my bucket list."

"You should do it then," Lisa says, eyes widening as she leans forward. "In fact, why don't the two of you run it together?"

Startled at the thought of running a full marathon and realizing the longest distance I've run is ten miles, I'm inclined to say, "Hell no." But then I actually reconsider when I see a glimmer in Kimmy's eyes. Perhaps if she had someone to train with, well, that might make a difference.

"I'm in if you are," I say before thinking out the ramifications to this commitment.

As I naively pledge to running 26.2 miles this upcoming November, the waitress arrives with our margaritas. She places a glass in front of each of us, expertly balancing the tray holding the pitcher, before she fills our glasses, which are laced with sea salt.

I lift mine in a toast. Lisa and Kimmy follow suit. "To the Philly Marathon," I say.

"Yes!" Kimmy agrees.

"What about you, Lisa?" I ask, giving my new friend a nudge on the shoulder.

"Aw, I'd like to join you ladies, but I have a bad knee from soccer."

"Lisa played Division One for Pitt," Kimmy proudly announces.

"What position?" I ask, happy the conversation has switched from running, as I'm beginning to second-guess my decision.

"Midfielder … center midfielder." Lisa's face becomes serene, hinting she misses those days.

"What happened to your knee?" I ask.

"During the third game of my senior year, I got slide tackled as I was making my way down the field. The sweeper went in for the foul to keep me from scoring. But I fell down hard and tore my ACL, ending soccer for me." Lisa's shoulders slump.

"But you were amazing." Kimmy places her hand on her sister's arm. "In high school, all of the best soccer colleges recruited Lisa ... Duke, Michigan, Penn State."

"Yes, but Pitt gave me a full ride," Lisa reminds her sister.

We stay at O'Malley's until ten thirty, sharing another pitcher of margaritas, two orders of chicken nachos, and a delicious chocolate lava cake. Full and happy, I can't remember the last time I've had so much fun with women my age. There was no BS, no gossip, no judgments, only real conversation.

As we leave O'Malley's and I head to my car, my spirit seems lighter than it has been in years, despite all I've eaten. Unlike the past several days, the spark inside isn't flickering on and off. Instead, it's becoming a more consistent light that seems to point me in the right direction. While I'm nervous about committing to a full marathon, something tells me it's the right thing to do. Before we left O'Malley's, Kimmy and I agreed to meet and run a few miles tomorrow afternoon. I guess this formally cements us as running partners. However, I feel as though I can help Kimmy, and she definitely needs *someone* right now. After all, nobody can lift themselves out of depression without assistance. I certainly know. As I pull out of the parking lot, I think of how pivotal Josie's been in my recovery.

Yet it wasn't only Josie. There have been more in my camp. I've got Gail and Susie. And now I can add Lisa and Kimmy to that list. Plus, Miles. I guess I am pretty lucky.

***

Josie's waiting at the door when I get home. This is the longest I've left her, and she's definitely happy to see me, or maybe she needs to go out.

As we take the last walk of the day, I reflect on how far I've come in such a short period of time. No longer am I self-quarantining in my apartment. I am beginning to trust myself and let go of my fears. But that's not all … I've adopted a golden retriever, met some nice women, and committed to running the Philadelphia Marathon. Plus, there's Nate, though I have no idea if he'll call me.

But the true test of my growth will be on Wednesday. I won't know for sure if I'm healed until then.

My thoughts are interrupted by a text coming in on my phone. Could it be from Nate? Excited, yet nervous, I pull my cell from my coat pocket. The message isn't from Nate, but it's the next best thing. The text is from Miles, and he says it's fine to bring Josie to Genesis. In fact, he thinks it's a great idea.

CHAPTER 22

Kimmy texts to let me know she'll be outside in a few minutes. I put on a light windbreaker then do some quick stretches in preparation for this afternoon's run. Josie looks at me, her head tilting back and forth, as if she's trying to understand what's going on.

"Josie, I'll be back in no time," I say as I take my apartment key from the small table and give her a quick kiss on the top of her head. A bit of guilt comes over me as Josie gets up and follows me to the door.

"No, Josie. We're not going on a walk," I say in my sweetest voice.

Sullenly, Josie retreats to her dog bed and begrudgingly plops down.

By the time I make my way out of the building, I see Kimmy jogging down the sidewalk. Her stride is natural, graceful, effortless. A part of me panics, conscious of how I am not that type of runner.

"Hey, Kimmy, how's it going?" I ask as Kimmy slows to a stop.

"Good." She offers me a brief smile before her face returns to its somewhat sullen state.

"Where do you want to go?" I ask, knowing I have no pre-planned route in mind.

"Why don't we head this way." She points to the left. "We can run to Lower Merion High School then do some laps on the track. It will break things up a bit."

I nod my head in agreement, and we proceed, side by side, down the uneven sidewalk. I'm careful to lift my feet to avoid tripping on the raised cracks. Kimmy's pace is faster than what I'm used to, causing my breath to quicken. However, I do my best to keep up.

"How long have you been running?" Kimmy asks.

After pausing for a moment, I say, "On and off for about seventeen years." It's the truth. I started running after my mom died. Unsure whether it was an escape or therapy, I only know running provided comfort.

"That's amazing," Kimmy says, a tone of wonderment in her voice. "I ran cross-country in high school. Then I guess I kept running because of how freeing it feels, as if there's nothing holding me back, keeping me confined."

Her last words stick with me, making me wonder if there's a deeper meaning to her statement. But instead of probing, I assume it's related to Luke. "Running's definitely healing."

"In so many ways," Kimmy responds.

And so we run, fast, without stopping. Sweat pours down my face, soaking the shirt beneath my jacket.

An hour and five minutes later, Kimmy and I say goodbye. The Garman on my wrist states that we ran close to eight miles. Damn, that was a fast pace. Wearily, I climb the stairs of my apartment building. When I unlock the door, Josie's waiting, her leash clenched in her mouth.

"OK. We'll go on a quick walk, but then I've got to stretch my hamstrings," I say as Josie bounds down the stairs. Slowly, I make my way to the door. But Josie's raring to go, anxiously pulling me outside.

***

I place Josie's bag by the door. It contains a fleece blanket, a collapsible bowl, some new toys, dog treats, and a roll of plastic bags. Tomorrow is Wednesday, April 1. April Fool's Day. Josie seems ready to go to work, but am I?

Staring inside my bedroom closet, I once again scrutinize the carefully chosen outfit for tomorrow: gray fitted pants, a white crisp button-down, and a tailored black jacket, all bought during the After Christmas Sale at Ann Taylor. My goal is to look sophisticated, polished, professional.

Before going to bed, I set three alarms to ensure I do not oversleep. But that is the least of my concerns. No doubt I'll be up throughout the night, as my brain is anything but tired.

I brush my teeth and wash my face, ensuring to properly moisturize, a new thing I'm trying to add into my routine. Then I crawl into bed, inviting Josie to join me. Readily, she jumps on top of her sheet.

"Tomorrow we're going to work," I declare to my dog, but the truth is, it's really meant for me to hear. It's no longer a choice; it's what *I'm doing*.

I nestle back into the pillow, thinking about the past two and a half months and how I transformed from a sniveling shrunken version of me to a more confident woman who is learning to let go and trust. I laugh as I reflect on my second run with Kimmy earlier this evening. Damn, that girl is fast. Well, she is five years younger than I am. Josie did the last mile and a half with us, and Kimmy seemed to enjoy having Josie along.

While sleep seems elusive, I do my best to relax as I play a sleep meditation from an app on my phone, hoping that will help.

***

Chirp. Chirp. Chirp. My first alarm sounds. It's 5:15.

Five minutes later, dressed in sweats and running shoes, I coax Josie off of the bed, where she is comfortably nestled, so we can go for a walk. She looks sleepily at me, but then she obediently hops off the bed and does a "downward dog" before she follows me into the living area. After hooking her leash to her collar, I grab my coat and we head outside. She's quick with her business, which is good because it's dark and chilly.

When we return, I feed Josie her breakfast, signaling this is the beginning of the day, then hop onto the treadmill and put in five miles before heading to shower. Surprisingly, my legs are not sore. My body must be adapting to the increased mileage. After showering, while my oatmeal simmers on the stove, I sit and meditate for ten minutes. This is my new routine, and I'm committed to making it a daily practice.

By 7:45, I'm ready, rather *we're* ready. But it's more than merely "ready"—I am fully prepared. Unsure if it was the morning run or the meditation that helped clear my head, I smile as I put my laptop and the folder with today's presentation into my Stuart Weitzman tote and sling it over my shoulder.

"Let's go to work, Josie," I say, picking up Josie's bag as my dog loyally follows me, a look of curiosity on her sweet furry face.

Ten minutes later, we're parking in Genesis's lot. After Josie jumps out from the back seat, she begins sniffing other cars, shrubs, and signposts, forcefully pulling me in different directions. She seems nervous. Perhaps she's absorbing my energy.

When we enter the lobby, a young woman holds the elevator door for us. She pushes the button with a five on it. I press the four button. The woman smiles at me then leans down and pets Josie. Josie sits there, attentive as her tail wags beneath her.

When the elevator doors open on the fourth floor, Josie looks at me for direction. I'm assuming she hasn't been in an elevator or an office building before, so I use soft words to encourage her out of the elevator before I turn back to the woman and say, "Have a great day."

The lobby's empty when we walk in. Actually, I planned to arrive early, hoping to use the extra time to get Josie settled. But to be honest, it was probably so I'd have a moment to center myself before engaging in the inevitable "welcome back" conversations with my coworkers.

I head straight to my office, encountering no one along the way. Once inside, I shut the door and look around. Everything looks exactly as it did in January, except now there's a gorgeous bouquet of pink tulips sitting on my desk. I read the card.

WELCOME BACK —MILES

He's such a sweetheart. I lean toward the vase, take a big inhale, then slowly allow the air to exit my lungs. Something tells me today is going to be OK—no, better than OK. I look down at Josie, who is eagerly exploring each nook and cranny in this small room.

"This is my office, Josie. Our office." I smile. "Let's get you situated." I take the report and laptop out of my tote and place them on my desk before unpacking Josie's bag. "Where would you like your space to be?" I ask as I eye the four corners of my office. "How about here?" I gently lay the blanket below the window.

Josie stops investigating her new surroundings then walks over and lies down, nestling into the soft fleece. I choose one of the new dog toys and offer it to her. Immediately she perks up and sniffs the furry rabbit. This toy has a crunchy paper sound, not a squeaker, something I feared might become bothersome if sound easily penetrates these walls. I put the bag of dog treats in my top left desk drawer, along with her leash and a package of rolled-up baggies, then I watch Josie play with her new friend. She looks happy.

After forty-five minutes of going through the files in my drawer, ensuring everything's where it should be, I decide it's time. Purposefully standing tall with my head held high and shoulders back, I pick up the report and laptop, clutching both tightly to my chest before turning toward Josie.

"I have a meeting now. You stay put, OK?" Then I turn on a television that sits on a corner table in my office, hoping the noise will keep her happy. I quietly exit and walk to the other end of the hallway.

Knock knock knock.

"Come in," the familiar voice says.

I enter. Miles, who is sitting behind his desk, stands up and walks over to greet me, offering a warm hug before inviting me to sit down.

"How are you? We've missed you, Ali."

"I'm good, really good," I say, meaning it. "Oh, and thank you for the flowers. They're beautiful."

"I thought you might like them. Did you bring your dog?"

"Yes, Josie's in my office. I'll introduce you to her later. She's such a sweetheart. I appreciate you allowing this. I hope it's not a problem with anyone."

"Are you kidding? With this crew?" Miles shakes his head and laughs before continuing. "Seriously, how are things going? Has the time away been helpful?" His face softens as he leans in.

"Well, I'm definitely not the person I was when you came to visit," I say, shaking my head as I remember my state when Miles unexpectedly stopped by in February. Miles smiles while I look down at the rug, slightly embarrassed. "For a while, I was stuck, unable to get out of my own way. I wasn't sure how to take the first step." And then I explain the Dog Walkers and how I noticed the one older man was missing from the group. "When I realized how concerned the two women were, I knew something was wrong. I couldn't ignore it. I had to offer to help."

"So the dog is what got you out of the apartment?" Miles asks, not mincing any words.

"Yes." Self-conscious of how crazy this sounds, I begin to twiddle my thumbs. "I had no idea what owning a dog entailed when I offered to take her," I admit, laughing aloud. "When she wanted out, I had to take her outside. It wasn't about me and my fears anymore."

"I'm happy for you Ali," Miles says. Then he sits up a bit straighter, fidgeting in his chair before asking, "How do you think you will be around David? He's still our counsel, so there will be times when he'll have to attend meetings you'll be at." Blunt, to the point.

Yet it's probably best to get this necessary conversation out of the way. "I've thought about that. And I've come to realize that while he was the catalyst, he wasn't the issue. I was." There, I said it.

"Good," is all Miles says. I think he's comfortable that I'll be able to maintain my composure while in David's presence. But am I?

"So how about you show me what you've been working on," Miles says, shifting his chair around his desk so he's now beside me.

I hand him a copy of the report then open my laptop, cueing up the PowerPoint, and begin to share the process I went through. I explain in detail how we can improve the bottom line for each product as well as increase marketability, supporting my reasons with statistics.

Forty minutes later, Miles leans back in his chair, interlacing his fingers behind his head. "This is excellent work, Ali. I knew you'd come up with solid recommendations." He smiles, pausing for a moment before continuing. "I am wondering, though … would it be possible to bring all manufacturing back to the States? I'd like to say our entire product line is built here."

This is why I love working for this man. He pushes me to be better.

"I'll do some research and see what I can find," I say, energized that I know my next steps.

"Perfect."

"Would you like to meet Josie?" I offer now that our business has concluded.

"I was waiting for you to ask me."

Miles and I leave his office and go to mine. When I open the door, Josie's curled up on the blanket, still playing with her toy. After she sees me, her tail emerges from underneath her body, and it begins to wag.

"Josie, this is Miles."

Miles slowly walks toward Josie, bends down, then begins to stroke her back. Within moments, Josie turns over, offering her belly to Miles, a true sign of trust.

"I now understand," Miles says, focused solely on my dog.

Just then, Carole, my administrative assistant, pops her head through the door.

"Ali, you're back!" She rushes over and hugs me. "We've missed you." No mention of why I was gone or if I am better. You have to love Carole.

"Miles said you were bringing your new dog." But before I can say anything, Carole's left my side and is down on the floor next to Josie. Slowly, more and more of my coworkers follow suit, and before I know it, my office is full, and Josie's become the biggest hit at Genesis.

"I'll walk her anytime, just let me know," Matt, one of the analysts, says. "I have a golden at home. They're the best."

"And if you need someone to watch her, like if you go away or something, I'll take her," Monica, our sixty-five-year-old receptionist, chimes in. "I've always wanted a dog like Josie." Her cherubic face radiates excitement as she makes this offer.

This exuberant "welcome back and meet Josie" party continues for the next fifteen minutes. Then, slowly, people file out of my office, returning to their cubicles, workstations, and offices of their own. I look at Josie.

"Everyone loves you, Josie. And to think I was worried about today," I say, releasing a big sigh. Josie moans back, as if to agree.

After realizing the time, I decide to take her outside, assuming she could use a short walk. Then I'll be able to dig into ways to bring all production back to the US.

As we walk toward the elevator, Monica says to one of the secretaries nearby, "Cover me, please. I'm going with Ali." Looking straight at me, she asks, "It's OK, right?"

"Of course. We'd love the company," I say, looking at Josie then Monica. Monica grabs the sweater hanging on the back of her swivel chair then rushes to join us on the elevator.

Something inside me shifts, releasing a piece of fear I had about returning to work. Everything is going to be fine. No one seems upset with me or looks at me as if something's wrong. Instead, it's the exact opposite. They've welcomed me back with open arms. And it feels so damn good.

***

After a long and exhausting day, Josie and I return to our apartment. It's a quarter to seven, so I decide to order takeout. Several minutes later, my phone pings. Wondering if the Thai restaurant has a question about my order, I quickly pick up my phone. But it's not the restaurant; it's Nate.

Nate: *Are you up for walking the dogs Friday after work? I can get off on the early side. How about I meet you at your place at 5:30?*

And the day only gets better …

CHAPTER 23

Sitting at my desk admiring the beautiful tulips Miles gave to me, I can't imagine my return to work going any smoother. I've completed the changes he and I discussed on Wednesday morning and am now investigating options regarding shifting production locations. It's good to be back.

I look at Josie, curled in a tight ball on top of her fleece blanket. All I need to do is say, "Time for work," and she's standing at the apartment door, leash in her mouth. She's been a huge hit with the staff. Even Miles seems to be smitten with her. But I must remember to make a note to buy a mini vac. She's shedding all over the place, and I'm embarrassed the cleaning service must deal with all of the dog hair. I figured if I did a quick vacuum at the end of each day, their job wouldn't be too difficult.

I'd be lying if I didn't admit I'm a bit distracted this afternoon. It's Friday, and in exactly three hours and twenty-seven minutes, Nate and Rocco will be outside my apartment building on the sidewalk, waiting for us.

Exactly what does one wear for a dog walk with a man who looks like Nate? I don't want to show up in sweats, but tight jeans and little kitten heels aren't called for either. Mentally reviewing the contents of my closet, I decide on a pair of yoga tights and a lululemon fleece. As the salesclerk said when I bought it, "You don't have to do yoga to wear our clothing."

Three hours later, we're home and I'm quickly changing into my "I look like I do yoga, but I don't" outfit. Glancing at the mirror, I adjust my hair before freshening my makeup. After all, it was seven this morning when I applied it.

"Josie, just so you know, this may kind of be more than a dog walk. I wouldn't call it a date or anything, but I need you to be on your best behavior, OK?" Josie's tail rapidly moves back and forth, and her tongue hangs out of the left side of her mouth. I clip her leash to her collar and wait, looking out the front window for signs of Nate.

Five minutes later, he appears.

"Ready? Let's go." Josie and I make our way down the steps and out the front entry. It seems absolutely ridiculous that such a minor movement was impossible two weeks ago.

"Hey," I say with a casual wave. Josie pulls to greet Rocco.

"Hi," Nate says with a big grin on his face as he steps toward me.

When we meet on the path, halfway between the door and the sidewalk, he gently touches my shoulder. "Good to see you. How was your day?"

Right then a breeze blows, and I instinctively push the hair from my face, somewhat flustered by his touch.

"Great," I say, "and yours?" I try to be cool and reserved, yet I know I'm anything but.

"I had a light case load today. Mostly reviews." He doesn't offer any more, but then again, he's in an extremely confidential profession.

We begin to walk. Josie and Rocco appear to be lifelong friends, as they happily lead us down the sidewalk. At first, the conversation is a bit awkward, but then it becomes easier as we begin talking about the dogs.

"So how are you and Josie doing?" he asks, seeming genuinely interested.

"She's been amazing. Mike must have trained her well. But I think it's more than that. She seems to get me even though it's only been two weeks," I say while keeping my eyes locked on the back of my dog, who is still walking side by side with Rocco, as if it's the most natural thing in the world.

"And she's good when you're at work?"

"Actually, Miles, my boss, lets me bring her to the office. I thought she might have trouble adjusting to being alone all day in my apartment. But luckily, Miles was open to the idea. So far, she's been pretty perfect. And, my coworkers love her. They're constantly stopping by my office to see Josie. Carole, my secretary, keeps bringing her toys, and our receptionist, an older woman named Monica who is kind of like a mom to everyone, baked homemade dog biscuits for her." I giggle remembering how excited Josie was after Monica gave her the special treats.

"What about Rocco? Is he OK when you're at the hospital? After all, you must work long hours. Do you have a dog walker?"

"Something like that," Nate says, but then quickly changes the subject. "Hey, I was thinking, I don't know about you, but after a long week, the last thing I feel like doing is cooking. If you don't have any plans for dinner, I thought we could grab a bite at White Dog Café later."

I literally stop in my tracks. Realizing how awkward that must appear, I quickly turn to Nate and say, in my most casual voice, trying not to sound too eager, "That would be nice. It has been a long week, and it would be great to relax and not deal with making dinner." Nate smiles. My heart throbs.

All this time, Josie and Rocco are happily walking along, seemingly oblivious to both of us and the nervous flirting that's occurring four feet behind them. Or maybe they realize what's going on and are allowing us space to figure it all out.

The wind picks up, and I visibly shiver. As if on cue, Nate puts his jacket around me. I do not resist in the least.

Ten minutes later, we're back outside of my apartment.

"OK if I pick you up in about forty-five minutes? That will give me time to feed Rocco."

"Sounds perfect," I demurely say before returning his jacket and heading inside.

"Oh my God, he asked me out to dinner." I pour a cup of dog kibble into Josie's bowl then do Mike's routine before presenting her with her meal. "Did you think he was going to do that?" I ask, looking at her, as if I expect a reply from my golden retriever.

Josie only wags her tail as she dives into her dinner.

What should I wear? Considering I struggled with an outfit for a dog walk, I wonder if I can figure out appropriate clothing for dinner.

But then, as I open my closet door, I spy a pair of dressy jeans and an embroidered top I'd bought at Anthropology this past January. I try on these brand-new clothes, looking in the mirror with a critical eye. But once I see the reflection, my shoulders soften.

Next, I go into the bathroom and scrutinize my face and hair. Since it's disheveled from the wind, I decide to sweep my hair back in a twist. After applying a touch more mascara, I lightly dab a bit of my favorite perfume behind my ears and untuck a few strands of hair before exchanging my simple earrings for another pair, ones that dangle a bit.

More confident with my look, I pull on a pair of boots and then transfer only the necessary items from my day purse into a smaller bag. I call for Josie, and we go for a quick walk to ensure she won't be uncomfortable waiting for me tonight.

Twenty minutes later, my doorbell buzzes.

I put on my leather jacket, give Josie a kiss on the nose, and head outside to meet Nate ... without Josie ... without Rocco. Tonight, it's only Nate and me.

***

He drives a Subaru Outback, which somewhat surprises me, but when I think about it, it doesn't. After all, there's nothing about Nate that seems pretentious or materialistic. While no doubt his salary would allow other options, he must have a ton of student loans to repay. This actually reassures me, indicating practicality.

As Nate opens the car door for me, something David stopped doing ages ago, I notice the scent of his cologne. I like it. But it gets better. After I'm seated and buckled in, I look up and right before he closes my door, he gives me the sweetest of smiles, looking deep into my eyes, as if trying to discover something about me.

***

The restaurant's not too crowded for a Friday night. However, next week's Easter week, so perhaps people are leaving for vacations, especially as most of the local schools have off for the holiday. The hostess seats us by the fireplace.

"This is one of my favorite spots," Nate says, and I concur. The ambiance from the fire only adds to this ideal first date environment.

"So did you grow up around here?" I ask as a busboy fills our glasses with ice water.

"No, I'm originally from the Pittsburgh area," Nate says. "Went to college in Bethlehem, at Lehigh, then med school at Johns Hopkins. I was in Boston for my residency and then moved to Philly when I began a fellowship at CHOP. I've been here since." He says this so humbly, as if everyone would be able to accomplish what he has.

"Wow, that's pretty impressive." But as the words come out of my mouth, his eyes cast down, and I realize that is the last thing he wanted to do, impress me. "I mean, that's great." He becomes more at ease with my rephrasing.

"Are you from this area?" Nate turns the discussion to me.

"Born and raised in suburban Philadelphia. Grew up in Upper Darby, attended the local Catholic school, then went to Villanova. After that, I worked downtown for a while before I met Miles, my boss. That's when I switched jobs and started working for Genesis."

"Who exactly is this Miles?" he teases as he brushes his hair off his forehead. This minor action makes my heart skip a beat.

"Miles founded Genesis. He's fifty-nine, bald, somewhat pudgy, and probably the nicest person I've worked for. He has been like a father to me. Gentle and kind. Miles challenges me, but at the same time is extremely supportive."

Nate smiles as he says, "You're pretty lucky. Not everyone has a boss like that."

I nod. If only Nate knew.

Right at that moment, our waitress appears, handing us each a menu. "We have some specials today. One is an elk burger topped with sautéed shiitake mushrooms, onions, and gruyère cheese. The other is halibut, pan sautéed with fire-roasted tomatoes, garlic, and cannellini beans. Both are delicious. While you decide, may I take a drink order?"

Nate gestures to me.

"I'll have a glass of pinot gris," I say, unsure what's the proper drink to order on a first date … because I've had so few of them.

"I'll have a glass of the house cab," Nate says then returns his attention to me.

"So you're from here. Do you see your family much?" he asks, ignoring the menu that was placed in front of him.

"To be honest, no. My mom died when I was fifteen, and, well, it hit my dad hard. He started to drink a lot. Our relationship went downhill quickly. When I got to college, I pretty much distanced myself from him. I had a scholarship, and I worked part-time as a waitress at a nearby diner, so I was able to take care of myself."

Nate frowns, not in disappointment, but perhaps in an attempt to process my life. "What about brothers or sisters?"

"I have seven of those, but they're much older. I was kind of an 'oops,' I guess. By the time my mom died, they were all out of the house. Three were in college, and the rest were married with kids of their own. No one lives in the area." I scrunch my shoulders then look down, as I do my best to explain my messed-up family. "We send Christmas and birthday cards, make an occasional phone call, but that's pretty much it. I know, it's sad." My eyes lift toward his, and I see he's visibly affected by my story. "Honestly, it's not that bad. You can't miss what you never had." My eyebrows arch. It's as if I keep reminding myself of this fact to soften the reality.

"But you never moved away? Why?"

My eyes squint as I look upward. "I have absolutely no idea."

We both laugh.

"I guess I like it here … four seasons, close to a city with good restaurants, not too far from the shore." As I profess these reasons, I begin to wonder if they are the truth or purely made up to justify why I've never risked venturing elsewhere.

"What about you? Why CHOP? Were there other places you could have gone?" I ask, hoping I'm not being too nosy.

"It seemed to be the right decision at the time," he says, but then becomes quiet.

Noting this shift, I decide to make light of his comment, as it's obvious I've touched on something sensitive.

"Isn't that always the reason?" I lightheartedly say, tilting my head, giving him my best smile.

***

I cannot imagine a better first date. We both order the elk burger special, and I think that impresses him. Perhaps he's used to women who only eat salad and salmon. Then, we split a piece of flourless chocolate cake afterward. Yet the best part is that there isn't a lull in our conversation, no awkward moments. We seem to jive.

I've *never* felt this way before, certainly not with David. There were often pregnant pauses when I wanted to ask something but assumed that I'd be crossing a line. So I held my tongue. But with Nate, I can be who I am. There's no need to hide.

When we pull up in front of my building, he puts the car into park.

"This was fun. Thank you," I softly say, trying not to sound serious, but wanting him to know how much I enjoyed the evening.

Nate's silent for a moment before saying, "I'll walk with you to your building."

Now it's me who is quiet as we head to the entryway of my apartment complex. Stopping in front of the door, I pause, unsure of what might happen. Nate turns toward me, takes a step closer, then gently places his hand on the small of my back, pulling me closer to him before he kisses me. His soft lips graze mine, but then, they become more deliberate. I melt as I lean into his warm muscular body that's now next to mine.

Several moments later, we separate.

"I'll call you," Nate says, walking backward down the pathway, a big grin on his face.

Somewhat flustered from this fabulous first kiss, I remain frozen by the door, my key in my hand. I stay that way, watching him leave.

"Goodnight," I call from the doorstep. He waves before getting into his car. I turn and unlock the door before sprinting up the steps. Josie must have heard me, as she's waiting patiently by the door.

"Oh, Josie, I had the best night," I say, as I grab her leash before the two of us return downstairs for the night's final walk. "He's amazing," I tell my dog. "Seriously, Nate's smart, incredibly gorgeous, and so kind. I didn't know they made guys like that anymore."

Josie nudges me with her nose, as if to say, "I know."

Ten minutes later, we're back inside. After hanging up my coat, I look at Josie. "So what do you think? Is he going to call?"

Josie gives a quick "ruff." Funny, I haven't noticed her bark before, except at mealtime. Could she be answering me? I look at my watch. It's nearly eleven. Kimmy and I are running tomorrow at nine. She wants to get nine miles in. Now I'm glad I had the burger and cake, knowing the extra carbs might be helpful in the morning.

CHAPTER 24

Bending over, I double-knot my new running shoes. Figured it was time to invest in another pair, especially now that I'm starting to put in more miles. Having a training partner is key. My commitment to Kimmy keeps me from cancelling on runs.

It's kind of ironic. Though I met Lisa first, I'm becoming closer to Kimmy. These two sisters couldn't be more different. While Lisa is deliberate, organized, and driven, Kimmy's tender, sensitive, and incredibly supportive. Kimmy's hinted at dealing with depression, but she hasn't mentioned Luke. All I know is what Lisa's shared. I cannot begin to understand the pain my running partner's endured. Yet, if she wants to talk about it, she will.

But I won't push her.

We meet halfway between our apartments. Since it's a longer run, we planned a loop route, not a back and forth, so we won't be able to get Josie for the last two miles. Josie will be disappointed, as she gets pretty revved up when I put on my running shoes. But I'll take her out tomorrow. I only plan to do a few miles then. If I go slowly, maybe she can join me for the entire run.

When I see Kimmy coming around the corner, I can tell something's wrong. Her face looks swollen, as if she's been crying.

"You OK?" I ask, coming to a stop when I'm within a few feet of her.

"I didn't sleep well; my mind was spinning all night." She's not making eye contact, so I don't press her. We begin to run.

Silence. There's only the sound of our feet hitting the pavement. After fifteen minutes, we come to a park. Hopefully, in this more serene environment, she'll open up. I decide to say something. "Kimmy, are you OK? You're never this quiet."

Kimmy doesn't respond. I turn my head toward her and see tears streaming down her cheeks. I reach over and touch her arm. My action, meant to support, only causes her to hunch over and dissolve into sobs. I stop running.

"I'm so sorry. I didn't mean to upset you," I say, not knowing what words would be helpful at this moment.

"No ... it's not you," she gasps between sniffs.

"What happened?" I place both of my hands on Kimmy's shoulders and lead her to a nearby park bench. When we sit down, she collapses in my arms. Unsure what to do, I hold her and allow her to cry. The intensity of her pain transmutes through her skin into mine, and it's as if I absorb part of her sorrow. Several minutes later, her sobs slow, and she pulls her head from my shoulder, looking up at me.

"Today ...," she sputters but then stops.

"Today's what, Kimmy?" I gently ask.

"Today's the day ..." Then the tears return.

"What happened on this day?" I ask, knowing it is April 4.

"Luke ...," she whispers.

I hold space for her, giving her the time she needs to proceed.

"It's when he died ... last April 4." The cries that follow cause people walking by to stop and stare. I ignore them. Instead, I cradle Kimmy, telling her it's OK, she's OK, she's going to get through this.

When it seems as though there are no more tears left for her to shed, she begins speaking in rapid phrases, spitting out facts. "I came home. We lived together in Manayunk … and saw him … lying there … blood everywhere. I called the police … but I didn't know he was in trouble … that people were looking for him."

I listen, resisting the urge to ask clarifying questions.

"I had no idea he owed so much. Sure, he bet on games, but so did all of his friends …"

"Oh, Kimmy." I can no longer refrain from speaking. "I'm so sorry."

"Later, the police told me he had received threats … telling Luke that if he didn't pay up, there would be problems."

I wait, allowing Kimmy the chance to share her story.

"The officer said he owed over $140,000. Why didn't he tell me? I could have helped him …" Kimmy stares at the ground as she grips her fingers into tight fists.

"Gambling's an addiction, like alcoholism and drug abuse." I feel as if I must say something.

"That's what all of the therapists said." She wipes her cheeks with her running jacket. "Apparently, Luke was also bipolar. Something I didn't know until his mother told me at the funeral service."

I take a deep breath, thinking that if her boyfriend would have shared this with Kimmy, things may have ended differently.

"Are you still going to counseling?" I ask, wondering how any person could handle this on their own.

Kimmy nods before saying, "Every week. And running helps." Her expression lifts a bit. Perhaps committing to run this marathon is the best thing for her.

"Well, then let's run," I say as I take her hand and pull her up off of the bench. "Come on." I nod my head in the direction of the path.

We start off jogging, slowly increasing our pace. At first, there's no talking, but then thoughtful conversation ensues.

"How long did you date?" I ask, hoping that engaging Kimmy is the right thing to do.

"Almost three years. We met at a bar downtown. He worked construction, made a lot of money. At the time I was living with some friends in East Falls. I was a hostess at Friday Saturday Sunday, you know, that restaurant downtown." She seems to look off in the distance as she then begins to tell me about their relationship. "In less than a year, we moved in together. He had this cute one-bedroom apartment in Manayunk. We were in love. Though sometimes we fought."

I nod, knowing no relationship is perfect.

"I didn't realize he was bipolar. I figured he had some depression issues. But it was much deeper than that." The stoplight turns red, and we come to a halt. I appreciate the pause as Kimmy's running fast, having increased the pace as she tells her story.

"Things were good for a while, but then he lost his job. Apparently, he mouthed off to the foreman. I told him it wasn't a big deal, that there'd be other jobs." The light turns green, and we begin running.

"Well, that was what I said the night before, and then, well, I came home from work the next day and found him …" She gulps.

The rest of our run is spent talking of their happier times. She shares how he brought her lilies on her birthday, took her on a carriage ride in Rittenhouse Square on Valentine's Day, and stayed up late with her to watch reruns of *Modern Family*. Somehow, talking about the good memories seems to soften the horrible image of finding him in their apartment. Our nine-mile run flies by, and before I know it, we're back.

"Ali, thank you," Kimmy says as she starts to cry again.

"You know I'm here for you," I say, meaning it with my entire heart.

Kimmy gives me a big sweaty hug before turning and running the last few blocks to her house. I head inside, knowing I promised we'd walk with Gail and Susie in twenty minutes.

I miss seeing them, and I think Josie also misses Joy, Will, and Grace.

After quickly changing into dry tights and a sweatshirt, Josie and I go outside and wait for Susie and Gail. When we see them approaching, Josie lets out another bark. I wonder if she's suddenly becoming communicative or if she spied a squirrel or chipmunk running on a tree branch.

"Ali, how are you?" Susie asks as she gives me a sweet motherly embrace.

"Great," I say, appreciating the warm hug. The dogs intertwine leashes, obviously happy to be together.

"Did the rest of your week go as well as you hoped?" Gail asks, getting right to the point. I had texted both of them to let them know my first day back was awesome. I believe they had concerns, and I didn't want Gail or Susie to worry. I had to laugh at the emojis Susie attached to her response. Gail only texted, "As I expected."

"But there's more," I begin. "I actually had a date last night." No doubt I'm blushing as I reveal this scoop to these women old enough to be my mother.

"Already? Where did you find him?" Susie asks, eyes wide, before Gail shoots her the look. "Well, I want to know." Susie wrinkles her nose at her sister-in-law.

"I met him while walking Josie," I say, thinking about last weekend. But then I add, "Actually, I'd seen him walk by my window ... before I met you." Admitting this lifts a weight from my shoulders. "But only once. And I saw him and his dog when Josie and I were walking. However, he didn't remember us. Yet, I kind of wondered about him ... who he was."

Gail and Susie grin, resembling a pair of Cheshire cats.

"So how was the date? Where did you go?" The words bubble out of Susie's mouth; she's unable to restrain herself.

"We went to White Dog, which is kind of funny, because he has a black lab and I have a golden retriever." It's only now I realize the irony.

"Do you like him?" Gail asks, eyes wide as if daring me to sugarcoat my response.

"I do." Returning to last night, remembering how Nate's lips felt on mine makes me blush. "He's smart, good looking, and incredibly sweet."

"What's he do?" Susie's questioning continues.

"He's a pediatric oncologist at CHOP," I say, knowing this will definitely elicit a response from Susie.

"Oh my God, a doctor! Well, this may be promising." Gail swats Susie's arm.

Laughing, I say, "Well, it's only been one date. Who knows if he'll call."

"Did he say he would?" It's Gail who asks this.

"Yes, after he kissed me goodnight." My cheeks become warm, signaling I'm turning bright red.

"Oh, he'll call, honey. I'd bet anything on that." Susie's got a dreamy look on her face, like she's returning to a distant memory.

As soon as we get home, the first thing I do is shower. My body seems to melt as the pulsating stream flows over my tight back and down my sore hamstrings. When I turn off the faucet, I hear the faint sound of my phone ringing. Fumbling out of the shower and trying not to slip on the tile floor, I run into the bedroom, looking for my phone. I see it on the bureau and quickly answer it.

"Hello?" I must sound like I've recently returned from a run, not stepped out from a relaxing shower.

"Hey, it's Nate."

My heartbeat quickens. He did call.

"Hey," I say, trying to sound interested, yet not too interested. Damn, I hate these mind games.

"What are you up to?"

"Just got out of the shower. I ran this morning then took Josie on a walk with two women from the neighborhood, the ones Josie used to walk with."

"It's a great day for that," he says, sounding like he's stalling a bit.

"Absolutely beautiful," I say, then add, "Were you out with Rocco?"

"Yeah, took him on a long walk this morning." Pause. "Hey, um, I don't know if you have plans tonight, but if you don't …well … um … do you want to come over for dinner? I went to the store and picked up some stuff." He quickly spits out the last words.

He's offering to cook for me? "Sure, I'd love to. Can I bring anything?"

"Only your beautiful self. I've got it all under control."

Nate now sounds more like himself. Wait, did he call me *beautiful*?

"How's seven?" he asks before giving me his address. "Oh, and feel free to bring Josie."

I hang up the phone and look at Josie lying on the purple sheet on top of my bed. "We have a date tonight, you and me, with Nate and Rocco. What do you think?"

"Ruff."

Damn, there may be more to this dog than I first thought. I bury my head in her fur, my sopping wet hair dripping all over the place. Yet I don't care. Nothing could bother me at this moment.

Then I get an idea. Though Nate doesn't want me to bring any-thing for dinner tonight, I can buy Rocco some dog toys and some-thing for Nate. But what do you take to a guy who's making you din-ner? Flowers? No. Chocolate? Wine? Tequila? Bingo. Tequila.

After dressing, I grab a quick lunch then head out to do some errands. But unlike before, there's no second-guessing myself, wor-rying about what he'll think. Something tells me it's all going to be good … no … much better than good, especially if last night's kiss and the fact that he's invited me to dinner at his place are any indi-cation. Yes, tonight will be special.

CHAPTER 25

Rummaging through my closet, I finally come up with the perfect "I'm going to a man's home for dinner" outfit: a loose cream blouse, short tan suede skirt, and boots. While anything but suggestive, it's definitely not my traditional go-to jeans-and-sweater look. Instead, it's more feminine and fun.

At 6:55, I call Josie and grab the two bags sitting on the kitchen counter; one's filled with dog treats and three squeaky toys, the other has in it a bottle of Patrón. Holding Josie's leash in one hand, the gift bags in the other, I head down the stairs and out the back door to my car. Several minutes later, I'm parked outside an inviting Tudor home. I look again at the note where I scribbled Nate's address. Yep, this is it. Somewhat surprised with how grown-up his house appears, I shrug the thought off as feelings of anxiousness begin to surface. I can't recall the last time a man cooked dinner for me. David certainly didn't.

"Ready?" I timidly ask Josie before exiting the car.

"Ruff." Her answer for yes. I love this dog.

The bright porch light allows me to fully see this quaint two-story home. I'm truly in awe. The house looks recently painted, and the shrubs are neatly trimmed. Daffodils fill the beds. Obviously, he, or someone else, takes impeccable care of this place. Not what I'd expect from a young single doctor. I ring the bell.

Within moments, the door opens, and there stands Nate, in jeans that fit him oh so well and a light blue chambray button-down shirt. He seems a bit flustered, more nervous than I would have expected. Maybe he's not much of a cook. Or perhaps, like me, he is new to this.

"Come in." While his smile's awkward, there's no hiding that simmer in those eyes. He bends down to greet Josie then gives me a quick kiss. Rocco comes running toward the door.

Immediately Josie's ears lift and her tail wags vigorously as the two take off into another room.

I hand him the bags as I look around at the beautifully appointed home. There's a gorgeous chandelier in the foyer with an elegant stairway leading to another floor. To the right is what appears to be a living room, expertly decorated, yet warm and inviting. Rich hues of blue intermix with grays and blacks, creating a sophisticated yet traditional look. It complements the outside of the house.

"Thanks." Nate's eyes light up as he looks inside of the one bag. "How did you know I love tequila?"

"A lucky guess." I shrug my shoulders, still pretty amazed with this man's home.

I hear a noise coming from another room, sounding like a child's television show. Unsure of what it is or where it's coming from, I look at Nate. That's when his expression changes.

"Come here," he says. "I need to tell you something." He leads me to a leather sofa located under a bay window in the living room. Nate gestures for me to sit next to him. I sense he's about to end our relationship, one that's yet to begin. But why would he invite me over if he didn't want to be with me?

"I wasn't going to share this with you tonight, but, um, some plans changed, so well, I need to tell you now." His face shows signs of stress.

The noise gets louder, and out of the corner of my eye, I see a little boy run into the room. The child has light brown hair, somewhat curly, like Nate's. The boy's blue eyes brightly shine, and he's grinning ear to ear.

"Daddy! Daddy! Watch Rocco and his friend play!" The little boy beams as he grabs Nate's hand, pulling him up from the sofa. My jaw drops as I realize Nate has a son.

"Just a minute, buddy. You go on in, and I'll be right there." Nate looks at me with the saddest eyes. "That's what I want to talk with you about."

"You have a son?" I ask, more intrigued than hurt that Nate hadn't mentioned this.

"Yes, Bobby. He's five." Nate takes my hands in his, then looks up at me before saying, "I didn't realize he'd be here tonight."

"Oh, that's not a problem," I say. "Was it his mom's night to have him?" I remember how David's ex would occasionally spring Caroline on him when we had plans.

"His mother is dead." Nate casts his eyes to the oriental rug below us. "My wife, Lynn, died four years ago … in a car accident. It was very sudden."

"Oh, my God, Nate, I am so sorry." Instinctively, I wrap my arms around him, pulling him into me. Unsure whether or not that was the correct response, I don't care.

He takes a big breath then pulls back. "Thanks, I'm OK— we're OK. It wasn't easy, but we're making it work." He sits up a little straighter, then continues. "I wanted to tell you last night, but I was afraid it might be a deal breaker for you. I mean you're so independent, I wasn't sure how you'd feel about me having a child."

At this exact moment, all I want to do is hold Nate and give him a reassuring kiss. Him having a son in no way changes things; if anything, it makes things sweeter. But, unsure whether or not Bobby will reappear from around the corner, I decide another approach might be better.

"Nate, I'm not sure how other women have reacted, but you having a son makes me admire you more. I mean, to raise a child on your own, after all you've been through ..." But Nate stops me from continuing.

"First of all, there have been no *other women*. You're the first person I've asked out since Lynn passed."

I look down at my hands, embarrassed I'd made that assumption.

"And second, I am not raising Bobby on my own. Both my parents and Lynn's have been incredible. There's no way I could do it without them." Nate pauses for a moment, as if to allow me time to fully grasp his situation.

"Both sets of grandparents live in the area?" I ask, trying to understand how he makes this work.

"Yes, Lynn's parents live in Haverford. And after Lynn's accident, my parents sold their home in Pittsburgh and bought a house in Bryn Mawr. I don't have any brothers or sisters, so Bobby's their only grandchild." Nate's warmhearted smile returns when he shares this. "And my dad, well, Bobby keeps him young." Nate chuckles, his eyes projecting a beautiful love for his family.

"And Lynn's parents help too?" I ask, then wonder if I've crossed a line by mentioning her name so casually.

"Jonathon and Elsa are older than my parents. At times it's tough for them to keep up with Bobby, but they do their best and are happy to watch him, especially the nights when I work late shifts. They were supposed to have him tonight, but Elsa has a cold and didn't want Bobby to catch it." Nate's eyes project an element of respect.

I shake my head, attempting to visualize the challenges Nate deals with on a daily basis.

"And Rocco goes wherever Bobby does. Both my parents and Lynn's have fenced in yards, so it's easy for them to have Rocco when Bobby comes. This way, there's one constant in Bobby's life."

"You are incredible," I say, squeezing his hands, which I am still holding. "Bobby's lucky to have so many people to love and care for him."

"But can that make up for losing your mom?" Nate asks, but then he flinches. "I'm sorry. For a moment, I forgot you lost yours." His baby blue eyes tenderly gaze at me as he tilts his head as if wondering how I managed.

"I was fifteen, not a baby, and I have many wonderful memories of my mom."

"All Bobby has is pictures," Nates says as he bites his lower lip.

I'm silent, wondering if he's about to share more about Lynn. However, Bobby bursts back into the living room, Rocco and Josie at his heels.

"Bobby, come here a sec. I want you to meet my friend," Nate says, eagerly pulling Bobby onto his lap. The dogs start playing by our feet, tugging at a toy rope.

"This is Ali."

"Hi, Bobby," I say, hoping he'll be open to me.

"Hi. Is this your dog? What's her name?" He seems much more interested in Josie than me.

"That's Josie. She's three. How old is Rocco?" I ask.

"Rocco's five, like me. Daddy got him right before I was born."

"Now that was a brave move," I tease Nate. "Having a puppy and a baby at the same time." Seriously, what were they thinking?

"Hey, we figured why not? We'd be home most of the time with the baby, so it seemed like a good time to get a dog." Then Nate turns his attention on Bobby as he grabs him then lifts his son above his head. "Man, you are getting big. I'm not going to be able to call you Little Guy for much longer." Bobby starts giggling as Nate drops him on his lap and begins to tickle him.

"Stop, stop … I won't grow any bigger, I promise." Bobby's grin is enormous as he wriggles around on Nate's lap.

"OK, but now I've got to start calling you Big Guy. You good with that?"

Bobby vigorously nods his head, the dimple on his chin, which mirrors his dad's, grows larger. Then, in an instant, he jumps down onto the oriental rug and begins to roll around with Josie and Rocco. Dog hair flies everywhere, but no one seems to care.

"I've got to check on dinner. Want to come with me?" Nate asks.

I nod, then Nate takes my hand and leads me toward the kitchen. On the way, he stops at the foyer table to grab the gift bags I brought. Meanwhile, Bobby and the dogs continue wrestling on the living room rug. I don't think I've seen Josie so happy.

Unlike the rest of the house, the kitchen is modern. Sleek stainless steel appliances are paired with jet-black granite counter-tops. White subway tiles adorn the wall above the gas range, and silver pendant lights hang over the island. The only color comes from the artwork. I walk closer to a piece to the right of the refrigerator.

"This is amazing," I say as I squint to read the artist's name.

"Thanks," Nate says as a serene look comes across his face. "Lynn painted that for my thirtieth birthday."

But Nate doesn't become upset or lost in thought. Strangely, he seems to be able to talk about Lynn without becoming distant, which kind of surprises me. He moves toward the two bags that are now sitting on top of the island.

"Rocco is going to love these," he says, eyeing the contents of the yellow paper bag. Nate then takes the bottle of Patrón from the blue bag. "Thanks, Ali. It's perfect. Let's save it for another night." Nate winks, then walks over to the cabinet and takes out two wine glasses. "Do you prefer red or white?" he asks.

"Either is great," I say as he bends down to retrieve a bottle from a wine closet. I can't help but notice how well his jeans fit. Damn. When does he find the time to work out?

Moments later, he hands me a glass of Shiraz, sharing a friend of his from med school recommended this bottle. "I hope you like it." In an expert fashion, he swishes the deep red liquid around in the glass before tasting it. At first, he frowns, but then, his expression softens, and a look of appreciation appears. It must be a good bottle.

"We're having lasagna. It's pretty much the only thing I know how to cook," Nate admits as he takes a sip of wine. "My dad's Irish, but my mom is Italian, and when I was little, she taught me how to make this recipe. Apparently, it's been in the family for a while." After putting on mitts, Nate takes a rectangular ceramic casserole dish out of the oven and places it on the stove top. Immediately, the room fills with the aroma of mozzarella and tart tomatoes. Inside the dish, red sauce bubbles beneath strips of gooey cheese. Something tells me Nate's more talented in the kitchen than he claims to be.

I clink my glass to his. "Cheers, or is it sláinte?"

"Nice, I forgot you're Irish too."

"Close to 90 percent," I say, a level of pride in my voice. "I thought I was all Irish, but apparently someone in my lineage screwed around." On a whim, I'd taken the Ancestry test and was surprised when I read the results.

"We all have a bit of mystery to us," he says, peering into my eyes as if to question mine.

Not wanting to share my story yet, fearful it might scare him away, I shift the conversation back to Bobby.

"Does Bobby go to preschool?"

"Yes, he attends Montessori," Nate says as he opens the fridge and pulls out a bowl filled with lettuce. "It's at Waldron Mercy Academy, located right around the corner. The school also has a kindergarten and goes up to eighth grade. This is his third year there. I started him early. Thought it was best." Nate opens a drawer, grabs tongs, and begins to mix the salad. He reaches for a bottle of salad dressing sitting on the counter then adds a healthy serving before continuing to toss.

"Does he like it?" I ask, not knowing much about Montessori or preschools in general.

"He loves it. And they have early drop-off and an after-school program. It works well for me, and the school is not too far from his grandparents'. Plus, unlike the nuns I remember from Catholic school, these Mercy nuns are pretty cool." He gives me an impish grin, and immediately I sense he was a bit naughty as a child.

***

Twenty minutes later, the three of us are seated around the wooden, Scandinavian-style table, devouring the lasagna, salad, and garlic bread.

"Ali, Ali," Bobby interrupts to gain my attention. "I made the bread. Do you like it?"

"It's delicious, Bobby," I say, as I take a big bite to show him how much I like it. "Yum."

"Do you want to know how I made it?" he asks, his little eyes growing wide. I nod my head yes.

"Well, first, Dad cut it in half. I can't use a sharp knife. But I did the rest. I took the butter and used a regular knife to spread it, real carefully, on both pieces of the bread." Bobby leans closer to me as if to ensure I'm paying attention to every detail. "Then, I got the garlic shaker and shook it seven times on each half. After that, I got the mossarella cheese from the fridge."

"It's mozzarella, Bobby," Nate interjects.

"OK, I got the *mozzarella cheese* and sprinkled it like this over the bread." His little fingers go back and forth as he demonstrates his method. "But Dad had to cook it. I'm not allowed near the oven." Bobby then pops off of his chair and runs to the fridge to refill his glass of water.

"Careful, Big Guy," Nate calmly warns. Bobby looks at his dad then rolls his eyes as he pushes his cup against the water dispenser on the refrigerator door. He stops, checks the water level, then adds a bit more, repeating this several times.

I first look at Nate, then at Bobby and laugh, amazed with how this evening is evolving. Never in a million years did I expect to be having dinner with a five-year-old, but I wouldn't change it for the world. This kid's awesome, making me wonder how much I've missed by not having kids. There's a small pain, deep inside my core, reminding me I'll probably never become pregnant and have a child of my own.

After dinner, I offer to do the dishes, but Nate adamantly refuses.

"No way, you're our guest. Dishes are my job. Bobby, show Ali your room. I'm sure she'd love to see your cool collection." Nate tickles Bobby in the ribs then slightly swats his backside as Bobby escapes and heads toward the foyer stairs.

"Come on, Ali. Follow me," he yells, motioning me to come upstairs.

"Dinner was delicious." I push my chair back and stand so I can go check out Bobby's room. But before leaving, I walk toward Nate's chair, bend down, and give him a soft yet sensuous kiss before saying, "Thank you."

Nate playfully grabs me, pulls me onto his lap, and kisses me back.

"Ali?" An impatient voice bellows from the other room.

I give Nate one more kiss. "Coming, Bobby," I say as I scurry out of the kitchen.

At first Bobby's room appears like any other little boy's bedroom. But it's not. There's a level of organization that seems unusual for a kid's room. Each item is perfectly placed, on shelves, on top of his bureau, on the perfectly centered small table. And this kid is definitely a Batman fan. The walls of Bobby's room are yellow, the bedspread of his twin bed has a black-and-yellow checkered pattern, and the pillow on top of his bed has Batman's face on it. On top of the shelves are small ceramic figures ... all the Batman villains ... the Joker, the Riddler, Catwoman, Poison Ivy, and the Penguin. A poster of Adam West and Burt Ward, the original Batman and Robin, hangs on the wall.

"Wow, Bobby, you must love Batman."

Bobby nods his head, biting his little pink tongue, which is visible through his teeth. His tongue is pushing against his one front tooth, which seems to be loose.

"I loved Batman when I was your age," I say, which is totally the truth.

"Do you see my collection of bad guys?" Bobby points to the figures on the shelf.

"I do. My favorite is Catwoman. Which one is yours?" I walk toward the shelf, admiring the figurines.

"The Penguin! He's so funny!" Bobby starts giggling as he imitates this character by wobbling back and forth and moving his arms. Then he says, "Do you know what else I collect?"

"I have no idea." Something tells me this is going to be good.

Bobby takes my hand and pulls me toward his closet doors.

"Are you ready to see something really cool?" he asks. "Shut your eyes."

I do as I'm told, then hear the closet doors open.

Bobby proudly sings. "Open them now!"

And there, on the shelves, are beautiful rocks—gemstones, actually.

"Oh, Bobby, they're gorgeous," I say, looking closely at the brilliance and intensity of the crystals. When I pick one up, my palm vibrates, as if energy is traveling from the stone through my fingers.

"They were my mom's," Bobby says, not in a sad tone, but in a proud, upbeat manner.

"Well, you sure are lucky to have such an awesome collection of rocks. I bet you take extra special care of them."

"I do." Bobby stands up straight and puffs out his little chest.

We then hear Nate call, "Who's ready for dessert?"

"Me, me, me, me, me," Bobby screams as he takes off, heading for the stairs.

Before returning to the kitchen, I take one final look around Bobby's room. In one corner is a little desk with an iPad on top. But it's the framed picture next to the tablet that catches my eye. Inside of the frame is a photo of a beautiful woman with long, wavy blonde hair and sparkling blue eyes. She's holding a plump baby dressed in denim overalls and a white long sleeve shirt. That must be Lynn. She's captivating, but in a mysterious way. Then my eyes focus on Bobby. As a baby, Bobby had his dad's dark, curly hair. My heart aches as I imagine the pain they've both been through. Forcing myself to leave, I take one last look at the picture, memorizing the peaceful look on Bobby's mother's face.

When I enter the kitchen, I see a large plate filled with chocolate chip cookies.

"They look delicious," I say as I wink at Nate.

"I can't take any of the credit," Nate says. "Bobby and his
grandma made these yesterday after school."

"Yep, me and Grandma Marney, not Grandma Elsa," Bobby
clarifies.

"What do you call your grandpas?" I'm curious.

"Grandfather and Pop Pop."

Nate continues to translate. "Grandfather is Jonathon, and
Pop Pop is my dad."

"Boy, you sure do have a lot of people who love you," I say as
I pick up a cookie and take a bite. The smooth chocolate quickly
dissolves in my mouth. "Bobby, you and Grandma Marney make
awesome cookies."

Bobby stands up and takes a bow. Nate and I both follow with
a round of applause.

After we've had our share of chocolate chip cookies, Nate
looks over at Bobby and says, "You've had a big day, so how about
you get into your pj's, brush your teeth, and then come down and
say goodnight."

"Do I have to?" His formerly chipper tone turns into a slight
whine.

"Yep. Remember, we're going to the Phillies opener tomorrow. So you need to get a good night's rest."

"OK." Bobby's mood brightens at the thought of baseball,
and he quickly disappears upstairs. Josie and Rocco trail behind
the little boy.

Five minutes later, Bobby's back, wearing Batman pajamas

and a red Phillies hat.

"Do I really have to go to bed?" Bobby asks again.

"Tell you what. How about if you crawl into my bed and watch Nickelodeon for a bit, because it's been a special evening." Nick looks at me. "But say goodnight to Ali before you go."

Bobby comes over to me, crawls up on my lap, and puts his soft little arms around my neck. Then pulls me to him, giving me a wet kiss right on my lips. I want to laugh, but instead I give him a big squeeze back and say, "Have fun at the game tomorrow."

Bobby then goes to Nate and repeats what I assume is his goodnight ritual before trudging up the steps.

"He's incredible," I say to Nate while he reaches for my empty wine glass.

"You're the incredible one," he says as his finishes the bottle of red, splitting it between our two wine glasses. "I had no idea how you would react. I wanted to tell you last night. But I didn't want to scare you away," Nate says as he sits down next to me.

"Scare me away? Are you kidding? I love kids." As I say that, I'm reminded that as much as I wanted to, I wasn't allowed to meet David's daughter. I take a sip of wine then set the glass on the table.

"My life's pretty complicated." Nate shrugs his shoulders.

"You must miss her terribly." I place my hand on top of his.

"Every day. But it's gotten easier, I guess. Nevertheless, it's surreal that she's gone." He looks down at our hands then interlaces his fingers with mine. "This is all new to me, so if I'm a bit awkward or include Bobby too much, you have to tell me."

I look at Nate, my heart a mixture of compassion for all he has been through and desire for the man sitting next to me.

"It's fun being with Bobby. Besides, this is who you are." I wave my free hand around the kitchen. "You aren't a single guy whose nights and weekends are his; you're a dedicated doctor who works long hours and then comes home to take care of his five-year-old son, whom you obviously adore, I might add."

"So it's not a deal breaker?" Nate lets go of my hand then runs his fingers through his hair, causing something inside of me to stir.

"Not at all." I lean closer to him. "I'll take both of you, gladly."

With that, he stands up and moves closer to me. As if on cue, I also rise. Placing his hand on the small of my back, he takes another step closer, leans down, then begins to kiss me. But this time, he doesn't stop. Apparently, he's no longer worried about Bobby walking in on us.

Instead, he seems solely focused on me. After several minutes, he leads me toward the living room, where we once again sit down on the couch. Soft, playful kisses swiftly turn deep, passionate with desire. Yearning fills my entire body. It's like I'm seventeen all over again. Everything with Nate is so different than it was with David. Nate's exciting, attentive, inquisitive. His lips travel to my neck, then down toward my collarbone. I find myself gasping, knowing there's so much more I want, need.

But now is not the time. As much as I do not want this to end, it has to, or I won't be able to stop.

"Nate. I, um, better be going. Bobby's upstairs. I, um …"

Nate sits up and heaves out a brief sigh.

"You're right. I'm sorry."

"No, don't be sorry. I don't want to go. But it's the right thing."

He pulls me toward him and kisses my forehead. "I'm the parent, and you're being the responsible one." He lets out a slight chuckle.

"Well, someone has to be," I say, looking seductively into his eyes.

I straighten my clothes, then call softly for Josie while Nate puts on a coat from the closet then helps me with mine before he walks me to my car.

"Thank you for coming over, for understanding …," he says while Josie jumps into the back seat.

I stop him from saying more as I place my fingers on his lips. "Shh … I told you I'm more than fine with everything."

That's when he kisses me, and in an instant, the passion returns, full force. But this time it's Nate who stops.

"I have to say goodnight, or otherwise, I'm going to take you back to the house with me."

Though inches apart, I can fully feel the intense heat emanating from his body.

"And I'd have trouble saying no." Reluctantly, I open my car door and get inside.

"I'll call you tomorrow, OK?"

Knowing he absolutely will, I grin before he gently pushes the door shut.

Nate watches as I drive away. Four minutes later, I'm parking the car in the back lot behind my building. I take Josie out for a quick stroll before calling it a night.

"Josie, what do you think? Things are happening so quickly. But, then again, isn't that the same way I found you?"

CHAPTER 26

"**I** don't know; it's all moving at warp speed." I tell Gail and Susie during Sunday morning's walk. I'm falling fast, and this scares me.

"Well, you are thirty-two," Susie says. "He's certainly not the first guy you dated." This makes me laugh, but Gail takes a much sterner stance.

"Susan, that is so out of line. Now, Ali, tell me about his son." Part of her softens, to a place I have not witnessed before.

"Bobby's amazing. He's smart, like his dad, and he has a curious spirit about him, which I believe he gets from his mom." It appears strange to talk about Lynn, yet something tells me she'd want me to. "There was a picture of him with his mom. She is beautiful— was beautiful." I hang my head slightly.

"How hard it must be for him to raise a son on his own," Gail says.

But then I explain the incredible support Nate receives from both sets of grandparents. "It sounds like they've developed a system that works for everyone," I say, impressed with the "all hands on deck" approach this family's adopted.

"And he cooks?" Susie says with a glimmer in her eye.

"Well, he makes lasagna. Said it was his mom's recipe. But I suspect he does fine in the kitchen. He seems to have a knack for a lot of things. And his house is beautiful. I'm sure his wife decorated it, but he maintains it, keeps it looking good." We momentarily stop, pulling our dogs to the side so two runners can pass by us.

During this brief pause, Gail asks the question I've been wondering since I first met Nate. "Are *you* ready to become involved again, so quickly after David?" Her delivery, direct and uninhibited, may be one of the qualities I love most about this woman.

"I don't know. I think so." I pause and tuck stray strands of hair behind my ear as I revisit this dilemma. "Being with Nate helps me see all that was missing in my last relationship. David kept me from meeting his daughter, but Nate *wants* me to spend time with Bobby. Nate's funny, and he's comfortable with laughing at himself. David was so serious, and he had to be in control at all times. However, their differences go past their personalities," I say, pausing for a moment. "Nate's home is warm and inviting. David's townhouse was sterile, sleek, cold. And, well, this may be too much information, but Nate is an amazing kisser."

"And was David?" Susie can't resist herself.

"Not so much, at least not that I remember."

"Well, a fading memory of a former relationship is a good thing. It means you are truly moving on." Gail pulls on Will's and Grace's leashes, signaling them to stop and sit while two men and their pug pass by.

I know those guys. I'd seen them walk by my house. The pug had a jean jacket on one day. Suppressing a giggle, I briefly reflect on who I was when I last saw these Dog Walkers. Though it was not so long ago chronologically, it seems like ages since I was that person. I smile at the trio as they pass by.

"If you ask me, which I know you are not," Susie begins, "you'd be a fool to let this one go." She merely purses her lips and struts straight ahead, totally avoiding her sister-in-law's glare.

"Ali will decide what's best for her," Gail strongly states. But then she turns to me and whispers, "Don't tell *her*, but I agree."

***

Around four that afternoon, my phone rings. It's Nate.

My heart flutters a bit when I answer. "How was the game?"

"We're on our way home. Bobby's asleep in the back seat. It was a big afternoon for him. A hot dog, soft ice cream, cotton candy … at first he was wired, but now he's sacked out, the crash after the sugar high."

I laugh, knowing I'd do the same if I had a son like Bobby. "Did the Phillies win?"

"Yes, it went three innings over, but they pulled through." The pride in his voice lets me know he's a true Phillies fan. "My parents volunteered to watch Bobby tonight, so I'm gonna take them up on their offer. Mom said she'd drive him to school in the morning," Nate says then pauses, as if waiting to see if I'll respond.

"Do you want to come over?" I ask. "I was going to make something simple for dinner." As I say this, I mentally scan the contents of my fridge and cabinets to determine if I need to make a grocery run.

"Thought you'd never ask." Said with confidence and gratitude. Damn, I love his voice.

"How's seven? Does that give you enough time to take Bobby and Rocco to your parents?" I ask, remembering Rocco goes wherever Bobby goes.

"Definitely. I'll see you then," Nate says before adding, "Can't wait."

"Me too … bye."

Now I must come up with a casual yet enticing dinner. Not wanting to do pasta, as we had lasagna last night, I decide to make chicken enchiladas. Because I know I don't have the necessary ingredients, I grab my purse and yell to Josie, "I'll be right back. Need to go to Whole Foods." I watch as Josie walks to her dog bed and lies down. Halfway out of the door, I turn around, go back into the apartment, and peer inside of the lower right kitchen cabinet. My bottle of tequila is practically empty, so I'll have to stop at the liquor store as well.

***

After feeding Josie her dinner, I take her out for a walk then quickly check myself in the full-length mirror hanging on the back of my closet door to see if I look OK. Dressed in casual jeans and a lavender long sleeve tee, I stand a bit taller when I see my reflection. My skin's glowing, and my face is relaxed, somewhat serene. I'm not sure where all of this is going, but I'm definitely falling for Nate Cavanaugh.

***

By 6:45, the enchiladas are in the oven and I'm mixing a pitcher of margaritas. With a few minutes to spare, I sit on the sofa and try to read. But it's no use. I'm too excited. When the doorbell buzzes, I spring off the sofa to answer it.

"Hi," Nate's voice comes across the intercom causing Josie's ears to perk up.

"Hey, I'm the first door up the stairs on the left, 2A," I reply as I buzz Nate in.

Then I unlock my door and wait in the hallway to greet him. Josie comes and sits by my feet, wagging her tail. When she sees Nate, she barks twice.

"Hey, Josie," he says and leans down to pet the top of her head before handing me a beautiful bouquet of purple tulips and a bottle of sauvignon blanc. He then steps closer to me and gives me a delicious hello kiss.

"Thank you. They're gorgeous. Come in," I say, taking his hand and leading him into my apartment. "It's small, but it works for us." I take a vase out of the cabinet, fill it with water, then add the flowers. After inhaling the fragrant tulips, I place the vase on the dining table and put the wine in the fridge to chill.

"I like it," Nate says as he takes in my living space. "You've got a great view."

I gulp, twice, knowing how I relied on my position at that window for so long. "Thanks, it kind of brings the outside in here." I fumble my words, hoping he doesn't notice.

"So what did you do today?" Nate asks, not picking up on my awkward response as I take the pitcher of margaritas from the fridge and pour drinks for both of us in the green glasses I brought back from a vacation in Cancún.

After handing him a glass, we sit down on the stools by the counter. "Josie and I kind of chilled today. I took her on a short run this morning, then we went for a walk with the two women who were friends of her former owner. She loves seeing them and their dogs."

Nate nods as he takes a sip. "This is good." He inhales the aroma coming from the oven. "Mexican tonight?" he asks, a glimmer in his eyes.

"How did you guess?" I playfully nudge his arm as I get up to bring the dish of chips and salsa sitting by the range top to the narrow counter in front of us.

"I love Mexican," Nate says, as he stares into my eyes.

"But I have to warn you, I haven't made chicken enchiladas before, so I hope you're a good sport if they're not right."

Nate doesn't say a word; instead he scoots his stool closer to mine and gives me the sweetest kiss, allowing me to taste the tequila on his lips. Playfully, I pull away as I ask a question I've wondered about for some time.

"So how did you end up with Rocco, and where did Randolf Octavious come from?" I would love to kiss this man all night, but I want to know more about him.

"Well, now that's a funny story," Nate begins. "While I was at Lehigh, we had this ridiculous fraternity thing. I think it all started one night when a bunch of us were pretty trashed. We had to pick a hard-to-remember name for our pledges to call us, at least two words long."

"But why Randolf Octavious?" I ask.

"I have absolutely no idea where I pulled those names from." Nate shakes his head. "I can only guess that I picked Randolf because I had cousins in Randolph, Massachusetts, and Octavious must have come from this history class I was taking that semester." Nate takes a healthy swig of his margarita then starts to chuckle. "If you think mine was bad, my best friend picked Fredericco Nimpho."

"That sounds like the name of a porn star," I say, totally amused by his story.

"Exactly. Every time his pledge uttered that name, there'd be all sorts of jeering."

"I definitely prefer Randolf Octavious over Fredericco Nimpho."

Josie comes over, wedging herself between our stools, then begs for a chip.

"You were in a fraternity?" I ask as I gently give Josie a tortilla chip, asking her to sit first.

"I was a Theta Sigma Kappa," Nate says, then lifts his shirt to show me the branding on his chest.

"Is that what I think it is?" I ask, shocked anyone would do what I believe Nate did—allow someone to burn a symbol of triangles on his chest. Still, my eyes linger. I can't help but hold my gaze a bit too long on his perfect pecs and abs.

"Yep. But it's kind of a secret thing. In fact, I'm not supposed to show anyone." He smirks as he lowers his shirt.

"But it's on your chest, so every time you go swimming, it's totally visible." My eyes are pretty wide, amazed this stuff actually happened. "Did they do that to everyone? Is that what your initiation was?"

"Oh, God no. This wasn't a rite of passage. It was more of an honor. You had to be an officer to have the option to be branded. Then, the house voted to see if you were worthy of the insignia."

"That is *so* different from the sorority I was in."

"You were a sorority girl?" Nate teases me.

"Yes, but they weren't a big deal at Villanova. I was a Delta Gamma, or DG." As I share this with Nate, I immediately think back to pledge shirts, Anchor Splashes, and candle passings. It seems so long ago.

I see Nate's glass is empty, so I refresh both of ours. We continue sharing bits and pieces of our past, mostly the events that later helped define who we are today, though at the time, we didn't realize their significance. I'm beginning to feel the tequila, but I don't mind. It takes off a layer of the armor I keep so tightly wound around me.

But then Nate asks, "So you know I've been married. What about you? Any serious relationships?"

I take in a big breath as I contemplate whether or not to go there. But after all Nate's shared with me, how can I be anything but honest? Plus, sooner or later, I'll have to explain the past few months. I take a big sip before I begin my story. "I had a pretty serious boyfriend in college. But after that, there was no one significant, a few guys, but nothing lasted more than six months. That is, until David."

Nate raises his eyebrows and waits for me to continue.

"David and I dated for a bit over two years. It ended in January." I pause. How much do I want to share? Will telling him my truth make him think I'm batshit crazy? But something inside tells me to trust, and so I do. I take another sip of my margarita, perhaps for extra encouragement.

"Actually, it was pretty rough afterward."

Nate leans closer, placing his hand gently on my knee, then asks, "What happened?"

"David's our legal counsel at Genesis. I met him there, in the elevator going to work one morning. He's thirty-nine and has a daughter, Caroline, whom he never let me meet." Embarrassed, I cast my eyes on the floor, avoiding Nate. Now I realize how important meeting Bobby was to me. Nate's hand gently squeezes my knee, encouraging me to go on. "Apparently David and I had different reads on the seriousness of our relationship," I say, swallowing hard. "I thought he was going to propose to me, when we were supposed to go to Costa Rica this past February."

"But he didn't?" Nate gently asks.

I shake my head and let out a slight laugh. "He cancelled the trip because his ex-wife decided to go away and wanted him to take Caroline."

Nate remains silent, holding space for me.

"I became upset, questioned why I couldn't meet his daughter. Things escalated. That's when he blatantly said he had no intention of getting married again. He liked things just as they were."

"Was he a bad guy?"

What a strange question, but then I honestly reply. "No, he wasn't." I believe this. "Afterward, when I had time to reflect, I realized David didn't say or do anything to make me believe he would propose. But because I wanted him to, I told myself it would happen. I guess that's because my entire life, whenever I worked hard enough at something, I'd achieve it. But that wasn't the case with David. No matter how much I worked on that relationship, it would never be what I wanted." There, I said it.

"And the breakup hit you hard?" No judgment or pity, only genuine concern.

"That's one way to say it." I hang my head. "I became upset that night, pretty much lost control, even sent a nasty text later. I'm not like that, and it terrified me that when I saw him at work, I'd react similarly." For a moment, the fear that inhabited my body during that time returns, but only for a second. I look up at Nate. His caring expression eases the pain, helping me to continue with my story.

"I had a presentation at work the following Monday. But I was physically and emotionally unable to do it. So I told Miles I was sick." I pause, still embarrassed about lying to Miles.

Nate waits, eyes solely focused on me.

"I was terrified how I would react if David was present at the meeting, which was possible considering I was sharing the final pitch for a new product and it would be totally feasible to have counsel there. I think the fear of losing control of myself frightened me more than the thought of seeing him." I stare at the floor, avoiding Nate's eyes, unsure of how he'll react.

"Did you go back to work?" Nate's tone is kind and soothing, not judgy at all

"No, I didn't." I sigh. "After two weeks, Miles came to my apartment. He was concerned. David had told him that we'd broken up, and that's when Miles figured out that I wasn't sick, at least not physically."

For the next five minutes, I continue to share what those two plus months as a recluse looked like. How dark it was at times, and then how I'd read, gain inspiration, and make a tiny step forward. I admit my inability to leave the apartment but also share the growth I made along the way. Finally, I explain the Dog Walkers and how I'd create backstories for those who passed by my window every day, sharing how these strangers became my lifeline.

Yet I don't end my story on a sad note. Instead, I give credit to the self-affirmations, books, meditation, visualizations, and of course, Josie for lifting me out of my quarantined state. Susie and Gail helped too. I admit my depression wasn't about my ex, owning I'd given my power away, no longer trusted myself, and had no idea who I'd become.

"I guess I needed the time and space to figure it all out."

"And you did ... that's what's so beautiful about your story." Nate takes my hand then softly kisses my fingers. "And when Mike wasn't with Susie and Gail, you knew something was wrong. Your concern for Josie was the final straw to get you to go outside?"

"Yes, she was the catalyst." My heart skips a beat as I look at Josie, sweetly nestled in her dog bed.

Continuing my story, I fill him in on meeting Lisa and Kimmy and how I'm now training for the Philly Marathon.

"Imagine being shot for owing money to the wrong people." Anguish sweeps through my body every time I envision Kimmy walking into their apartment and finding Luke dead, in a pool of his own blood. But then I'm reminded of the pain Nate experiences on a daily basis.

"Then some of the people whom you had watched actually became your friends?" Nate asks.

I shake my head yes.

That's when Nate's expression shifts from concern to curiosity. "Did you see me walking Rocco?"

His eyes widen, but I flinch, as though the wind's been knocked out of me. If I answer honestly, will he think I'm a stalker? But if I lie, then I'm not being true to myself.

I inhale deeply, look Nate in the eyes, and admit, "Once. I couldn't see you. But I recognized Rocco."

"And now, like the others, I'm also in your life, for real." He gently grazes my cheek with his fingers.

Instantly, I relax, knowing my being truthful did not cause him to get up and leave.

Still, I sense a shift in his demeanor as he leans back in his chair.

"So did you create a backstory about me?" Nate is grinning ear to ear. Then he bites into a tortilla chip and washes it down with a swig of his margarita.

"You won't make fun of me?" Suddenly my cheeks blush, and I'm mortified I bared my soul to him and now about to reveal the ridiculous story I devised.

"No, I am curious. Let's hear it." His tone is definitely light-hearted, nonjudgmental, perhaps somewhat taunting.

I take it that he's challenging me, so I accept. I lower my voice as I begin to reveal my imaginary Stephen. "Because I only saw you once, I thought you did something like worked for the CIA and came here sporadically to visit your mom." I scrunch my nose before burying my face in my hands.

Nate becomes hysterical laughing. "Why on God's earth did you come up with that explanation. Did I look evil, devious, shifty? Or was it my debonair good looks?" He raises his eyebrows, gives me a sly look, then finishes off his margarita. I take a big sip of mine.

"No ... you were wearing a hoodie. I couldn't see your face." As mortified as I am, I begin to laugh along with him.

The timer goes off, saving me from further humiliation.

As I get up to take the enchiladas out of the oven, Nate follows me into the kitchen and takes the wine from the fridge.

"Glasses are in the upper left cabinet," I say as I plate our meal.

When we sit down at the table, we continue our conversation. Though Nate is no longer teasing me. He seems interested in how I dealt with the solitude.

"In hindsight, it wasn't that long, a bit over two months. But it felt like forever," I admit as I devour a forkful of the spicy chicken covered in cheese.

"Yet you learned a lot about yourself, something that would have taken years to do without the isolation."

"I guess so. I'm not saying I've figured it all out. I only know what parts of me I wanted to leave behind as well as the areas that need growth. Fear is a pretty powerful thing. So is being alone. Yet it makes you stronger, in a weird way. Do you know what I mean?" Verbalizing this sentiment, my confidence rises, and I'm glad I decided to be honest with Nate.

"After Lynn died, I couldn't deal. My heart was shattered. I didn't struggle with losing myself; I just didn't want to live anymore, not without her. So I shut down, pushed people away. Yeah, I knew everyone was trying to help, but I guess I didn't want to feel better." Nate's eyes dim a bit as he shares his truth.

"Your pain kept you connected to Lynn?" I ask, unsure if I'm on the right track.

"That, or in denial. Bobby was a baby, less than one, and I worked nonstop, especially as a resident. Lynn knew Bobby, his schedule, everything. But she died so suddenly, she couldn't share a thing with me … about our son or what his needs were. Losing her nearly killed me, and then the thought of being a single dad, well, I was scared shitless. There was no way I could take care of Bobby on my own." Nate takes a big breath as he stares into space.

"But you did it, and Bobby's amazing." I take a sip of the wine; a hint of grapefruit lingers on my lips.

"He is pretty special." Nate relaxes a bit as he reflects on his son. "But it's not because of me. With the help of our parents, I finally believed I could be a good dad. Sure, things weren't going to be better overnight, but I knew Bobby and I would be OK." Nate's face brightens a bit. "But dating, now that is something I stayed away from," he says as he gives me a devilish grin.

"So why me? Why now?" I ask, unsure whether or not I truly want to know the answer.

"I have no idea." Nate cuts into the enchilada and takes a bite, chewing while he appears to gather his thoughts. "Do you remember the first time we passed each other when walking the dogs? Not the night we spoke, but the one when you said your remembered seeing me and I didn't recall anything?"

"Yes," I say cautiously, wondering where he's going with this.

"Well, that was our anniversary. We would have been married for seven years. I was pretty much a mess the entire day." Now it's Nate who casts his eyes down toward his lap.

I gently take his chin in my hand and lift it tenderly, allowing me to look into his eyes.

"You and Lynn had something incredibly special. I can't begin to understand why you lost her, but now you have Bobby to keep her memory alive." I pause for a moment before adding, "He showed me her gemstones."

Nate's eyes widen. "He did? Bobby rarely talks to me about those rocks." His face relaxes a bit. "He must trust you."

"Do you?" I ask, but I have no idea why I say this. Yet I want to know.

"Yes, I do," Nate speaks softly. "I guess that's what makes you different. Some of the women out there, they exhausted me, assumed I'm needy. But Bobby and I don't need anything right now. We're figuring things out."

I continue to gaze at Nate, in awe of how he's been able to keep it together.

"But something changed when I met you. I began to want again … but that's different from needing. It's like a part of me I'd forgotten started to wake up."

"But I'm not special. In your position, there must be tons of women after you," I joke, but I do wonder. I can only imagine how beautiful some of the female doctors and nurses are at CHOP.

Nate gives me a look, frowning a bit. "It's your genuineness that makes you beautiful—that and your amazing legs." He gives me a tantalizing wink. "When we first met, I sensed that you're completely comfortable with who you are. And now that I'm getting to know you, I can tell you don't do things merely because you assume you're supposed to. You seem to trust yourself. It's refreshing."

Embarrassed, I blush because the woman he describes is who I am aspiring to be, not the person in quarantine nor the Allison who dated David. I begin to play with strands of my hair, avoiding Nate's eyes.

"From what you've shared, it seems like you lost a piece of yourself in your last relationship. And I'm guessing you aren't going to let that happen again."

I look up and nod. "The cost is too high," I say as I lean in toward Nate. "If I've learned anything during that time, it's that we can love others and share ourselves with them, but ultimately, we must be true to who we are. Because in the end, that's all we have." No doubt Nate understands, as this also applies to losing Lynn.

Without breaking our visual connection, Nate stands, pulling me into his arms. We begin to kiss. Slowly yet deliberately, softly yet with promise. My heart rate quickens.

As if on cue, he guides me to the sofa. Leaning back into the soft cushions, I feel the warmth of Nate against me. The touch of his hands on my body combined with his musky scent arouse my senses to a new level.

He can read me … what I want … what I need.

I'd forgotten. But Nate instantly knows. Being with Nate is natural, so different from David. Yet everything flows perfectly. It's as if there are no barriers between us to shelter our vulnerable selves. Instead, we share a genuine connection, an unselfish desire, an unspoken language.

I cannot say how long we lay on the couch. All I know is at some point, we rise, leaving half-eaten plates of chicken enchiladas on the table next to partially empty glasses of wine. He takes my hand, and I lead him to my bedroom.

CHAPTER 27

I wake before my alarm sounds, totally disoriented. After opening my eyes, I look to my right for confirmation this was not a dream. The comforter's pulled back and the pillow shows the indentation of his head, but there is no Nate.

A horrible pit forms in my stomach causing me to curl into a tight ball.

He's gone, left without saying goodbye. But what did I expect? It happened too soon.

We should have waited.

I let out a deep exhale as I pull the covers over my head, sinking deep into the safety of my bed. But then the door opens. I peer out from underneath the comforter to see Nate holding a cup of coffee. He places it on the side table next to my bed.

"Good morning," he says, looking chipper. Then he bends down and gives me the most heartwarming kiss. "I have to be at the hospital for early rounds, but I didn't want to leave without saying bye."

Slightly embarrassed by my initial reaction, I breathe him in, returning the kiss. "You have to go?" I ask, though I know the answer.

"Just for now. But are you up for having pizza with Bobby and me tonight? Monday evenings are designated pizza nights," Nate explains as his blue eyes penetrate into my soul.

"I love pizza on Monday nights." My eyes remain locked on his.

"We'll pick you up at six thirty, OK?" Nate's lips turn upward right before I pull him in for one final kiss.

I hear the apartment door shut as I slowly sit up in my bed. Coffee in bed? How amazing is that? With my pillow propped behind my back, I slowly sip the rich roast as I replay last night. Never had I been with a man who felt so good. Nothing was awkward, not in the slightest. Yet it was more than how naturally we flowed and anticipated what the other wanted—it was the depth of passion I've never experienced before. Not that I've been with many men, but the few I have slept with, well, nothing comes close to last night. Struggling to identify the exact feeling, I lack the words to capture this emotion.

Then the word *complete* comes to mind, but quickly I remember Renée Zellweger's famous line in *Jerry Maguire*: "You complete me." That's not the correct word, for I am complete without any man. Nate makes everything clearer, crisper, brighter. But I will never need any man to complete me because I know I am already whole.

And I'm seeing him tonight … with Bobby. I can't understand how my feelings can be so strong for a man I've just met.

Keep perspective. I don't want to fall too fast or change who I'm becoming. I've made too much progress to return to needing a man. And I'm certainly not going to allow whatever this is to stop my healthy morning routine. I get out of bed and quickly put on running clothing, take Josie out, then feed her before hopping on the treadmill and putting in a quick four miles. Then, after I shower and grab a light breakfast, we head to work. Yet, as much as I try, I cannot shake the thought of Nate nor how good his body felt.

The morning flies by. Before I know it, Valerie, an engineer who first began as my intern last year, knocks on my door.

"I'm going to Hymie's Deli. Do you want me to order any-thing for you?" she asks. Hymie's has been around forever, and to do that in this town, you have to be good.

Food sounds good. In fact, I'm suddenly famished. "I'd love a turkey on rye with lettuce and tomatoes. And a side of coleslaw, please. Let me know the amount, and I'll Venmo you. Thanks, Val."

This has become our routine. Val picks up lunch on Mondays, and I do Thursdays.

I head to the office's kitchen, deciding a cup of coffee is in order. I need something to keep my eyelids open. As I put a pod in the Keurig, Kathleen, an analyst, walks in.

"It's good to have you back," Kathleen says, a bashfulness in her voice. "And, um, well, I'm sorry about you and David." She quickly looks down at the floor.

"Thanks. It's great to be back. And regarding David, well, it wasn't meant to be," I say as I take the filled mug from the Keurig and discard the used pod.

Instantly, her head springs upright as she quickly spits out, "You do look, well, beautiful, and happy, which I didn't expect, con-sidering everything you've been through."

"You know, I'm actually glad we're no longer together. And I am happy with how everything's turned out." I keep my eyes on Kathleen as I stand tall, shoulders back, with my chin slightly lifted.

Perhaps Kathleen expected a different response. Yet, while I assume her intentions are pure, her reaction makes me wonder.

"Of course, I'm so happy you're happy," she says in an unusu-ally high-pitched voice as she scurries out of the kitchen.

Shaking my head, I return to my desk and dive into an in-dustry marketing report while slowly sipping my coffee. The topic is about possible solutions to prevent the hacking of smartphones.

Twenty-five minutes later, Val hand delivers my lunch. I inhale my sandwich, except for several pieces of turkey, which I give to Josie, all while diligently reading and dissecting the report.

Before I know it, it's after four, and I still have a pile of paper to sift through. If I can't finish in the next hour, I'll bring the work home with me and tackle it after "Monday Pizza Night." Merely thinking of Nate, something I've had trouble not doing, creates a glow within. I begin to drift back to last night, to the assuredness in which he moved, how he knew what would please …

"Hey, Ali, do you have a minute?" Miles is at my door, which is slightly ajar.

"Sure," I say, "come on in."

Miles takes a seat across from me. "So how's it going? Everything OK?" he asks in a fatherly tone. Josie walks over and sits down at Miles's feet. It's as though she, too, has deep admiration for him. Perhaps instinct tells her he's the reason she's allowed to come to the office each day.

I lean toward my boss. "Miles, things are great. I love being back at work. And having Josie here, well that's huge." At the mention of her name, Josie wags her tail.

Miles scratches the side of his head then says, "You look good, especially today. You're actually beaming. I hope I'm not crossing lines, but what's going on?" His question's laced with concern and curiosity.

"I do?" Does it show on my face? And then I think about the encounter in the kitchen earlier today.

"Yeah, you look, um, blissful. I guess I'm used to seeing you super focused, serious."

Blissful … *that's* the word I was searching for earlier this morning. I can finally attach a word to my feeling … immersed in a state of peaceful bliss.

"I've met someone," I admit, causing Miles to sit up straighter.

"Already? Who is this guy?" he asks in an interested tone.

And so, after Miles promises to keep this information to himself, I share the basics about Nate. I tell him how we met and that he works at CHOP as a pediatric oncologist. Then I include the bombshell: he is a widower with a five-year-old son.

Miles is speechless, something I haven't seen before. But after a few moments, he leans down to pet Josie, saying to both of us, "Wow, you two are certainly forging a new life together. I have to tell you, Ali, you're surprising the hell out of me in more than one way. Besides seeing how you're doing, I wanted to stop in to let you know you haven't missed a beat. In fact, the quality of your work has never been better. And everyone's happy you're back. Plus, Josie's a big hit."

Chuckling, I say, "I can't begin to tell you how many people stop by my office to see Josie. I'm constantly getting offers to take her on a walk. Monica even asked if she could watch Josie if I wanted to go away."

As Miles stands up to leave, he looks at me with solemn eyes. "I'm proud of you, Ali. When I visited you in February, you were not in a good spot." His forehead wrinkles with this pronouncement. "I was extremely concerned. In fact, I wanted to make it a condition that you receive professional help in order to return to Genesis. But Madeline told me to give you a chance to figure things out. She felt you had the fortitude to pull through on your own. I'm glad I listened. She was right."

I get up from my chair, walk to Miles, and give him a warm embrace. "Thank you for believing in me. Not many people would have. I'm not so sure I believed in myself at that point."

"Well, apparently all you needed was some time, and maybe some prodding from Josie." He winks as he leaves. "Oh, and if this thing becomes serious, I want to meet the guy," he says before shutting my door.

Blessed to have such an incredible boss, who luckily listens to his wife, I reflect on the common messages from all of those books I've read. It all boils down to trusting, letting go, and allowing, the exact process I am going through. And then I remember the second major lesson, in order to love another, we must first learn to love ourselves. And that is what I am doing … learning to embrace who I am, the good, the bad, and the ugly.

I exhale, proud that I allowed my vulnerability to show when I shared my story with Nate last night. He didn't judge me. Instead, he stayed, held space for me, and loved me for who I am.

***

Apparently, Monday Pizza Night takes place at Narberth Pizza, voted the "Best of Mainline and Western Suburb Pizza" in 2013. We sit at an orange laminated table, Nate and Bobby on one side, me on the other. It's a great view. I love watching Nate interact with his son. It's as if they have a nonverbal language of their own, a code of sorts, which only they understand.

"We always order a white pizza pie with pineapple and bacon. It's so yummy," Bobby says, saliva practically dropping from the corners of his tiny mouth as he describes their weekly meal.

"But please, get whatever you want. You don't need to eat that," Nate says, rolling his eyes. "The toppings are a bit unusual." Then he grins as he begins to tickle Bobby, who is mimicking him.

"Stop it, Dad," Bobby pleads between giggles.

"Pineapple and bacon sound delicious, Bobby," I say, closing my menu and placing it on the table.

Twenty minutes later, the server, a thin, pimply teenage boy with dark-rimmed glasses, appears with a gigantic white pizza, dotted with pineapple slices and bits of bacon. He then places two Caesar salads on the table, one by me and the other between Nate and Bobby.

I watch as Bobby kneels on the orange seat and begins to pull a slice of pizza from the round serving pan. But after placing one in front of himself, he takes another plate, puts a slice on it, then sets it to his left. I guess he must like to eat pizza from clean plates. But then he explains.

"That's for Mom," Bobby casually announces. "I like to include her."

My eyes move from him to Nate, reminding me that their loss remains a fixture in their daily life, something that will never disappear. A lone tear falls from my eye and down my cheek. Quickly, I wipe it away, but not before Nate sees. Then I feel his hand gently squeeze my knee beneath the table, as if he's comforting me.

"Well, I think it's a beautiful idea," I tell Bobby, who is digging into his pizza. A tiny piece of cheese hangs from his chin.

During the course of dinner, I learn that at school today, Katie deliberately tripped Bobby at recess because she likes him. He also shared how he got in trouble for talking, but it wasn't his fault; it was Katie's, because she was the one talking to him.

"By chance is Katie pretty?" I ask, causing Bobby to turn crimson.

"No, she's an idiot," he says, scrunching his little nose.

Nate and I cannot help but laugh.

The piece for Lynn remains untouched. Later, Nate asks the server for a piece of foil, apparently for Bobby to take the extra slice home.

"Sometimes Mom doesn't finish her piece, so she lets me eat it later," he explains as his dad carefully folds the foil around the paper plate.

As we wait for the server to bring the bill, Bobby starts to tell me about their plans for Easter.

"Every year, we go to the shore for Easter. We stay with Grandma Elsa and Grandfather ... at their house on the corner." Bobby continues, giving the details about building sandcastles on the beach with Nate, going for ice cream with his grandfather at the stand five blocks from his house, and how Grandma Elsa promised they will dye Easter eggs on Friday.

"Hey, Ali, why don't you come with us?" Bobby blurts out.

"Oh, Bobby, that is your special time with your grandparents." I flinch when the five-year-old son of the man I just slept with invites me to spend the weekend with them ... at his deceased mother's parents' home.

"Come on, Ali. We'd have fun. I bet Grandma Elsa would let you dye eggs too," Bobby pleads.

As I'm about to come up with some lame excuse as to why that isn't possible, Nate surprises me by supporting Bobby's request.

"Bobby, what a great idea. The house is huge. In fact, my parents are coming on Saturday. I know everyone would love to meet you."

While flabbergasted at this invitation, it's Nate's tone that catches my attention. He means it. He honestly thinks his parents, as well as his former wife's parents, are open to meeting me. My prior experiences have taught me the exact opposite ... the guy rarely wants to introduce you to his family. But not this one ... no, he imagines everyone getting along beautifully. Lynn's parents will welcome me, with open arms, into their home, not thinking twice about their son-in-law bringing another woman to their beach house. Yeah, right.

Nate must understand my struggle with this concept. "Please, think about it. We can talk later," he says as he glances down at Bobby.

"Ali, you've gotta come. And bring Josie. Then Rocco will have someone to play with." Said so simply, in a matter-of-fact fashion only a child can get away with.

Thank God the teenage server arrives with our bill. Nate puts two twenties on the table. "We're all set. Let's get you home, buddy. It's a school night." Bobby hops off the bench, but not without first grabbing the foiled package.

In a few minutes, we're parked outside of my building.

"I'll be back in a sec. I'm going to walk Ali to the door, OK?"

Bobby nods as he reaches for Nate's cell and begins to play a game on the phone. We walk slowly down the path, knowing we only have a few moments to ourselves.

"About this weekend, I want you to come." Nate sounds serious.

"But this is Lynn's parents' house. What will they think? Do they really want to meet me?" My voice strains as I attempt to have Nate see things from my position.

"Are you kidding? Bobby called both sets of grandparents first thing on Sunday morning and told them about you. I wouldn't be surprised if Elsa planted the idea in Bobby's head."

"You mean your in-laws *want* you to date again?" My eyes pop from my head when I ask this question.

Nate smiles and says, "Of course. They want me, and Bobby, to be happy. I guess it seems strange, but it's not like I left her. She was taken from us." Nate pauses for a moment. "I will always cherish that part of my life, but it doesn't mean I have to spend the rest of it alone," Nate says, placing his hands on both of my shoulders. Then, after tilting his head, he leans toward me, kissing me ever so softly. My knees become weak as I melt in his arms.

"Bobby …," I say, worried he'll see us.

"Shhhh, he's glued to the phone." Nate continues kissing me. When we stop, he looks me in the eyes. "You're going to have to meet them at some point. Why not get it over all at once? Plus, the weather's supposed to be in the midsixties and sunny." He raises his eyebrows as if to tempt me to accept his offer. "And Josie's invited. They have a fenced-in yard ... with a pool. What retriever wouldn't love that?"

I remain silent, mentally rehearsing all the reasons why I cannot commit.

But then Nate says, "I want you to come with me." His look is beyond seductive, and I can barely contain myself.

"When would we go?" I whisper, contemplating whether or not this is a good idea.

"I'll pick you up around 5:30 on Friday. Elsa and Jonathon plan to leave first thing that morning. Bobby and Rocco will go with them. My parents don't arrive till Saturday. So you'll have time with Johnathan and Elsa first, which I'm guessing is your biggest concern." Nate's on a roll, not stopping his pitch. "The house is pretty fabulous; it's on the beach, not far from town. We'll go crabbing, take walks on the beach. And mini golf should be open because of the holiday."

I stand there, visibly struggling with this unusual invitation.

However, Nate is relentless. "Did I tell you Elsa's an amazing cook? Plus, I'll make sure we're back Monday afternoon, plenty of time for you to be ready to go to work on Tuesday." Nate looks at me with puppy dog eyes.

"You promise me I'm not imposing?" I let out a big sigh, acknowledging defeat.

Nate pulls me into his arms and hugs me tightly. Apparently Bobby is now watching because I hear the car door open before he loudly yells, "Hey, stop it, OK?"

Startled, I look over, mortified, only to see the biggest smile on his little face.

"I don't think I'm the only Cavanaugh who's falling for you," Nate says, his lips grazing my forehead before he returns to his son.

CHAPTER 28

Unconsciously, I twirl strands of hair around my left pointer finger. Glancing at the pad of yellow paper on my desk, I see it's covered with spirals of red marker. Doodling's a habit I picked up in college. But I'm not sitting in a lecture, bored and restless. No, I'm at work and my mind's drifting all over the place. I keep thinking of Nate, what he's doing, imagining the children he sees each day, the trauma he deals with, the prognoses he must give to grief-stricken parents. But I'm also reminded of how he tasted, felt.

Then my mind does a 180 and shifts to this upcoming weekend. I hope to leave the office by three tomorrow. That will give me an extra hour or so to settle myself before I depart for a weekend at the shore with Nate, Bobby, his parents, and his dead wife's parents. I must be nuts, imagining how awkward these three days at the beach might actually be.

Last night, I called Susie to let her know I couldn't walk this weekend because I'll be away with Nate and his family. In typical Susie fashion, she pressed me for details, making me promise I'd call her as soon as I got back.

"Things are moving quickly, Ali," she said, her voice filled with promise yet tinged with a bit of motherly concern.

"I know. I wasn't going to say yes, but Nate assured me we'll have an incredible time." I became silent for a moment. "Susie, I'm scared."

"I know you are, honey."

"I've come so far, realized so much about who I am and what I need." I paused before continuing. "I don't want to lose myself to him."

"Then don't. You have the power. You always have. Remember, you chose to give your power to David. I doubt you'll do that again," Susie coached.

My monkey mind drifts, but this time, to more practical things. I'm mostly packed. All that's necessary is for me to fill the cooler with some items I've purchased for Elsa and Johnathan: specialty cheeses, salami, berries, and such. And I found a beautiful serving dish that will hopefully go with their decor. From the description Nate gave me, I think it might. I also have a small Easter basket for Bobby. It's the first time I've assembled one. I chose yellow grass, to match the walls in his bedroom, and filled it with chocolate eggs, malted balls, gummy bears, and jellybeans. In the center, I placed a miniature Batmobile, complete with a tiny Batman and Robin sitting inside of the car. But I'm most excited about the gemstone. I hope I haven't crossed a boundary.

Actually, I got this idea yesterday while treating Kimmy to lunch for her twenty-eighth birthday. We met at a café on Lancaster Avenue in Bryn Mawr, not too far from work. I can't remember when I last took time away from the office to have lunch with a friend. But considering all Kimmy's been through, I thought I'd break my rule. In an effort to make lunch extra special, I'd called the restaurant in advance to order a birthday dessert for Kimmy. She was totally caught off guard when the waiter appeared with a lemon raspberry mini cake, topped with a sparkling candle!

As we were leaving the café, I saw a toy store across the street. By the lavish Lego display in the front window, I knew that this place would have something for Bobby. Upon entering, I was drawn to the superhero section, and that's where I found the Batmobile. But then, after making my purchase, I noticed the rock shop next door. Before I knew it, I was standing in front of a shelf of beautiful uncut amethyst.

Pulled toward one particular rock, I picked it up and instantly felt a vibration in my fingertips.

Then I heard the voice.

Buy it.

And so, on impulse, I bought it for Bobby's Easter basket, along with a blue apatite bracelet for me. I put the bracelet on immediately and haven't taken it off since. The store's owner shared that this gemstone helps increase personal power, ease social anxiety, stimulate personal truth, and promote mental wellness. Could there be a better stone for me?

I have no idea who this voice belongs to. It's certainly not mine. But so far, it's always pointed me in the right direction.

***

The noise of an incoming email breaks my trance-like state. It's Miles asking that I stop by his office before I leave today. I look at my watch. It's 4:45, so I take the next twenty minutes to finish up the few remaining items on my desk before I tell Josie I'll be back in a moment.

"Have a seat, Ali," Miles says after I peek my head through his open door. His face looks more serious than usual. I wonder what's up. Knowing that when Miles is in business mode, there's no small talk. I take a seat in the chair across from his desk and wait for him to proceed.

"Tomorrow morning, we have our monthly budget meeting," Miles begins, matter-of-factly.

"Yes, you received the summary I sent regarding my portion of the meeting?" I ask, 99 percent sure I had sent it to Miles yesterday.

He softens a bit and gives me a brief smile. "Yes, excellent as usual. But that's not why I asked to speak with you." Miles pauses and takes in a big breath before he bites his lip. "I wanted to give you a heads-up ... David is coming to tomorrow's meeting. I didn't want you to be blindsided." Miles seems to exhale as he delivers the message I'd inevitably need to hear.

"I see." To my surprise, I'm not panicking.

"Is that going to be a problem?" Miles tilts his head, waiting for my response.

I sit up straighter, pressing my spine into the back of the chair. "No, everything will be fine."

"Good, that's what I was hoping to hear," Miles says as he smiles and stands, my cue that our meeting is over.

We say goodbye, and I head toward the door. But I stop and turn toward my boss before leaving. "Miles, I'm curious. Have you talked with David? Is he going to be OK with me in the room?" I ask with a broad grin emerging on my face, wondering if Miles will reply to the bait.

"Get out of here," Miles banters right back. "Have a good night. I'll see you tomorrow."

***

Later, after I'm all packed and Josie's travel bag is ready, she and I take our evening walk. Nate's working late tonight, so while we've texted here and there, I'll have to wait till tomorrow's car ride to let him know about the meeting and seeing David. Nate's asked me about David, and I've answered his questions, but I sense there's a bit of unresolved business with my ex. Maybe that's why I haven't said much about David. To be honest, between seeing David and meeting Nate's parents and in-laws, I'm more concerned with the latter. Yeah, I know it will be awkward seeing David, especially in front of everyone at work, but strangely, I'm not worried. However, the true test will be tomorrow, when we're actually in the same room.

CHAPTER 29

My five o'clock alarm blares, jolting me out of bed. I'd set it thirty minutes earlier than normal so I can get an extra two miles in on the treadmill. Running eases my mind, and today, I need to be thinking clearly.

My monkey mind's racing, going a hundred miles an hour, much faster than the 7.7 mph displayed on the digital panel. Mentally reviewing today's meeting agenda, I'm relieved I'm not the first to present. It will allow me time to center myself, ensuring I'm calm and focused ... with David there.

An hour and forty minutes later, Josie and I confidently stride into the lobby. I push the Up elevator button. Within moments, it arrives and the doors open, allowing us to enter. As I turn around to face the closing door, I hear his voice ... the voice of the man whom I'd desperately longed to please, who wouldn't allow me to meet his daughter, and whom I'd given my will to in an attempt to secure his love.

"Please hold the elevator." Each word is perfectly enunciated.

I tell myself to breathe as I press the Hold button. David rushes inside but freezes in his tracks when he realizes who held the elevator for him.

"Allison," he says, as if he's seen a ghost. Perhaps he has, as the Allison he knew is no longer. Instead, Ali is now controlling the elevator panel, allowing him to enter.

"Hello," I say, as I look my ex up and down with unforeseen curiosity. Yes, he still is extremely attractive, in a sophisticated and polished sort of way. I focus on his face, perfectly clean shaven. And David's hair is meticulous, so different from Nate's tousled curls. Then I stare into his eyes, the deep green eyes that used to make me quiver. But they do nothing to me now.

Seeing David for who he truly is, I stand tall, assured of who I have become.

David appears to be taking me in at the same time. His face softens as he leans in to give me an awkward hug. "You look great, Allison," he says, taking yet another step closer to embrace me. Then he looks at Josie. "Who's that?"

"Josie, my dog." I offer no further explanation. It's none of his business.

The elevator sounds as its door opens, announcing our arrival. Monica, the receptionist, stops what she's doing when David and I emerge from the elevator. Her eyes widen in my direction, but I nod my head and smile, signaling I'm fine. I head down the hallway. David follows. However, when we come to the conference room, I do not pause. Instead, Josie and I continue to my office, leaving David behind. I don't need to turn around. I'm sure he is standing alone by the door, confused. It's amazing to have my power back.

When it's time for the meeting, I gracefully walk into the conference room, my head held high. Poised, I take my seat next to Miles. There's a tenseness in the room. No doubt my coworkers are wondering how David and I will behave. Perhaps they're unsure how I'll handle myself. But I'm not worried.

Ninety minutes later, the meeting is over. As I stand up to leave, I turn to look at my boss.

"Well done, Ali." While Miles does not embellish, I pick up on my mentor's satisfaction. I smile in return, grateful for my relationship with Miles. He gets me, and I seem to understand him.

As I'm about to leave the conference room, David approaches, looking more animated than usual. I watch as the stiffness leaves his face, and instead, a bright smile appears. Not expecting another conversation, I pause, curious as to what he wants.

"Allison, I was wondering ... if you're not doing anything this weekend, perhaps we could—" he says in the sweetest voice, one that I have not heard for ages.

But I cut him off. "Thanks, but I don't think that's the best idea. Good to see you, David."

I give my kindest "fuck you" smile then abruptly turn and walk into the hallway.

The rest of the day flies by. Work becomes effortless. And now, I am now ready for my next challenge ... spending Easter weekend with Nate and his family.

***

Looking at the number of bags, I realize I packed too many clothes. Nate said it was completely casual at the shore, but his definition of casual might not match Lynn's parents'. I'm still concerned about meeting them. It's one thing to say they want Nate and Bobby to be happy, but it's another to actually spend the weekend with the woman your son-in-law is now dating.

At five thirty sharp, the buzzer rings. Josie gives a quick "ruff" when Nate knocks on the door.

"We're only going for three days," he teases when he sees the pile of bags by the door.

Playfully, I pull Nate into my arms, enveloping him in kisses.

"Keep doing this, and you can bring as much as you like," he says, grinning.

After gathering everything, the three of us head to his car. As we walk out of the building, Nate peers inside the tote with the tray and nonperishable edibles. "You didn't need to do that."

"I wanted to get something for Jonathon and Elsa. After all, they've invited me into their home. And I bring a gift whenever I'm a house guest."

Nate looks at me, his eyes widening a bit as if he suspects more.

"OK, maybe I went a bit overboard. I guess I kinda feel like I'm *the other woman*," I say as I shrug my shoulders. While I'm trying to make a joke, there's nothing funny about it.

He stops, setting the bags on the pavement by the car. "Listen," he says, taking my hands after he lets Josie into the back seat. "Lynn will always be a part of Bobby and me." He furrows his forehead. "But it's been four years. It's time for me to move on with my life. It's taken some time, but I'm ready. It was Elsa who made me realize this." The lines on his forehead relax.

"She did? They're OK with you and me?" I need to hear Nate say the words.

"Yes." His tone is definite as he looks straight into my eyes. "And Bobby's been talking about you nonstop. Do you know how happy that makes them?" A wide smile brightens his face.

Feeling a tiny bit more secure about this weekend, I pull Nate close to me, inhaling his musky scent. Slowly, the muscles in my neck soften and my shoulder blades return to their proper position. Yet, as much as I want to believe Nate, something keeps telling me the Jansens may feel differently.

***

Thirty minutes later, as we begin to cross the Ben Franklin Bridge, I decide to share this morning's encounter with David. But I'm surprised when Nate becomes silent.

"This doesn't bother you, does it? It's not like I wanted to see him. It was inevitable we'd bump into each other at work." I don't mean to sound defensive, but I might be coming across that way.

There's an awkward silence. Finally, Nate asks, "Did you have any feelings for him?" His voice cracks a bit. Could he actually be jealous of David?

"God no." I gently squeeze his thigh, hoping to alleviate any concern. "I didn't need to see David to confirm there's nothing between us." Yet I appreciate having that fact validated.

"I guess I knew you'd bump into him. But I wasn't expecting it to happen so soon." Nate takes my hand then kisses my fingertips.

"So what about you? There must be tons of women chasing you around the hospital." I arch my eyebrows as I finally ask the question that's been lurking in the back of my mind.

Nate clears his throat. "There might be a nurse or two." He smirks as he keeps his eyes straight ahead on the highway. "But there's nothing to worry about." Nate turns toward me and winks. I believe him.

We leave the serious conversation behind and play music, singing along to "Love Shack," "Bohemian Rhapsody," and "Chicken Fried." While Nate has many notable qualities, keeping a melody is not one of them. Looking over at the man driving us to the Jersey Shore, I could not be happier. While I adore Bobby, having Nate to myself is pretty sweet.

It's when we make our way onto the island that Nate lowers the windows, allowing the brackish saltwater scent to fill my nostrils. This reminds me of earlier days spent at the shore. Josie perks up, loudly sniffing as she leans her head out of the open back window.

It's been a couple of years since I've been to Stone Harbor, and I cannot believe the construction that's occurred. Classic old upside-down shore houses have been demolished, replaced by amazing summer homes resembling mini mansions.

As we get closer to our destination, Nate explains the Jansens built this home after Jonathon sold his funeral business to his sons, allowing Elsa and him to spend summers at the shore. Lynn's grandfather began this business in the 1960s. But it was Jonathon who grew the funeral home to a point where they had over seventy employees and increased operations to include a crematorium, cemetery, and mausoleum.

"And his company did Lynn's funeral?" The thought pains me.

"Yes," Nate says as he shakes his head. "I never knew how he survived it. Actually, that's the last service he personally directed. But he wouldn't allow anyone else to do it, wanted to make sure everything was perfect." Nate exhales then makes a left turn onto 118th Street.

"So this beach house is relatively new?" I ask, the inflection in my voice rising, a sign of uncertainty and perhaps insecurity.

"Yes, Lynn was never here, if that's what you're asking." Nate gives my hand a gentle squeeze.

"I'm sorry. I'm just terrified of saying or doing the wrong thing this weekend," I admit, rubbing my forehead.

"Ali, please try to relax. I think once you meet them, you'll understand." That's all he says as he pulls the car in front of a stunning house on the corner of 118th Street and Second Avenue.

This house is much bigger than I imagined. Adorned with gray shingles, the beautiful white home has a wraparound porch complete with rocking chairs and gorgeous pots filled with yellow and purple pansies. I can see there's a gated area in the back.

"Nate, you said the house was nice, but this place is amazing."

My mouth drops as I take in the grandness of the home. With its impeccably appointed exterior, I can only imagine how incredible the inside is.

"Jonathon's business did well," Nate casually says as he takes the keys from the ignition. Josie begins to whine. He looks at me, raising his eyebrows. "Stop worrying and trust me, OK? I wouldn't have invited you if I thought anyone would be uncomfortable."

Bobby comes running out the front door. Nate hops out of the driver's side, scoops up Bobby, and gives him a bear hug.

"Did you have a fun day?" Nate asks.

"Grandma Elsa and I dyed eggs, then Grandfather and I went to the beach and built a big sandcastle. And then we took Rocco on a long walk into town, and I got a twisty!" Bobby looks at me, then leaves his dad's side and gives me a hug.

"Where's Josie?" he asks.

I point to the back seat. Bobby releases his arms from me and opens the back door. Josie goes flying out to relieve herself. Bobby laughs.

Then when she's finished her business, he yells, "Josie, come over here. Rocco's waiting for you in the backyard." And with that, they disappear.

"He's like a tornado," I say and laugh as we begin to unload the car.

When we reach the porch stairs, an elegant woman opens the front door. She has light gray hair pulled back into a short ponytail and is wearing a pair of khakis with a powder-blue sweater set. I had no idea what to expect, but my body immediately relaxes as this graceful woman steps toward us.

"I hope it was an easy trip," she says, embracing Nate.

"Super easy," Nate says, and then he turns toward me. "Elsa, this is Ali."

Extending my hand, I give my best smile. But she'll have none of that. Instead, she motions me to her, then gives me a gentle hug.

"It's so good to meet you, Ali," she says, her lips covered in bubblegum-pink lipstick, like my mom used to wear. Expecting Elsa to eye me up and down in order to compare me to her daughter, I've assumed incorrectly. She only exudes pure warmth, acceptance, and ease in my presence.

A deep voice calls from inside the house. "Are the kids here?"

"Yes, Jonathon, they've arrived," Elsa says loudly as she takes my hand, leading me toward the door. "Drop your things on the porch. The men will bring everything inside." Despite appearing delicate, Elsa most definitely runs the show.

As we walk inside this beautiful shore home, a tall lean gentleman, whose thick dark hair is speckled with streaks of gray, comes down the stairs.

"You must be Ali. So happy you could be here." He says as he, too, pulls me in for a hug. But his arms are strong, not delicate like his wife's.

"It's so nice to meet you both," I softly say, amazed by their genuine warmth.

The two only look at one another and then smile. Jonathon puts his arm around his wife's waist. "How about we have a drink, and then I'll put the grill on, OK?"

Elsa nods at her husband before saying to me, "Come, let me show you to your room." Elsa heads up the stairway. I follow, grabbing the tote with the Easter basket in it … can't let Bobby see that.

At the top of the landing are four bedroom suites. This house was definitely built with guests in mind.

"I thought you would like this room," Elsa says, pointing to the door on the far right. "It has a beautiful view of the beach; none of the houses between here and the dunes block the view."

Eager to see the ocean, I cautiously peek inside the room before venturing in. Decorated in shades of yellow, the bedroom's hardwood floors are partially covered with a light gray rug. Directly across from the elegant queen bed is a huge bay window facing the ocean. I walk across the room so I can take in the view.

When I turn around, Elsa remains standing in the doorway, smiling as she observes my reaction.

"Thank you, Elsa, truly."

And then, for some unknown reason, what's been on my mind suddenly blurts out of my mouth. "I can only imagine how hard things have been for you. To lose a daughter so suddenly ..." Tears begin to fall down my cheeks, slowly at first, but then uncontrollably. Before I know it, I'm in Elsa's arms, and she's comforting me. We stand there for several minutes as I release a flood of unexpected emotions.

"Honey, we loved Lynnie with our entire heart. And Nate is like a son to us. Then when Bobby came along, well, we couldn't have been happier. But things changed." Elsa pauses before continuing. "I didn't think I was capable of feeling such pain." I lift my head and see the face of a mother who lost a piece of her heart.

"But how can you accept me so quickly?" Once again, my fears surface.

Elsa takes in a big breath, places her hand on my cheek, then says, "Bobby talks about his mom, but he doesn't remember her at all. He was too young. But Nate, well, it was difficult for him. I think the hardest part was that he could never say goodbye to Lynn."

I stand there, listening to this lovely woman bare her soul.

"But recently, there's something different about Nate. He has a lift to his voice. And Bobby, he can't stop talking about you. It's 'Ali this' and 'Ali that.'" Elsa grins as she shares this. But then her face becomes serious. "We can't bring Lynnie back, but we can hope

Nate finds another woman who can make him happy." Elsa blushes a bit after this statement.

"Tell me about your daughter. What was she like?" I ask, genuinely wanting to know more about Lynn. "Bobby has a picture of his mom in his room. She was beautiful." I remember how her long blonde hair appeared to fall so gracefully, framing her delicate fair skin. Yet it was her captivating blue eyes that seemed to be alive, dancing with laughter.

"Oh, you and Lynnie would have gotten along quite well, I suspect." Elsa's face beams as she makes this pronouncement. I can see Lynn inherited her glow from her mother. "Lynnie had an ethereal way about her, yet she had the heartiest of laughs and a wicked sense of humor. She didn't have a lot of friends. Lynnie claimed so many of them were frivolous and caught up in unimportant things. But the friends she had, well, they were loyal. We continue to stay in touch."

"What did she like?" I eagerly ask, grateful to be having this conversation, right here, right now.

"She loved being in nature, flowers, and gardening … and gemstones." Immediately, I think of the collection in Bobby's room.

"Bobby showed me. They're amazing."

"Yes, she felt they had energetic properties, carried different stones for different reasons. I believe this fascination began while she was in college." Elsa seems to drift a bit, as if there is more to this story.

"Where did she go to school?" I ask.

"Berkeley." Elsa laughs. "Her father had a fit when she announced that she'd been accepted. He wanted her to stay in the Northeast, attend a solid, conservative school. But that wasn't her style. She had wings and needed to fly."

"But she came back to Philadelphia?" I ask, wondering if that was due to Nate.

"Yes, she and Nate were newly married and living in Boston while he was finishing up his studies. But then, after he received the offer at CHOP, Lynnie discovered she was pregnant. And so they decided to return. I couldn't have been happier …"

Nate appears at the door, carrying the rest of my bags.

"Hey," he says, looking pleasantly surprised that we are deep in conversation and oblivious to the somewhat dried tears on my face. "I'm supposed to take drink orders." He sets the totes by my bed.

"My usual, please, Nate," Elsa says then whispers to me, "Gin and tonic."

"I'll have the same," I call out.

"Coming up," Nate says as he walks out of the room.

"You get settled, and I'll see you downstairs. I'm so happy we talked." Elsa pats my hand before standing up and heading toward the door.

But before she leaves, I go to Nate's mother-in-law and hug her tightly, softly saying, "Me too."

She only nods, blinks back a tear, then heads downstairs.

✳✳✳

After hanging up a few items in the closet, I brush my hair and wipe away the mascara that's bled onto my face. Then I take the bag with the tray and add the missing perishable items from the cooler before joining Nate and his family downstairs.

Everyone's in the kitchen, which is located in the back of the house and looks out onto the pool area. Nate and Jonathon sit at the dark gray granite island while Elsa casually flits around, putting the final touches on dinner. At a small seating area to the right of the kitchen, Bobby busily digs through bins of Legos, building some sort of monster-looking creation on top of the glass coffee table. Josie and Rocco are resting nearby. It all looks so natural, like it is supposed to be, making me wonder if I am also to be part of this picture or if my presence will upset things, alter the flow.

When I walk into the room, Nate comes over and places his hand on the small of my back, then offers me a seat on the stool situated between Jonathon and him. This display of affection in front of Jonathon and Elsa is somewhat awkward, causing my cheeks to feel warm. But before I sit down, I walk toward Elsa and hand her the gift bag.

"What's this?" she asks.

"Just something to say thank you for having me to your home this weekend. Really, it's very kind of you."

"We are so happy you could join us, Ali," Elsa sincerely responds as she begins to take out the cheeses, salami, berries, and other food items. When she comes to the gray, yellow, and navy ceramic tray, her face lights up. "It's perfect. How did you know?"

Thankful that my instincts were correct, I say, "I asked Nate about the colors in your kitchen, and then when I saw the platter, well ... I hoped it would work." Somewhat relieved that Elsa seems to like the gift, I take a seat on the stool between Jonathon and Nate.

"So, Ali, Nate says you design software for telephones. That sounds fascinating. What got you interested in that?" Jonathon asks, his eyes looking into mine, genuinely intrigued. Slowly, I open up, becoming more and more comfortable with each question he asks.

While Jonathon and I continue our discussion, Nate disappears outside with a plate of strip steaks. Josie and Rocco follow. Elsa takes a tray of roasted vegetables from the oven, placing it on the stove top. Moments later, she adds a sweet potato casserole next to the roasted veggies.

"Please, what can I do to help?" I ask as I watch Elsa turn her focus to a bowl of greens she retrieves from the refrigerator.

"Enjoy yourself," she replies, smiling sweetly as she begins to combine ingredients into a bowl, expertly whisking them before pouring the contents on top of the salad.

A few minutes later, Nate returns with a plate of sizzling steaks and two dogs at his heels.

"I think we're ready," Elsa says.

And then, as if on cue, Jonathon asks me, "Red or white wine with dinner?"

"Red, please," I say, "if it is open."

He chuckles as he heads to the bar and uncorks a bottle. "We got this in Napa last fall. Want to give it a try, Nate?"

"Sounds great," Nate replies as he assists Jonathon by taking four wine glasses and placing them on the table. The interaction seems so natural.

"Please, grab a plate and help yourself," Elsa says, having assembled a beautiful display of food.

Bobby drops a handful of Legos and scoots to his grandma. She takes a steak, cuts it in half, and places it on his plate. She then spoons a healthy serving of potatoes and several roasted veggies on her grandson's plate before handing him the dish.

"Do I have to eat asparagus?" he asks, evoking a less than sympathetic look from his grandmother.

Once we're all seated around the table, Jonathon offers a prayer of thanks, and Bobby chimes in with a loud "amen" at the end. I look at the four people surrounding me, wondering how and why I'm here. Everything's happening so quickly. Yet, though it's been a whirlwind, it seems so right.

It's at this exact moment the voice reappears.

Believe.

CHAPTER 30

Rays of sun stream through the magnificent bay window, coaxing me awake. After my eyes adjust, I climb out of the cozy bed and move to the source of light, gratefully absorbing the serene view in front of me. The distant water rises and falls in a calm, rhythmic pattern. I survey the surrounding homes, amazed none block this gorgeous seascape. Returning to the Atlantic, I'm humbled by the enormity of this ocean. Josie stirs in the corner of the room where she's been sleeping on top of a beach blanket. She walks over to me, wagging her tail. I lean down to pet my dog as I take a deep breath, feeling blessed for all that's come into my life.

Nate was right. Elsa and Jonathon could not be more welcoming. After my initial discomfort, which was quickly eased by Elsa, it became evident how much they love Nate and Bobby and want both to be happy. They beam whenever their grandson is in the room. I guess they see parts of Lynn in Bobby. I watched as Elsa's eyes glimmered when he dug into her homemade apple pie. And observing Jonathon build Legos with Bobby after dinner, well, it helped me see how beautiful families can be together. Immediately I think about my father and how he will never experience such joy. My euphoric mood temporarily halts, but then it shifts again when the door suddenly opens.

"Ali, Ali, it's time to get up. You have to see the seagulls!" Bobby yells. Rocco comes running in after Bobby, causing Josie to perk up. Then Rocco greets her with a butt sniff. Nate quickly appears.

"I hope he didn't wake you," Nate says, frowning at Bobby who's now headed toward the stairway. Josie looks up at me before following Bobby and Rocco out of the bedroom.

"No, I was only admiring the view," I say as I look toward the ocean.

"Well, so am I." Nate walks to the window then pulls me into his arms. "Good morning," he says after giving me the dreamiest kiss.

"Hi," I answer back, locked on those baby blue eyes.

"Sorry about the separate bedrooms." Nate blushes. "I wasn't sure how Elsa was going to handle it," he says, turning a bit redder.

"Are you kidding? Staying in the same room would have been so wrong."

"But I can visit." Nate's voice picks up, filled with hope. "Elsa and Jonathon's room is downstairs."

"But Bobby's across the hall," I remind him. Yet it might be possible. "We'll have to wait and see," I tease as I kiss him, hoping for a nocturnal visit.

***

After a breakfast of fresh pastries and bacon, apparently Bobby's favorite, Nate and I go for a run.

We start off south, running to the end of the island. When we turn around to head back toward town, the strong wind stings my face.

"I didn't realize you were a runner," I say, admitting how little I actually know about this man.

"Retired. Ran in high school and my freshman year of college ... cross-country," Nate says as he sprints ahead to the end of the block, where Second Avenue intersects with Eleventh Street. Then he jogs backward down Eleventh toward the beach, playfully laughing as he waits for me to catch up.

This explains his lean body build. No doubt I'm bound to learn a lot more about him, as well as his family, this weekend. But why wait? Why not take advantage of our morning run to find out a bit more about the man I'm now seeing?

"What else don't I know about you? Any dark secrets hidden in closets? Tell me now before your parents arrive and I start asking questions." I give him my best "so what's it gonna be" look.

"You want to know about my past?" Nate taunts me as we turn left on First Avenue. Now parallel to the beach, I see the ocean and the dunes to my right.

Inhaling the sea salt air, I readily admit, "Yes, I do."

"Well, then ask away." Nate speeds up his pace a bit, making a game of this.

"OK, I will." I continue running, focused on keeping stride with Nate. After another block passes, I ask, "Who was the first girl you kissed?" I start out easy on him.

"Jenny Parker … first grade … during recess?" Nate then provides some frivolous details. He seems to enjoy playing this game. "You?" he finally asks, a block later.

"Girl?" I laugh.

"If that applies," he says, raising his eyebrows, before he reaches out and gently pinches my bottom.

I shake my head. "Matty Brown," I reply. "Right before he pulled my hair. OK, the next question will be a bit harder," I warn as I vigorously pump my arms, realizing it's getting difficult to keep up with Nate. "Who was the first person you slept with?"

"Wow. Big jump from kissing Jenny in the first grade." Nate pauses, then says, "Andrea Parker, during the fall of my freshman year at Lehigh. I think she was 'the first' for a few of the guys on my hall." Nate cracks up as he continues to run effortlessly. "OK, your turn. Tell the truth."

I make him wait a bit before revealing my first love. "It was during my sophomore year at Villanova. His name was Matt Peterson. We dated for close to three years, broke up right after we graduated and he moved to LA," I say, momentarily returning to such a distant time in my life.

There's a pause, perhaps I'm stuck in a memory, but looking at Nate pulls me back.

"What else have you got for me? Bring it on." His eyes light up as if he's issuing a challenge.

But my real question isn't about anything frivolous or rites of passage. It's much deeper—something that, considering where I'm at, is important for me to know.

"Tell me about Lynn," I say as I try to keep up with Nate's pace. "How you met, fell in love, where you got married, what it was like when she had Bobby." There is so much more I could have said, but by the look on Nate's face, shock softening into understanding, I know he will answer my questions.

Nate stops running and takes my hand. We walk silently down 103rd Street toward the sandy wooden walkway that leads to the beach. Passing through the dunes speckled with short grasses slowly rising from the sand, I inhale the crisp air, hoping Nate's OK with answering my question.

After several minutes, Nate stops and sits down on the beach, gently guiding me next to him. He wraps his left arm around my shoulder and pulls me into him, resting his head on top of mine as he gazes at the crashing waves.

"I met Lynn during my residency at Johns Hopkins. It was a Friday night, after a particularly grueling week at the hospital. My buddy and I were meeting for a beer at a neighborhood bar. It was early summer, but I remember it being hot and humid that night.

"I first saw her sitting at an outside table with a group of women. She had thick, wavy long blonde hair and deep blue eyes, but it was her clothes that caught my attention. She looked like a hippie chick, so not my type. Yet she intrigued me. It took about three Heinekens for me to get the courage to talk to her. But once I did, well, that was pretty much it for me." Nate's eyes become distant as if he's reliving this moment.

"Love at first sight?"

"I guess so. Sure, she was gorgeous, but after talking with her, I knew she was so much more, unlike any of the women I'd dated." Nate pauses, seemingly searching for better words to relay his emotions. "Lynn had this way about her. She could sense how others were feeling, what they needed. I'm not sure if she was born this way or what."

"Was she intuitive?" I ask, cognizant of her passion for gemstones.

"She told me she was. But it was more than that. It's how people, even animals, acted around her, as if she had some sort of magic over them." Nate runs his fingers through his hair as if he's still trying to process everything.

"Did you date for a long time before you got married?"

"I was about to start my final year of residency when we met. The following March, I was offered a fellowship at Dana Farber Cancer Institute in Boston. It was too good not to accept it, but it meant leaving Lynn. When we talked about it, she said she'd move with me, claiming she could easily find another job in Boston."

"What did she do?

"Lynn was a high school counselor. Worked at one of the poorest schools in Baltimore. But the kids loved her. She told me they seemed to trust her, felt safe in her presence. That's how every-one was with Lynn."

"So you moved to Boston?" A huge wave crashes on the shore, spritzing us with salt water.

"Yes, but not before I proposed. I didn't think it was fair to ask her to leave her life and follow me unless we had a commit-ment." Nate looks into my eyes before continuing. "We found an apartment in Brookline, not far from the hospital. Lynn applied for a counseling position at a nearby high school. They were impressed with her résumé, but I'm guessing it was the interview that landed her the job. The next summer, we got married in Philadelphia." Nate pauses for a moment, and I envision how enchanting Lynn must have looked in a wedding gown.

"Then, as my fellowship was coming to an end, I started ap-plying for jobs. That's when the head of CHOP's Pediatric Oncology Department reached out to me, offering me an incredible position."

"How did Lynn feel about moving back to Philadelphia?" I ask, wondering if the free spirit in her had been hesitant to return to her hometown.

"Well, that's right about the time she found out she was preg-nant. After a lot of tough discussions, we decided it was a good move, for both of us and for the baby. Of course, Lynn's parents were ecstatic. Not only would they become first-time grandparents, but they'd also have Lynn back in the area."

I now better understand the big picture, though Lynn wasn't in Philadelphia for that long before her accident.

"And Bobby, was it a tough delivery?"

"God no, Lynn was a pro … no meds, totally natural delivery. She took to mothering right away."

A bit of jealousy rears, as I've always wanted a child of my own, and giving birth is something I'll probably never experience.

"And Bobby has no memory of his mom?"

Nate lifts his head from mine then stares into the ocean, swallowing hard before responding. "He talks to her all of the time. Says she answers him back." Nate heaves out a big sigh. "But the only memories he has are from the stories we've told him and the pictures he's seen."

I turn to look at Nate, who remains lost in the water's motion. "Maybe he does talk with her." My voice is solemn. "He's not the only person who has said this. And kids, well, it's easier for them. Their souls are pure; they haven't been told things like that can't happen."

Nate turns then shifts his body closer, his eyes searching into mine. "I hope he can talk to her. I want him to have some connection with his mother, even if I can't understand it."

I kiss his forehead before grabbing his hands and pulling him from the sand. We've had enough serious talk for now. "I'll race you to that lifeguard stand," I say, taking advantage of a head start. Sprinting furiously, I feel sand fly beneath my feet.

Nate plays along, letting me win. When we arrive, he encircles his arms around my waist then pulls me up, onto the raised wooden structure. His lean muscular core presses against me, our bodies becoming one.

"I guess we should head back," Nate finally says. "My parents are supposed to arrive around eleven."

And so we begin to jog on the firm sand by the water's edge. We're silent most of the way, perhaps both adjusting to what we are becoming—a couple. Meeting Elsa and Jonathon was so easy. They've genuinely welcomed me, as if I were part of the family. But then I start to wonder what Nate's parents will be like. Will they like me? He hasn't told me a lot about them, especially his dad.

"Give me a quick 'what I need to know about your parents' tutorial before I meet them," I say between breaths.

Nate laughs. "Mom's the super nurturer. She loves to take care of people. I guess that could be due to her nursing background," Nate says. "And my dad, well, he's a staunch Republican, meat-and-potatoes guy. He rarely misses a Pirates or Penguins game, but it's the Steelers that own his heart. He lives for football. Think he's having some trouble adapting to all of the Eagles fans in his neighborhood." Nate rolls his eyes, hinting he doesn't share his dad's intense passion for football.

"Your dad's retired?" I assume so, as I know they moved to Bryn Mawr shortly after Lynn died.

"Yes, he was a cardiologist at University of Pitt Medical Center in Shadyside. He could have worked a few more years, but when his younger brother died suddenly of a heart attack, the same thing that killed his own father, well, that's when Mom insisted he slow down, take time to enjoy life." Nate pauses before continuing. "Their plan was to downsize and then spend winters in Florida. But all of that changed," Nate says as we run over the wooden plank walkway through the dunes, taking us to Elsa and Jonathon's street.

Moments later, we see a silver Cadillac pull into the Jansens' driveway.

"There they are," Nate says as his face brightens. We begin to walk the rest of the way. "Hey, guys," Nate yells as the car door on the driver's side opens and a medium-sized man with thinning gray hair appears and turns toward us.

"Nate," he says, his tone deep but filled with emotion.

Then I hear, "Hi, honey." I see a short, curvaceous woman with mid-length dark brown curly hair come from the other side of the car.

"Mom, Dad, this is Ali," Nate says as soon as we come within feet of his parents.

Immediately his mother approaches me. "I'm Marney, and this is Pat," she says, motioning toward her husband. "I am so happy to finally meet you," she says, emphasizing *so* and *finally*, causing me to blink. Nate and I met less than two weeks ago. Then she engulfs me in a warm embrace; the top of her head only reaches my chin.

"It's so nice to meet you, Marney." I smile, pausing for a moment before turning toward Nate's dad.

But with him there's no hug, not even a handshake. I get an emotionless nod and a curt, "Good to meet you." That affection in his voice when he greeted Nate completely vanishes when he looks at me.

Elsa appears on the porch. "Pat, Marney, welcome! Please, come in. Jonathon took Bobby crabbing, but they should be back in a bit." Rocco and Josie come running toward us.

Immediately, Nate picks up his parents' luggage and follows his mom up the stairs into the house. Marney turns back to Pat. "Honey, will you please grab the coolers from the back seat?"

"Sure thing," he replies.

"I'm happy to help," I say, unsure of what role, if any, I have in this situation.

"I've got it." Direct and final.

I take a step back as Nate's dad opens the rear car door and disappears inside. I stand there, waiting to see if I can be of assistance. Several moments later, he steps away from the car with three insulated bags in his hands. As his eyes briefly scan mine, I offer a smile, hoping he'll show some sign of acceptance. Instead, he diverts his glance and heads for the stairs.

Stunned, I remain on the pebbled driveway and watch Nate's father trudge up the wooden stairs and into the house. This weekend was going so well. What have I done to upset this man?

CHAPTER 31

After devouring Elsa's homemade chicken soup and oatmeal raisin cookies she and Bobby made earlier in the morning, we head to the Cape May County Zoo. It's been years since I've visited the zoo. While small in comparison to the Philadelphia Zoo, this local zoo hosts a variety of animals, perhaps my favorite being the monkeys.

But it's the giraffes that Bobby gravitates toward. On our way out, via the gift shop, he begs for a stuffed version of this animal. I silently giggle as all four grandparents practically squabble over who will purchase the toy giraffe for Bobby.

After returning to the house, Jonathon announces that cocktails will be at five on the back porch prior to our six thirty dinner reservation at Via Mare. Luckily, the weather's unusually warm, permitting us to sit comfortably outside for a drink before we head to dinner.

I watch as Pat carefully observes me throughout the entire evening, seeming to notice my every move. Marney appears to pick up on it as well. Our eyes connect for a moment too long, perhaps in confirmation.

Afterward, when we return to the house, Nate tucks Bobby into bed, with his new stuffed giraffe, before heading downstairs. Jonathon offers Pat and Nate cigars, and the men retreat to the back porch. Meanwhile, Elsa opens a bottle of chardonnay and pours three glasses.

Conversation flows easily, and I forget the unease I felt in Pat's presence. We talk about Bobby and all of the mischief he gets into. Then the focus shifts to gardening and which perennials Marney wants to add to her yard this spring.

A half hour later, the men return, reeking of cigar smoke. Elsa orders Jonathon to immediately change and put his clothing in the laundry room. Marney gives a little smirk, then excuses herself and Pat, saying they had an early morning and are headed to bed. Jonathon and Elsa follow suit, leaving Nate and me alone in the kitchen.

He opens the container of oatmeal cookies. "So what do you think of my parents?" he asks as he bites into a cookie. Obviously, he's clueless about his dad's behavior

"They're great," I say reflexively. Then I add, "Your mom is so sweet."

"And my dad?" Nate looks at me, as if hoping for an equally positive response.

"I like him." I reach for a cookie. "Though I'm not so sure how he feels about me," I say, wondering if I'm being too sensitive.

Nate shrugs his shoulders then says, "With my dad, what you see is what you get. He doesn't have any hidden agendas. It's difficult for him to mask his feelings." Nate grabs another cookie from the tin. "But he's the real deal. He's been an amazing father to me, never missed any of my games or meets, and he's awesome with Bobby."

We stay up and talk for a bit, but then Nate says, "Oh, I promised Elsa and Mom I'd put the Easter baskets for Bobby out before I went to bed. Want to help?" I nod then we head into the laundry room and pull various baskets filled with colored grass and all sorts of treats from the upper cabinets, where they were stored safely, out of Bobby's sight.

Together, we place the baskets behind chairs, in nooks, and on a top kitchen shelf, hidden behind a plant. We are deliberate to ensure that neither Josie nor Rocco, who are carefully watching from the braided hallway runner, are able to reach any of these Easter presents.

"I made one too," I finally say, hoping none of the grandparents will care. I run to my room then quickly reappear with the basket, showing it to Nate. "Is it OK?"

He pulls me into his arms, providing the affirmation I need. Before heading upstairs, we carefully place this basket behind the television in the family room.

That night, after everyone's asleep, I hear my door open as Nate carefully makes his way into my room. It's only Bobby, Nate, and me upstairs. His parents are in the guest suite on the first floor. He assures me it's fine, promising he'll leave early in the morning, as he sets the alarm on his watch. With Nate next to me in bed, life is perfect.

**

The next morning, Nate's alarm sounds at five thirty. He kisses me before quietly returning to his room. But I cannot fall back to sleep, so after forty-five minutes I get up, throw on sweats, and head downstairs, prepared to start the coffee maker.

But when I enter the kitchen, the rich aroma of freshly brewed coffee fills my senses. Marney's up, and she looks about ready to pour herself a cup.

"Good morning. Would you like some coffee?" she offers with a warm tone to her voice. I smile and nod as she takes a mug from the tree of mugs sitting next to the coffee maker.

"Cream and sugar?" she asks.

"No, thank you," I say.

After she hands me the cup of black coffee, I look toward the deck. The sun is beginning to rise.

"There are blankets in that closet." She points to the closed door to the right of the pantry. "Let's grab two and head outside, so we don't wake the others."

I go to the closet and find fleece blankets on the middle shelf. After taking two, I follow Marney outside. We sit down on chairs facing east. While we cannot see the ocean from the deck, we can certainly smell the pungent salt water and hear the crashing waves and seagulls.

"You know, he likes you—Pat, I mean." She quickly adds in clarification, as if I might think she is talking about Nate. "But he's worried." She pauses. "We all are."

I look at Marney, and the cheery expression I've become accustomed to transitions to one of sadness.

I take a sip of my coffee. "I can only imagine how strange my being here is for everyone." My throat tightens. Will this conversation turn awkward, like my interaction with Pat when they first arrived?

"No, it's not strange at all, Ali. It's wonderful. Perfect, actually. The way you both connect, and you with Bobby. It's all so natural. I just …" She stops herself from saying more as she stares into her mug.

"What, Marney? Tell me." I reach over to her and place my hand on her arm.

Her eyes look up and then she takes a big breath before blurting out, "I don't want to see Nate get sick again." Then she loudly exhales, and as the breath leaves her body, she appears to shrink before my eyes.

"What do you mean 'sick again'?" I have no idea what she's talking about. Nate didn't tell me he was ill. My pulse races.

"I shouldn't have said anything," Marney starts to chastise herself. A grimace forms on her face, and she clenches her hands around the blanket on her lap.

"No, please, tell me what happened?" I want to know. I need to know.

"OK. It's probably best you're aware." She stands up a bit then shifts the chair beneath her so she's now facing me. "As you can imagine, things were incredibly difficult after Lynn passed," she begins, her voice constricting somewhat. "Here Nate was, with a newborn, in a brand-new house, a demanding job with ridiculous hours … and then Lynn died in that horrible accident. No good-byes, no closure, nothing … I think it was the suddenness that was the most tragic."

"And Jonathon did her funeral?"

"Yes, that poor man … I do not know how he oversaw his daughter's burial. They say losing a child is the hardest thing. And Lynn, while she and her parents were not that close, well, they adored her." Marney sees my reaction to her last statement.

"Lynn was a beautiful spirit, an old soul, so to speak. But her parents were pretty rigid and old school, must be the German and Dutch in them." For a moment, Marney's face relaxes. "Bobby's definitely softened them. They've changed in so many ways since we first met. From what Nate's shared, Lynn was the black sheep of the family. She went to the beat of her own drummer."

"Like going to Berkeley?"

Marney smiles. "Yes. She was determined never to return to Philly. She claimed it was stodgy, old school, too conservative for her." I silently chuckle, as I've often thought the same. "Yet, when Nate received the offer from CHOP, and she was unexpectedly pregnant, well, I guess the practical side took over, and they came back."

I nod, better understanding Lynn now that Marney's shared this information.

"When she died, Nate fell apart. Lynn did mostly everything for him and for Bobby, and she managed the household. After all, Nate was barely home. But that wasn't it. Lynn was Nate's world. They didn't have close friends nearby, as they'd recently moved to Pennsylvania. I guess they were each other's best friend. Pat and I lived over four hours away. We'd visit, but we didn't want to impose." Marney looks down and shakes her head before continuing. "It was about a month after the accident. That's when we got the phone call. It was late, about one in the morning."

I sit up straight, intently focusing on Marney. Unable to refrain, I ask, "From Nate?"

"Yes, but we could barely understand him. He'd taken pills, a lot of them. And he was rambling about not wanting to live anymore." Tears begin to fall down her cheeks, but she continues. "Pat immediately called 911 while I stayed on the phone, kept Nate talking. It took less than five minutes, but it seemed like an eternity before we could hear loud knocking in the background. I made him answer the door, and then an EMT got on the phone, assuring us that Nate would be OK and that they were taking him to Lankenau Medical Center. Pat and I left immediately, driving straight to Lankenau." Marney becomes quiet.

"He was OK?"

"Yes, but Pat and I knew he was incapable of dealing with everything. So I stayed with Nate and took care of him and Bobby while Pat returned to Pittsburgh and put our house up for sale."

"And that's when you moved to Bryn Mawr." I nod my head, another piece of the puzzle falls into place.

"Yes, Elsa connected me with her friend's daughter who is a realtor, and she found a beautiful home for Pat and me. There's some property, so Bobby has a yard to play in, and I have a place to garden. But it's not overwhelming, like our home in Fox Chapel was."

"How did Nate get better?" I ask, returning the conversation to him.

"Counseling, and I'd like to think help from the four of us, and Bobby. The little child who he barely knew became his main focus. He continued working at CHOP, but only after taking time off, about six months. They understood; after all, he'd been through so much." Marney's eyes brighten as she shares the happy outcome to her story.

"It was all of your love that brought him back?" I ask, seeing the strange parallel with my own recovery. This explains why Nate so easily accepted my story and self-isolation.

She nods.

The porch door opens, and Pat appears. "Do you want to go to the early church service?" he asks Marney. She nods, then says as she rises, "Would you like to join us? Jonathon and Elsa stopped going, but I think Nate and Bobby are coming." There is no pressure in her offer, only a warm gesture.

"I would," I say, as I get up. "I only need a moment to change."

As I walk past Pat, I lean up and kiss his cheek. "Good morning." The skin on his face is rough; no doubt he's taken a beating throughout these past five years. Now I have a better understanding as to why he's been so cold to me. Pat can't bear the thought of Nate—or maybe even himself—getting hurt again. It all makes perfect sense.

Pat doesn't say anything, but as I sense his body soften with my kiss, I hear the voice.

He approves.

***

After church, we come home to a house smelling of sausage and eggs. The table's set for brunch, but first things first.

Bobby bounds into the kitchen, eyes wide. "Can we begin the hunt?"

Elsa sweetly smiles, signaling he may. Josie and Rocco follow him as he runs about, searching behind chairs, under tables, and in closets. After ten minutes, Bobby's recovered seven baskets, each unique with something of special interest to him. Eagerly, he explores the contents, gingerly popping jellybeans into his mouth before biting off the ear of a dark chocolate bunny. When he comes to the basket I made, he stops, first picking up the Batmobile. He runs his fingers over the comic book car before testing out the wheels on the hardwood floor. Immediately Rocco runs after the speeding toy car.

"That's so cool!" Bobby laughs as he chases after his dog.

"I think there may be more in there," I say before looking at Nate.

Bobby returns to the basket and begins to dig into the yellow plastic grass.

"Wow!" His hand holds up the uncut amethyst. "This is amazing! Mommy must have told the Easter bunny to put it in there."

The room falls silent, Elsa takes a deep breath, then looks at me and mouths "thank you." The adults see this and knowing Lynn's mother is OK with me continuing her tradition of giving Bobby rocks, everyone relaxes. I keep my eyes on Bobby, but I feel a hand on my back. I look up and see that Pat's come to sit next to me. He remains silent, but from the way his eyes glisten, I can tell he does approve, like the voice said.

That's when it hits me. Could this voice be Lynn's? Is she guiding me, helping me navigate her family, so I can be comfortable in Nate and Bobby's world?

While this concept would have haunted me in the past—Nate's dead wife's voice inside of my head—I now realize it's not there to scare me or keep me away from Nate. No, it's the exact opposite. She wants me to be with Nate and Bobby. She is encouraging me, coaxing me forward. I look at Nate. He seems so happy. Do I tell him or keep this to myself? I decide to wait; there's plenty of time. And who's to say he'd believe me.

***

After Elsa's delicious brunch, everyone but Marney heads downtown for a game of miniature golf. She's staying behind to begin preparations for Easter dinner. This is *her meal*, and according to Nate, she always makes the same thing—Sicilian Timballo and braciole in ragù sauce and for dessert, limoncello tiramisu and Italian knot cookies, with sprinkles, for Bobby. I offer to stay behind and help, but she practically pushes me out of the kitchen. So I promise I'd be in charge of cleanup, a gesture she seems to appreciate.

We play two rounds of miniature golf. Nate wins the first round, and Pat, the second. Afterward, we head to Springer's for ice cream. Unsure whether or not this iconic ice cream shop would be open on Easter, we take a bet, and as luck would have it, there's a line of people waiting to order ice cream cones from the famous Springer's.

***

When we get back, the house smells amazing. Continuing to refuse help, Marney scurries about the kitchen, shooing everyone away. Jonathon and Pat go to the enclosed side porch and play cards; Elsa takes a walk on the beach; and Nate, Bobby, and I go for a bike ride.

By five o'clock, everyone's showered and assembled for drinks before we begin dinner.

"I'd like to propose a toast," Jonathon says, raising his glass. "To Ali ..."

"Hear, hear." Glasses clink, including Bobby's plastic cup containing white grape juice, the only juice Elsa allows in her house.

Shocked and embarrassed, I offer a small smile while Jonathon continues. "I don't know how Nate found you, but we're all so happy he did." Nate comes over and kisses me on the cheek. Bobby laughs.

Then I have an urge to respond, to those around me whom I've only recently met, but who have opened their home and hearts to me.

I raise my glass. "Thank you. This has been amazing ... you are amazing ..." But then I begin to choke up.

Nate continues in my place. "For the first time in so long, things seem so right. Cheers." Then he kisses me once again, but not on the cheek.

CHAPTER 32

When I wake up, Nate's gone.

Stretching my arms over my head, I inhale deeply, not wanting this weekend to end. Yet I know it must. Spending time with Nate's family has been amazing. I'm in awe of how easily they've accepted me, and I'm beginning to comprehend the nuances of their relationship.

Nate and I go for a morning run, savoring the solitude of the quiet beach. Nate promises that when we next return, Stone Harbor will be filled with families retreating from the Philadelphia heat. In an attempt to postpone our departure, I urge Nate to run farther. But we both know we're only delaying the inevitable. We can't escape the fact it's soon time to pack the car and say goodbye.

But the goodbyes are only momentary. Marney's invited everyone over for dinner next Sunday. She promised to make lasagna, the same recipe Nate made for me.

***

Later that afternoon, as we drive north on the Garden State Parkway, Nate and I talk quietly while Bobby, seated between Rocco and Josie, watches a movie on his iPad. I learn more about each of the grandparents and their role in Bobby's upbringing. I refrain from mentioning my conversation with Marney. That is between us. Nate will tell me when he's ready, if he ever is.

But if he chooses to keep this to himself, I certainly understand. For two months, depression held me in its grips, and I only ended a relationship ... I didn't lose a spouse. Unable to imagine Nate in that state, I merely gaze at him as he drives, his curly dark hair, which soon needs to be trimmed, falls slightly in his eyes. I reach for his hand. And as our fingers intertwine, the voice appears.

It's me.

Instead of jarring me, the voice confirming her identity only provides a sense of calm. It's reassuring knowing Lynn's been guiding me, leading me to Nate. I say a silent thank-you, hoping *she* hears *me.*

***

In less than three hours, Nate parks his car in front of my apartment. Josie seems reluctant to leave Rocco and Bobby. I know how she feels.

Nate helps me with my bags, but we stop outside of the apartment building. He can't leave Bobby, asleep, alone in the car.

"I have to work late tomorrow and Wednesday. Bobby will be with my parents. Is it OK if I stay here both nights?" He looks at me, a deep longing in his eyes.

"I wouldn't want it any other way." I kiss him one last time, then unlock the door to the building's foyer. But as Josie and I are about to go inside, Nate stops us.

"Wait, there's something I want to tell you," Nate says, his voice slow and deep.

Carefully, I place the bags against the opened door then turn to face Nate. He moves toward me, placing his hands on my shoulders. He pauses, looks deep into my eyes, and whispers, "I love you."

"I love you too," I say softly before our lips connect.

We remain locked in our embrace. Finally, I hear Josie's whimpers, apparently impatient with Nate's and my long goodbye. Nate gives me one last kiss then says, "I'll see you tomorrow, sometime after nine."

***

While driving to work the next day, I notice the tulips are in full bloom. The sun's shining brightly, and I've got a song in my heart. I can't help it. I'm in love. Monica gives me a funny look when Josie and I exit the elevator.

"Morning, Ali," she says, her head tilted as if she's trying to figure out something.

I settle in at my desk, and Josie falls asleep in the corner. I think she's exhausted. Bobby kept her and Rocco running around most of the weekend. She's not used to being with a five-year-old.

About an hour later, there's a knock on my door. It's my secretary, Carole, carrying a large bouquet of bright pink peonies. "These arrived … for you," she says, eyes wide, as if waiting for me to share my secret admirer with her.

But I don't; I only rise from my chair and graciously accept the flowers and place the vase to the left of my computer screen. As soon as Carole leaves, I open the card.

Thank you for saying yes to last weekend.

I love you.

Nate

My heart flutters. Hearing him say he loved me yesterday afternoon sent me flying, but now as I read this card, I'm able to savor each and every letter of those three perfect words.

I try to focus on work, but my mind is elsewhere. I text Kimmy to confirm our running date later today. She replies that she's looking forward to it, then asks if I want to grab a quick bite afterward with Lisa and her to catch up. Knowing Nate's working till nine, I readily agree. I haven't seen Lisa for a bit, and unlike when I was with David, I don't want to give up my girlfriends, no matter how much I like, or love, Nate.

**

Six hours later, Kimmy and I are running down Lancaster Avenue. She's drilling me with questions about my weekend. I give her brief answers but request we wait till dinner so I can tell both her and Lisa at the same time. Reluctantly, she agrees, and we spend the rest of the time talking about her week.

Later, as I shower before meeting the sisters for dinner, I acknowledge how positive and upbeat Kimmy's becoming. I haven't heard the self-doubt talk that consumed her when we first met. As I throw my hair into a ponytail and apply a touch of makeup, I wonder if it's the spring weather outside or if it's something else in the air. After all, it's not only Kimmy who's making huge strides. A mere month ago, I was an utter mess. But then, I found Josie … and Nate.

**

I meet Lisa and Kimmy for Thai, and as we're waiting for our dinner, I fill them both in on my weekend at the shore.

"You were so brave," Kimmy says. "I can't imagine how nervous you were going to his wife's parents' home." Her eyes are wide in disbelief.

"I know, but they couldn't have been sweeter. They made me

feel so welcomed." I reflect on Elsa and Jonathon's kindness, and a part of me melts in gratitude.

"What's Bobby like?" Lisa asks, and I share his characteristics as well as his antics. But then she digs deeper. "What does he think about you?" Kimmy nudges her, as if to insinuate she's out of line.

"No, it's OK," I say as I take a moment to consider her question. "You know, I've never done anything alone with Bobby. Nate's always with us. Maybe I'll see if Bobby wants to do something this weekend, just the two of us. And I bet Nate would appreciate the free time."

***

Later that night, after Nate's arrived and we're cuddling on the sofa watching television, I ask, "Do you think Bobby would want to do something alone with me this weekend?"

Nate sits up and turns toward me. "Are you kidding? He'd love that. What were you thinking?" He takes my hand, then begins to kiss my fingers.

"Well, I could take him to The Franklin Institute or the Please Touch Museum … or the Camden Aquarium."

"Ali, you don't need to do anything like that. And, besides, his grandparents have taken him to all of those spots."

Hearing this response deflates my spirit.

"Spend some time with him. Take him to the park or out for ice cream. You know, the normal, everyday stuff kids like."

That's when I realize how much "normal" Bobby is missing. Yes, he has four loving grandparents who spoil him dearly and take him all over the place, doing whatever they can to help fill the void Lynn left. But that is only part of it. Is it possible to give him something else he needs?

"I get it," I say, tracing my finger over Nate's lips, down toward his collarbone and beneath the vee of his scrub shirt. "Bobby wants to do the kind of things kids do with their mom, not a grandparent."

As the words escape my mouth, I realize my intent could be misconstrued. But I don't think it is because Nate sweeps me into his arms, his mouth traveling down my neck to my clavicle and then, after unbuttoning my shirt, to my breasts. His tongue continues downward, and before I know it, my breath quickens. Taking my hand, he leads me into the bedroom. Josie can wait for her final walk.

***

Waking up next to Nate is pure heaven, something I could definitely become used to. On Thursday morning, as he kisses me goodbye before leaving for the hospital, I ask if he, Bobby, and Rocco would like to come for dinner that night.

"Are you sure you're up for the three of us?" Nate asks, most likely conscious of the size of my apartment.

"Absolutely. It will be fun," I say, anxious to make dinner for Bobby and Nate.

"Then we'll see you tonight." One more lingering kiss, then he's gone.

***

I leave work early knowing I must stop at the store on the way home to pick up ingredients for dinner. I want to make something Bobby will like. After mulling around some options, I decide on spaghetti and meatballs, my favorite when I was his age.

At six thirty, the door buzzes. That reminds me, I want to

give Nate my extra set of keys. Moments later, the two, rather three of them—I can't forget Rocco—arrive. Josie and Rocco start doing laps around the dining table. Bobby jumps in, chasing the large dogs as dog hair flies everywhere. Josie's tail's wagging and her tongue's hanging out of the side of her mouth as she rounds the corner of the table.

During the chaos, Nate, who seems unfazed, takes a bottle of cab from a brown paper bag and uncorks it. As he pours wine for both of us, I ask Bobby if he'd like something to drink.

"You got any grape juice?" he asks, a bit breathless from the constant running.

Knowing that is his favorite, I'd bought a large jar at the store today. "Coming up," I reply. Nate shakes his head and smiles as he watches me fill a plastic glass with white grape juice from the fridge.

"You are amazing," he says.

"Wait till you hear what I have planned for Bobby and me on Saturday," I say, in a somewhat taunting voice.

In ten minutes, the three of us are seated at the table, plates of Italian bread, salad, and spaghetti and meatballs in front of us. Nate takes a paper towel and tucks it into Bobby's shirt while Rocco and Josie sit attentively by his feet, as if waiting for a stray meatball to come their way.

"So, Bobby, I was thinking you and I could do something on Saturday," I say, curious if he'll show any interest.

"Really, Ali? That'd be awesome," he says as he shoves a twirled forkful of spaghetti into his mouth. Red sauce drips down his chin.

"What would you think about having a picnic?" I ask as I go to the closet and return with a large bag. "The weather forecast said it is supposed to be sunny, but windy, so I thought we could try these out."

I hand him the bag, and he jumps off his chair, moving away

from the table so he can see what's inside.

"Wow!" He pulls out both kites, closely examining the pattern. "This one's mine, right?" he asks, pointing to the Batman kite.

Nate puts his fork down and reaches for my hand.

"Yes, that's yours, and the yellow-and-purple one is mine."

"Can we try them now?" Bobby asks, looking at Nate.

"No, buddy, it's too late. And besides, there's no wind," Nate says as he points to the still branches outside of the bay window.

"But we'll go on Saturday. I promise." Bobby's face lights up as he unwraps his kite.

***

Later that night, after Bobby's inhaled three chocolate peanut butter brownies, he falls asleep on the sofa, his face laced with traces of red sauce and chocolate icing.

"Kites … what a great idea," Nate says as he helps me with the dishes.

"Glad you like it," I say as I teasingly grab him from behind. My hands linger, wanting, but knowing that won't happen tonight.

Nate looks over at Bobby and both dogs, who are still lying by the sofa.

"Dinner here was awesome. Thank you." He gives me the sweetest of kisses. "But you know what would make everything better?" he asks, whispering softly in my ear.

"What?" I'm curious, willing to play his game.

"If there was more space." He grins. I'm confused. He's not criticizing my apartment, but I'm unsure where he's going.

"Your apartment is perfect … for you … but it's not only you anymore, is it?" he asks, as he kisses my neck.

"I guess I could find another place to live …"

"No, move in with me, with us," he says, becoming serious.

Suddenly my throat tightens, and a stifling sensation comes over me.

"Nate, it's too soon, and what about Bobby and your parents … and Elsa and Jonathon?" I ask, coming up with every reason why it's not right.

Nate takes my hands then ushers me into the bedroom so we can talk in private. Sitting on the side of the bed, he says, "I don't want to spend a night without you, and that's impossible … because of Bobby." He momentarily glances through the open door into the other room, where Bobby remains asleep on the sofa. "But if you moved in with us, well, we could be together every night … and morning." He looks deeply into my eyes, as if pleading with me to consider.

"Nate, as much as I want to, I can't pack up and move in with you and Bobby. I know my apartment's small, and if we're all here, it's definitely cramped. But we haven't known each other for an entire month. Moving in would be irresponsible." While a part of me is tempted, I cannot say yes.

"You can tell yourself that, but you know what we have is different." Nate's voice strains a bit, as if hurt, something I haven't heard before. He takes a big inhale, then exhales before saying, "But I don't want to rush you. I guess I'm being selfish, torn with wanting to be with both you and Bobby." Nate looks down at the floor, and I have a sudden urge to change my mind, to make him happy. But I don't.

"There's no rush. I can stay over some of the time, but I can't move in." I want to say more, tell him how I worked to find myself again, that I'm afraid that if we take things too quickly, I'll lose everything I fought so hard to regain. But I don't.

Nate only sighs, his forlorn eyes locked on the carpeted floor.

281

"I promise you, we'll make this work," I say, placing my hand on his thigh.

Yet, not only does Nate shut down verbally, but I can also feel a tenseness in his leg where my hand rests. We sit there in silence, neither of us willing to say what we feel. The space between my eyes begins to throb as if warning me that this is too much too fast. I cannot stop my personal development to jump in where Lynn left off. I love Nate, and Bobby, but I will not automatically turn into a wife and mother just to make Nate happy.

As I begin to muster the courage to share these thoughts, I hear faint noises coming from the living room. Then, all of a sudden, there's crying.

"Daddy, where are you?" Bobby yells.

I look at Nate, and the expression on his face practically kills me. Bobby cries louder, and we both get up.

"Coming, buddy," Nate says after clearing his throat. I watch as he goes to his son. After picking up Bobby, who is now sobbing as he clings to the bag of kites, Nate looks at me, shrugs, then calls for Rocco to follow them out the door. Josie nudges Rocco on the nose before they leave. I remain standing in the doorway to my bedroom, watching as the most perfect man and his beautiful little boy exit my apartment. Am I letting go of what I should be holding onto?

Should I reconsider Nate's offer?

I wait to hear the voice, craving her guidance. Yet there is nothing, no wisdom of her words, no encouraging prompts. Only silence.

***

An hour later, my cell rings.

"Bobby finally settled down. I think it startled him waking up in a strange place without me." A big sigh comes across the phone.

"Yes, this is a lot on him too." I pause and wait. I want to know what Nate's thinking right now.

"I think you two spending time together on Saturday will be a good thing," Nate finally says.

"I hope so." Doubt begins to invade my mind. I've never been alone with a five-year-old boy before. But that's not what I'm concerned about. It's how Nate and I left things. While I wouldn't call this a fight, it's the first conflict we've had, and as of now, there does not seem to be a resolution that works for both of us.

After a bit of awkward conversation, we say goodnight. Josie and I take the night's final walk. I feel how much my jaw is clenching. There's so much I want to say, but I'm afraid to speak up. As we near the turnaround point of our walk, I look at my golden and ask aloud, "Was I right to say no? I love him, and I know he loves me. But is this real love? How do I know for sure?"

Trust, let go, allow.

She speaks. Her words smack me in the face. Have I answered my own question, or has she?

CHAPTER 33

Sweat beads on my chest, soaking through my long sleeve T-shirt. The sun's shining, and there's a light breeze. It's perfect running weather. My Garmin watch shows I'm about to hit nine miles, but today's goal is eleven. Kimmy's out of town, so I'm on my own for this week's long training run. But I don't mind. Actually, pounding the pavement solo is therapeutic.

The Red Hot Chili Peppers' latest song streams through my headphones, providing a background of sorts for me to objectively analyze my relationship and Nate's request that I move in with him.

Yes, I love Nate. He's amazing. And Bobby, well, my heart floods with joy when I think of that child. But living together? It's too soon, and after all that's happened these past months, I don't think I'm ready for this next step. Moving in with someone is a big commitment, especially when there is a child involved. The last thing in the world I would want is for Bobby to become attached to me and then Nate's and my relationship not work out.

But then as I approach mile ten, it hits me what's most troubling. Does Nate love me, or is he looking for a replacement for Lynn? That's what I really need to know. This question alone causes my throat to constrict, so I quickly put it out of my mind.

And that voice, *her* voice, is it me, or could it really be Lynn? Is she guiding me toward Nate and Bobby, and if so, is that what I want? And, what does her message mean? Trust, let go, allow. Am

I to trust my reasons, let go of Nate, and allow our relationship to end, or am I to trust my heart, let go of my fears, and allow love to happen? I don't know.

I can see my apartment building ahead. The run's done, but I haven't figured anything out.

***

After a quick shower, Josie and I congregate on the sidewalk, waiting for Susie and Gail. After all, it's Saturday, our weekly time to walk and talk.

"Oh, Ali, he loves you!" Susie's ecstatic, and Gail, who's normally cautious, is brimming with questions as I fill them in on my weekend.

It's as if these two are vicariously living through me. But then I share what happened Thursday evening and how we spent last night apart because Nate was working late. Plus, I told Nate I wasn't feeling well and needed to rest ... and I'd see him Saturday when I picked up Bobby ... all because I wasn't ready to continue the conversation, the one that needs to be had. But he seemingly believed me, didn't question my need for a night alone. Maybe he, too, required some distance.

"Ali, you have to be honest about your feelings," Gail chides.

"But what do I say? I don't want to hurt him, but I can't move in with him. How can he expect me to do that? It's all happening too fast." I stop walking and bury my head in my hands; my hair tumbles over my face as tears fall.

It's Susie who moves next to me, placing her arm around my waist.

"Honey, what do you want? Where do you see yourself? If time were irrelevant, what would you do?"

"You mean if there were no timelines? If it wasn't all happening so fast?" I snivel, trying to understand what she's asking.

"Yes, if it was ten months from now, or two years, what would you say to Nate?"

"I don't know," I say as I look up, my face moist from crying.

Gail then speaks: "I think what Susie means is maybe it's not about how quickly the relationship is proceeding. Perhaps the real question is whether or not Nate is who you want to spend your life with."

Instead of responding right away, I take a breath to consider the question. *Is Nate the one?*

My mind travels back to how our relationship developed and how I so quickly became a part of his world. Did it feel right? Was it what I wanted?

At this exact moment, there's an intense flash throughout my body, and it seems as if there's a string attached to the center of my heart, pulling me upward, expanding my chest. The armor I've so carefully wound tightly around me begins to crumble, slowly falling away. Now, without the cold metal shielding my heart, all I can do is feel. And that feeling is love, pure love.

But if the sensation coursing throughout my body is not enough, the voice returns. She speaks in a tone of strong conviction. *Commit.*

I freeze, shivers going up and down my spine. Do I tell Susie and Gail, who I trust and respect, about this voice? But who hears their boyfriend's deceased wife talking to them? Yet I desperately crave another's input about what's happening inside my head. I need to know if it could be real or if it's merely my messed-up imagination. That's when I allow my need for another's opinion to outweigh my fear of being judged as crazy.

"There's something I have to ask you." I pause, wiping my eyes. "I don't want you to think I'm nuts or anything, but do you ever hear voices ... of dead people?" I spit it out quickly then stare at Josie's leash, hoping I don't look up to find them laughing at me.

But when I finally lift my eyes toward their faces, they look as though they've seen a ghost.

"Ali, whose voice do you hear?" Gail asks placing her hand on my shoulder.

"I ... I'm not sure ... but I think it might be Lynn's, Nate's wife." Gail and Susie are familiar with Lynn, and earlier I filled them in on some of the things Elsa had shared with me about her daughter.

"Let's have a seat." Gail motions to a nearby park bench, and the three of us sit, the two women flanking me. The dogs take their cue and settle down on the grass, not pulling, perhaps happy to have a break from our walk.

Now I'm beginning to panic, afraid they might think I've totally lost it. After all, they know how depressive and reclusive I became after David. But this is different.

"Ali," Gail begins, "when did you first hear this voice?"

I think back. "It was in the middle of March. Before I had Josie. Before I met you. The voice said, 'Stay here. Stay safe.'" I take a moment and dig deep into my memory. "And then I remember hearing it the first night I had Josie; it told me to go outside." I gasp. "It was the night I first ran into Nate." I keep searching my memory. But then, it comes to me, clear as can be. "'Window.' It said to go to the window ... and that is when I first saw Nate walk by ... when he was one of the Dog Walkers." My body trembles and goosebumps form on my arms.

"Oh, dear," Susie says, stroking my hair in a comforting manner as her eyes stare at my forearm. "While I would have believed your story, your physical reaction definitely confirms it."

I look at the goosebumps. Susie only nods.

"But why would you so readily believe me?"

Susie lets out a long sigh, then begins, "After Gail's Walter died, my husband, Henry, started hearing from Walter."

Astounded, I turn to look at Gail who nods then says, "It's true. At first, I didn't believe him. I thought it was merely a reaction to losing his brother, whom he adored. But Henry kept insisting Walter would speak to him." She stops.

Susie continues the story: "The three of us went to see an expert in these things. I guess she was like a medium of sorts. Anyway, she confirmed Henry was correct. Walter had been communicating with him. While my husband was unable to correctly interpret everything his brother was saying, this medium connected with Walter and filled us in with the missing information."

"How long did it go on?" I asked, unsure as to whether I want this to continue or stop all together.

"For several months, until all of Walter's affairs were in order. He loved Gail, but Walter was a controlling man, and he wanted to ensure everything was taken care of after he died. He didn't want to burden Gail with it, so he reached out to Henry." Susie stops talking and looks at Gail who is staring at her hands folded upon her lap.

"And Lynn's doing the same thing? She wants to make sure Nate and Bobby are taken care of … and she found me to do that?" The words come through my mouth without me realizing they are mine. Perhaps, once again, Lynn's guiding me to see the obvious.

"Had it not happened to Henry, I would not have believed it was possible," Gail admits as she reaches down to pet Grace who's moved next to her feet. "Knowing Walter only wanted what was best for me after he was gone, well, it helped me move on and live my life." Gail smiles.

"Does that ease your guilt?" Susie asks, patting my hand.

"I suppose it does. And after meeting Lynn's parents and Nate's, well, it seems like everyone is OK with how fast things are happening." I bite my lip as if trying to digest this unfathomable concept.

"But are things moving too fast for you?" Gail asks as she looks me directly in the eyes.

"It seems like we should be taking things more slowly," I admit.

"*Should* is a word that does not benefit anyone. What do *you* want, Ali?" Gail's precise with her words, forcing me to acknowledge my unspoken guilt with how quickly Nate and I have fallen for one another.

"I don't want it to be a rebound, for either of us," I say as I clench my eyes shut and my voice begins to crack. "Nate's amazing—perfect, actually—and the way I feel about him, well …" I blush, causing both women to giggle. "And Bobby, he's so adorable, and he needs a mom."

Gail and Susie exchange a quick smile then Susie says, "I think you know exactly what you want. But are you afraid to own it?"

"Why don't we finish our walk," Gail says as she rises from the bench and motions to Will and Grace to follow. Susie and Joy also stand, leaving me sitting alone on the bench, Josie at my feet.

While I'm not questioning my love for Nate, I am stuck on whether or not I am ready to fill Lynn's shoes. My thoughts are interrupted when Josie pulls on her leash and gives a quick bark, causing me to stand up and join the others.

The rest of our walk centers on small talk, recipes they've recently tried, the unusually warm summer predicted, and Oprah's latest podcast. By the time we get back, it's five after eleven, enough time for me to make our picnic lunch and pick up Bobby by noon. However, I can't shake the meaning behind the voice.

***

Less than an hour later, I grab the picnic basket and blanket. I look for the kites, then remember Bobby took them with him on Thursday night. Since Nate worked the late shift last night, Bobby stayed with his maternal grandparents. Elsa promised to drop Bobby off by eleven this morning so Nate could get him ready for me by noon.

I knock on the door. Nate answers, still in a pair of red plaid pajamas, and instantly my heart melts.

"It's nearly noon, sleepyhead," I say, running my fingers through his thick hair. Seeing him isn't as awkward as I thought it might be. I've most likely exaggerated the situation.

Bobby comes bounding down the stairs, holding the bag of kites, followed by Rocco. "I'm ready, Ali!"

I look over at Nate's son and see he's combed his normally unruly hair, a rarity, and is dressed in jeans and a Lehigh sweatshirt. "Look at the sweatshirt Dad got me at his college reunion." Bobby's smile is a mile wide. I turn to watch Nate, who is proudly gazing at his son. There is no hiding how much he adores Bobby.

Bobby runs out the door toward my car. Rocco goes to follow, but Nate grabs his collar. "Stay, Rocco. I'll give you some of my pancakes." I catch a whiff of the delicious smell coming from the kitchen.

"We'll be back before four," I say after giving Nate a slow and sumptuous kiss. "We can talk then, OK?"

He nods. Despite his late night at the hospital, I can tell he's feeling better about what happened Thursday night. However, there are things I now need to say. I want to tell him I'm readier than I thought. But I'm scared of losing myself, and I have to take things slowly.

But now is not the time. I blow him a kiss as I watch that impish grin of his return. He's not upset. It's all going to be fine. I turn and jog toward the Volvo, giving my entire attention to the little boy who's now climbing into the back of my car.

***

"Where are we going?" Bobby asks.

"It's a place called West Mill Creek Park," I say, focusing carefully on the road. I glance in the rearview mirror. Bobby's looking at the cell phone that Nate apparently gives to him whenever they're apart.

"What are we going to do?"

Oh my, this is going to be a form of Twenty Questions, a game I'd play with my mom anytime we drove anywhere. Could Bobby be a bit nervous to be alone with me? I think he trusts me, but he's so used to his dad and grandparents. This is all so new to both of us.

Fifteen minutes later, I'm parking the car, and Bobby's unbuckling his seatbelt, raring to go. He hops out of the back seat, clutching his phone and the kites, while I grab the blanket and the picnic basket.

"Hungry?" I ask.

Bobby vigorously nods his head up and down.

After entering the park, we find a flat spot by the creek. Immediately, I see Bobby's eyes light up when he discovers the large boulders at the water's edge.

"Let's have lunch then check out the creek, OK?" I place the picnic basket on the grass and then spread out the blanket.

"What's in the basket?" Bobby asks as I sit down on the blanket. His eyes widen as I lift the lid and then take out aluminum-wrapped packets, giving Bobby one and putting the other in front of me.

As he opens the foil, he looks at me. "Peanut butter and marshmallow? That's my favorite!"

I remember Elsa sharing that with me, and it stuck, because when I was little, I loved peanut butter and marshmallow sandwiches too. "There's also apples and grapes," I say, knowing the last thing I want is a kid hyped up on sugar. I hand him a bottle of water and a napkin, anticipating the stickiness of the sandwich.

We talk about bugs, school, the beach, mostly what I'd expect interests five-year-old boys. I learn his Pop Pop snores, his dad hates liver, and Grandma Elsa used to be a librarian.

"That's why she's *always* reading books to me."

He continues to tell me his favorite ice cream flavor is chocolate peanut butter, he only eats Captain Crunch cereal, and the most delicious candy bar is M&M's. That's when I question whether M&M's actually count as a candy bar because they're really bits of candy, not a bar. He laughs, becomes silly, then asks what's for dessert.

"Let's see what's there." I can't wait for Bobby to find the treat I made.

He takes out both plastic containers, then two spoons, and extra napkins. He hands me one of the plastic Tupperware containers and a spoon then looks quizzically at his.

"Open it, silly," I say.

When he does, he starts giggling "Ohhh … that's gross!" He drops the spoon on the blanket, and then with his chubby little fingers, pulls out a gummy worm from the chocolate pudding covered in crushed Oreos.

For the next ten minutes, while I eat the pudding with my spoon, picking around the gummies, Bobby's completely quiet, totally fixated on devouring his dirt dessert.

When he's finally done, his face is covered in chocolate. Luckily, I brought along wipes.

"Good?" I ask, perhaps fishing for a compliment.

"It was delicious!" Bobby slurs the *s* a bit, something I've noted about his speech.

"Let's check out the creek, OK?" Bobby pops up and follows me to the water's edge. "Look carefully by that big rock. Do you see the tadpoles?" I point to several tiny amphibians moving quickly in the water.

Bobby's fascinated, his eyes locked on the tadpoles as he asks, "Those are baby frogs?"

"Yes, and if you wash out your dessert container and fill it with creek water, I bet we can take some back with you. Then you can see for yourself if they do turn into frogs."

Together we return to the blanket to fetch the plastic container. Carefully, Bobby washes it in the creek, removing all chocolate remnants before filling it with fresh water from the frigid stream.

"Now the trick is to be fast." I demonstrate, cupping my hands to capture some of the squirming tadpoles. Bobby watches intently, then tries. While not successful at first, he persists, snagging a few, which he carefully places inside of his plastic container.

"I can't wait to show Dad." His face beams with pride, causing my own chest to swell with love.

I look at my watch, noting it's after two. "How about we try flying those kites?"

"Sure," Bobby yells. "I'll go get them." He heads to the blanket, and I watch as he carefully places the container on top of the basket before returning with his kite.

"How do you make it fly?" Bobby asks, unfolding his Batman kite.

I show him how to run with the kite, then, after it catches some wind, I model how to slowly let out the string. He watches, eyes wide, as his Batman kite starts to fly through the air. I pull it back down.

"Your turn," I say, handing him his kite. I take a step back and allow him to attempt it on his own. Seeing how difficult it is for him, I go to the blanket, grab the other kite, which is still folded, then move next to Bobby, demonstrating with my own kite. It takes me a few minutes, but before long, the purple-and-yellow kite's flying high. Bobby follows my lead, and the Batman kite soars below mine. He's done it!

But then, I look at my kite. There's something wrong with it. Did the salesclerk give me one with a defect?

"Ali, what's it say on your kite?" Bobby giggles, causing me to pull the kite in so I can better examine it.

Once it's within ten feet, the lettering becomes crystal clear. MARRY ME

At that exact moment, Nate appears, and Bobby starts jumping up and down. I look at the kite, and then I look at Nate, who is walking toward me.

When Nate's less than a foot away, he goes down on one knee, reaches for my hand, and says, "Ali, marry me." Then he looks at Bobby, who is slowly inching his way closer to us. "Marry us," Nate says as he takes a small gray velvet box from his pocket and opens it. Inside, nestled in the crushed velvet lining, is a magnificent square-cut diamond ring in a platinum setting.

I'm speechless. It's all happening so fast. But then my mind returns to this morning, when Gail asked what I wanted. That is when I knew ... it's Nate ... and Bobby. Then, as if to confirm any suspicion, the voice returns.

Say yes.

But I don't need the voice to tell me what to do. I kneel on the ground, in front of Nate, and whisper, "Yes." Tears stream down my face.

"Put the ring on, Ali!" Bobby yells.

"So this is how it's going to be?" I ask as I hold my left hand out and Nate easily glides the ring on my finger.

"You bet. Never a dull moment," he says as he pulls me into his arms, holding me tightly.

As I'm thinking, *don't ever let me go*, another set of arms squeezes the side of me, but the hands are little, and sticky. I turn and kiss Bobby on the forehead.

"You knew about this?" I give him a devilish look.

"Yep! That's why Daddy gave me the cell phone ... so he could find where we were."

I laugh, shaking my head in disbelief at the lengths Nate went to surprise me. "You could have been a CIA agent," I tease, reminding him of "his backstory." Nate raises his eyebrows and shrugs his shoulders. Bobby gives us a confused look.

"Never mind, buddy. It's a joke between Ali and me," Nate says, taking my hand and leading me back to our picnic area.

"And what do we have here?" he asks, picking up the container on top of the basket.

"Tadpoles. They are going to turn into frogs. Ali showed me how to catch them," Bobby proclaims, in an authoritarian voice. "And we had peanut butter and marshmallow sandwiches ... and dirt for dessert."

Nate looks lovingly at me. "You knew what he needed."

I gulp and nod my head as I tussle Bobby's hair. But he quickly takes off running toward the creek.

We spend the remainder of the afternoon at the park, checking out the trails and climbing rocks. Afterward, Nate and Bobby follow me back to my apartment. When we get inside, they walk Josie while I pack an overnight bag.

***

That night, Bobby eats pizza in front of the TV while watching *Aladdin,* his favorite Disney movie. Nate and I grill salmon and vegetables, open a bottle of chardonnay he's been saving, and talk about our future. Though there is no rush to get married, we choose the month of October.

Right as we're finishing dinner, the doorbell rings.

"Wonder who it is?" Nate says, but something tells me he already knows.

As he answers the door, Marney, Pat, Jonathon, and Elsa come bounding in.

"Congratulations!" Elsa says, kissing my forehead as Jonathon hugs me then hands Nate a bottle of champagne.

Marney gives me a bouquet of beautiful yellow roses before pulling me into her for a hug. "Welcome to the family," she says, a huge smile on her lovely round face. I return the embrace with loving affection. It's then I see the huge cake she's brought. Something tells me I'm going to have to start watching my calorie intake around Marney. That, or keep training for marathons.

Then Pat approaches and gives me a bear hug. He whispers in my ear, "Thank you ... for loving my son." I hear his voice crack a bit as he starts to become choked up.

I look up at Pat and promise, "I always will."

Together, the six of us celebrate with huge slices of cake and champagne, followed by toasts, well wishes, and embarrassing stories about Nate, told perhaps to make sure there are no secrets. However, there's still one he hasn't shared.

Later that night, after everyone's gone and Bobby's sound asleep, we sit alone at the kitchen table, a bit tipsy from the wine and champagne. Both dogs sleep at our feet.

"There is something I've never told you." Nate's eyes narrow, as if he's debating whether or not to proceed.

I say nothing, allowing him the time he needs.

"After Lynn died, well, it was really tough for me." He stops, looking closely into my eyes before continuing. "I lost my will … to live. I was in over my head, alone, had a baby to care for. I couldn't do it." He stops talking, diverts his eyes downward, and hangs his head. I hold his hand, hoping to give him the strength to continue.

"One night, when Jonathon and Elsa had Bobby, I stopped at a bar on the way home from the hospital." He looks up at me, his eyes about to overflow with tears. "Guess I had a few too many, barely made it home. And then, when I did, well, that's when I decided I couldn't stand it any longer … I had some pain pills, from a knee surgery. They were still in the cabinet…" The tears begin to fall. "I don't want this to change your mind about me, but you need to know," he says in a barely audible voice.

"Shhh," I say, as I gently place my finger to his lips. "Your mom told me … at the beach."

His expression shifts from sadness to confusion to anger.

"Don't be upset. She … everyone … they worry about you. They didn't want me to hurt you. That's all." And then I proceed to tell him about the conversation.

"I'm really sorry my mom told you before I could," Nate says, his voice quiet.

"No, it's good she did. It showed me how much they all love you and Bobby. Plus, well, you knew about me … after David … when I went through my thing. And you accepted everything, without once judging me."

"That was totally different. You didn't try to kill yourself."

"No, but I thought about it. And you can't compare our losses. Nate, the point is we're both good, we've survived, and we've healed. Sure, there's still some pain left, but we're better and we found each other. That's what matters"

Slowly, this seems to sink in. Nate's face softens, then he shifts his chair closer to mine and pulls me into his arms.

"Tired?" he asks.

I nod, then he takes my hand and leads me upstairs to his, what will soon become our, bedroom.

The room has pale gray walls and off-white woven blinds, which have been lowered. There's a wicker chair and ottoman in one corner, a few standing plants, a bureau, and a queen bed. I move toward the bureau, looking at the framed photos, perhaps expecting to see pictures of Lynn. But there are none. There are only pictures of Bobby and one of Nate's parents.

I turn and look to Nate.

"I've scrubbed every memory of her from this room—don't worry," he says, giving me his tender smile, yet there's a slight sadness in his eyes. I can't expect that to disappear; I can only hope it lessens.

He pulls back the indigo quilt, motioning me to sit next to him. As I follow his lead, he wraps his arms around me, and in the gentlest way, he eases me back onto the pillow and slowly, we begin to make the sweetest love. There is no frenzy, rather something else, something better. Our every movement seems to flow, in unison, as one.

Afterward, as we hold one another, we share our hopes and dreams, as individuals, and also as a couple, one with a child. We acknowledge possible roadblocks ahead yet are confident they can be overcome. I hear his soft breath become rhythmic. Nate has fallen asleep.

Before shutting my eyes, I take my hand from under the covers and gaze at the ring on my finger. Nate told me that when I said it was too soon for me to move in with him and showed hesitation about losing myself in the process, he realized how much he wanted me to be part of his life. He could have waited, but he didn't want to waste any time. He'd been miserable for so long, and now that he had found me, well, he knew that was it.

Tonight, I agreed to move in, but slowly, more for Bobby's sake than anything else. I don't want him to think I'm trying to replace his mom. Plus, he and Nate need their time. After all, like Josie was to me, Bobby is who ultimately helped Nate overcome his debilitating grief ... he had a son to raise.

Suddenly, I have an urge to check on Bobby. Careful not to wake Nate, I crawl out of bed and quietly leave the bedroom, walking toward Bobby's door. As I open the cracked door and peer in, I see his night-light is on. Bobby's soundly sleeping, his arm clutching the giraffe from our visit to the zoo. He looks peaceful, content. I stay there for a while. I watch Bobby breathe, purse his lips, and heave out little boy sighs. Fully aware I'm not only marrying Nate, I'm also becoming a mother, something I used to dream about but assumed was no longer possible. How wrong I was.

I take a step back, readjust his door so it's only a few inches open, then return to Nate. As I crawl under the covers, I know the woman I have become is ready for this step. I no longer need to prove anything to anyone. I am fine as I am. I trust myself.

CHAPTER 34

It's been five weeks since I married Nate and became Bobby's "New Mom," a term our almost six-year-old devised. And now, on this damp Sunday morning, a light drizzle falls as Kimmy and I run down Kelly Drive, approaching the final mile of the Philadelphia Marathon. While a bit wobbly, my legs are still somewhat strong. No doubt our thorough training is paying off. When we round the turn, I see Boathouse Row. The finish line is right after that, at the entrance to the Museum of Art.

As my legs automatically turn over in a less than even rhythmic pace, I permit my mind to wander for a bit. It takes me to the day I became Mrs. Ali Cavanaugh.

***

I now laugh at how I took up half of the limo. I always thought my wedding dress would be plain and simple, yet mine was elegant. Its intricate lace bodice hugged my body perfectly, and the smooth silky fabric softly fell around me.

It seemed natural to choose Lisa and Kimmy as my maids of honor. These sisters have renewed my faith in female friendships. While my relationship with each is unique, together we have a special bond, built on trust, companionship, support, and fun.

Susie and Gail also participated in the wedding. These two women have become surrogate mothers during our past months together. While no one could replace my mom, they've both provided me with unconditional love and guidance. Without a doubt, they've been an intricate part in my healing process. And they led me to Josie. Of course, they squawked when I asked them to be bridesmaids, declaring they were too old to take part. But once I assured them how important it was to me, and that I'd choose appropriate dresses, they agreed, though reluctantly.

We weren't sure where to have the ceremony. Neither of us are religious, but we wanted a priest to marry us, as we knew it would be important to Marney and Pat. Elsa and Jonathon graciously offered their shore home for the wedding, but I couldn't accept, which of course Nate understood. Miles suggested a wedding venue in Glen Mills. We loved it, but it was booked for over a year. But then, we received a call, sharing there was an opening on October 17. This shocked us, as mid-fall is prime wedding season. Apparently, a couple had cancelled, something about the groom sleeping with the bride's sister. While sad for them, we loved the space and were thrilled to be able to have our wedding there.

Marney was critical in the planning. Nate shared how much she wanted to help. When he married Lynn, Marney was not included in the plans and felt left out. I think she hoped that me not having a mother would open the door for her. Honestly, I was thrilled to have her assist with the wedding. But the true gift was spending time with my future mother-in-law. She's pretty amazing, all five feet two of her.

At first, I wanted to invite my siblings and dad to the wedding, anticipating that perhaps this event might bring us together. But when I reached out to let my brothers and sisters know I was engaged, it became evident everyone was too busy to have a decent phone conversation, let alone travel to Philadelphia for a wedding. When I spoke with my dad, he was pleasant on the phone, but I could tell he'd been drinking, an insight my siblings confirmed when I spoke with them. But in a strange way, I was fine with it all. They were once part of my life, but I'm no longer the girl they knew. While a part of me regrets I stopped interacting with my biological family, I am blessed to have found others who have more than filled that role. And that is why I asked Miles to give me away on my wedding day. He accepted with pleasure, and I smile as I replay the conversation we had that day.

"I couldn't be happier for you," Miles said as we paused for a moment before following the procession.

"Thank you," I said then kissed him gently on the cheek.

"What was that for?" His eyes twinkled as the lines on his face softened.

"For believing in me when I couldn't. You knew all along, didn't you?"

Miles leaned closer before softly whispering, "You are like a daughter to me. It killed me to watch you lose yourself when you started dating David. But I couldn't tell you. You had to realize the truth for yourself."

✳✳✳

That day, my heart could not have been fuller, for if it were, it would have burst. Never did I believe I'd meet and marry a man like Nate. In fact, I thought men like that only existed in movies. And Bobby, well, he's like a cherry on top of our sundae ... he makes the entire dessert sweeter. I wondered if the voice would speak to me that day, as I had not heard her words since Nate proposed. But maybe Lynn, or whoever the voice was, finished what she set out to do. The voice led me to Nate, and now, I no longer need her guidance. But strangely, a part of me misses her.

***

Kimmy, who is gracefully running next to me, has come so far since we first met. She and Lisa still live together, but Kimmy's now creating a new life on her own. Recently there is a guy whom she seems to like, and he appears to be interested in her.

Our long runs these past months have been therapeutic for both of us. I've helped her sort through some of the demons she's carried since Luke's death. Slowly, she's releasing the pain and guilt she assumed for not recognizing his gambling addiction. In no way is her suffering gone, but she's now able to function better, slowly regaining her life.

And I stopped worrying that my relationship with Nate happened too quickly. After all, when you know, you know. But being a mom to a little boy, well, that evoked all sorts of apprehension. Over the many miles we've traveled together, Kimmy's given me encouragement when I felt inadequate about being Bobby's "New Mom." There's something about pounding the pavement with a good friend that seems to ease life's challenges.

Kimmy looks at me. "Think we can finish in less than four hours?" she asks. I nod yes and reach for the carnelian crystal I now carry with me when I run. It is supposed to help motivate and increase self-confidence. The woman at the rock shop said it assists with focus and manifesting successful outcomes. I thought it was the perfect gemstone to help get me through this marathon. And I continue to wear the blue apatite bracelet I bought in April. I say a quiet thank-you to Lynn for opening my mind to the healing power of gemstones.

We both quicken our pace, weaving between the people ahead of us as we keep a close watch on the time. Pushing ourselves past the point of comfortably talking, we continue, gaining momentum. The crowd cheers, air horns blare, and a band plays "Philadelphia Freedom."

Then I start to scan the hordes of people waiting at the end of the race. While I know it will be impossible to find them, I desperately want to see Nate and Bobby.

Kimmy picks up that I'm losing focus. "We're almost there. Don't slow down." She pats me on the back as if to offer encouragement.

Suddenly it's become apparent that the Philly Marathon is not the only race I've trained for. This entire year has been a marathon of sorts. So much has occurred over the past ten months. I'd lost myself, slowly rediscovered who I was, adopted Josie, met true friends, and then found Nate and Bobby. And each step of the way, I've grown, pushed past uncomfortable limits, allowed others to support and cheer me on, yet trusted myself to finish *my race.*

And that is exactly what I do. I cross the finish line. Holding Kimmy's hand high in triumph as we complete our goal, one which has helped us both in different yet similar ways.

That's when I hear the familiar scream, "Ali! We're over here!"

I turn toward the voice and see Bobby on top of Nate's shoulders. Lisa and her boyfriend, Robbie, are also there. There's another guy talking to them, but I haven't met him before.

After they remove the timing bracelets from our ankles and hand us space blankets, Kimmy and I hobble over to our cheering squad. Marcus, the guy Kimmy's been talking about, is standing with Nate, Bobby, Robbie, and Lisa. Marcus wanted to surprise Kimmy by showing up to watch her finish the race.

Eventually, we say goodbye and walk back to the car. Bobby runs ahead, but I slowly limp behind. Now I can definitely feel the impact this race has had on my body. Thank God there's a hot bath in my future.

***

Later that afternoon, while Nate and Bobby watch the Eagles play the Cowboys, I slowly make my way upstairs and prepare my long-awaited bath. As I open the linen closet, searching for a bath bomb, I see the test, the one I bought last week, sitting on a shelf. I'm never late. I figured it's been all of the running and the excitement about the wedding. After all, it's been anything but "regular" around here lately. Yet, right before I'm about to ease my way into the tub, I hear the voice, the one I thought I would never hear again.

Have faith.

Instead of stepping into the foamy bath I've been dreaming about all day, I listen to the voice, the one I've trusted all along. Slowly, I remove the stick from the pink box and then head to the toilet. Moments later, I look at the window on this plastic device, wondering if two lines will appear, or only one. Suspecting the latter, I place it on a tissue by the sink. The box says results occur in three minutes. I look at the clock on the granite counter. The second hand seems to be ticking slower than normal.

Though I want to stare at it, I won't allow myself to do so. Instead, I pick up a magazine and try my best to flip through the pages.

Finally, I can't wait any longer. It has to have been three minutes. I put the magazine down on the counter, turn my gaze toward the stick, and allow myself to look.

Two pink lines ...

I don't scream in joy or call for Nate. No, this is something I want to languish in before I share it with my husband. While I'm thrilled to become Bobby's "New Mom," a part of me longed for the infant and toddler stages. But now, there's a high probability I'll have a chance for that and so much more.

Easing my sore body into the sudsy hot bath, I sigh as the foamy water envelops me and the lilac scent of the bath bomb permeates my senses. I permit myself time to relax and absorb the magnitude of these two pink lines.

"Hey, Ali, can I get you anything?" Unexpectedly, the door to the bathroom opens. Nate pops his head through the doorway, careful not to let out the steamy air. "Thought you might like ..." But then he stops mid-sentence, his eyes fixate on the stick lying atop the counter. Quickly, he comes inside, shutting the door behind him. After turning his head from me to the stick then back to me, he asks, "Is two good or bad?"

"Good." A huge grin appears on my face. I can no longer suppress my joy.

Nate's eyes light up as he kneels next to the bathtub, pulling my wet body into his strong arms. He tenderly strokes my hair and whispers, "And it keeps getting better." Then, without warning, my husband climbs into the tub with me. Water overflows all over the tile floor as we both laugh aloud, consumed by the blessing of the two pink lines.

If someone had told me last February that in less than ten months, I'd be married, with a stepson, and newly pregnant, I would have declared that person delusional. Yet it was me who was lost, unwell, in need of healing. Only by letting go and trusting in myself was I able to regain my life. And in the process, I received more than I could have ever imagined possible.

Now, my world is crazy, exciting, beautiful, and totally out of my control. And for the first time, I feel free. I take my hands and cup my husband's face. Looking deep in his eyes, I realize that while our future is unknown, we have everything we need. There is no more searching. I am complete.

ACKNOWLEDGMENTS

Authors may write books,
but publishing novels requires a collaborative spirit.
It is with heartfelt gratitude that I thank my all-star team …

> Julie Swearingen—for her brilliant editing skills
> Alison Cantrell—for her gift of precision
> Lieve Maas—for her graphic design and publishing talents

LIST OF CREDITS

Made in the USA
Columbia, SC
10 March 2024

32387208R00188